Whole

by

J L Wilson

A Remembered Classics Romance, Book 6

Whole

Cover Art by *Kim Mendoza*

The Wild Rose Press, Inc.
PO Box 708
Adams Basin, NY 14410-0708
Visit us at www.thewildrosepress.com

Publishing History
First Crimson Rose Edition, 2019
Print ISBN 978-1-5092-2882-9
Digital ISBN 978-1-5092-2883-6

A Remembered Classics Romance, Book 6
Published in the United States of America

Someone jerked me to my feet so hard I was sure my arm was broken. The blond guard shifted his grip to my hair and pressed a gun to my head, his eyes fixed above us where Asa stared down, rifle on his shoulder.

"I'll kill you," the guard said, tugging my head back, exposing my neck. "Call him off or I kill you."

I tried to pull away but his hold was tight. When I shuffled my feet, they touched some obstruction and I realized it was Chessy's body. My stomach lurched and I longed to be sick, longed to drop to my knees and puke. Instead I drew in ragged breaths, trying to form words.

"Tell him," the guard said. "Tell him." He inched backward, his eyes focused upward. The gun didn't shift an inch from where it pressed into the side of my forehead.

I hazarded a glance at Dodge, who was frozen in place, his eyes on me. His gun was in his hand but he didn't have a shot.

The blond guard holding me pulled his gun away slightly so he could whisper in my ear. "He won't shoot. He won't risk you."

I stared into Roberta's eyes. I think she saw my answer before I spoke. "It isn't a risk." I smiled at the house and managed to tilt my head slightly to the left. "Take the shot."

Dedication

To the Ladies of the Turtle,
who help me find these stories

Chapter One

I walked onto the screened porch of our house and peered at the dock in the distance, one hand shading my eyes from the sun glinting off the water. Mike had called from the lodge to tell us a visitor was here.

I glanced at my husband who sat with his long legs propped up on the hassock, his laptop balanced on his knees. "Company coming."

He frowned at me. "I told you I don't have anything to say."

"And I told you that reporters would probably find us, sooner or later. We should talk to this one, tell the whole story."

He shrugged, one shoulder lifting his faded red T-shirt. I've known him most of my life, and he's always appeared deceptively thin, at least until you saw his muscled arms and strong thighs. I have always envied him his tall slenderness because I'm short, barely five-feet tall to his six-feet. In my youth I was thin, but time and gravity have taken their toll and now I was a somewhat plump and matronly sixty-six-year-old with graying brown hair and a few more wrinkles than I liked to see.

"You're perfect just the way you are."

I was startled out of my musings. "How did you know what I was thinking?"

He took my hand and rubbed it against his neatly

trimmed gray goatee. "You get that funny little frown, the same one you get when you stare at yourself in the mirror and you don't like what you see." He pulled me to him and our lips met in a lingering kiss. "I love what I see."

I straightened, running my hand over his thick gray hair, tied back today in a pigtail that snaked down his back. "You always know the right thing to say."

He peered beyond me, to the expanse of lake beyond the screened porch. "I have no idea what to say to her. I think I'll let you handle it."

I didn't blame him. We had successfully evaded reporters for twenty-plus years mainly because we were recluses here on our private Minnesota lake. We bought the lake, the island, and the lodge when we fled the Twin Cities in the late 1990s, and we settled in as wealthy early-retirees. Our friends knew, but they wouldn't tell. We kept their secrets and they kept ours.

"Be careful," he said. "She might be cleverer than we think." He snapped his fingers and our French bulldog, Dina, raised her head. As always, she sat not far from him, in a spot where she could keep an eye on his comings and goings. "Take the hound with you. She'll protect you."

"I doubt I'll need protecting." Still, it might not be a bad idea. Dina was deceptively petite with mostly white fur and fawn-colored splotches on her sides. She had the typical fawn mask on her face with white jowls and chin and big ears that pricked toward me now. "Come along, Dina. I can use the company."

She sprang to her feet and trotted to join me. Although only a foot tall, she was solid and compact with thick muscles and an air of firm determination.

She put on a good front, but only we knew what a clown she truly was. "I'm not worried," I told him. "I trust your instincts."

"My instincts haven't always been right."

I squeezed his shoulder. "I'm sure they're right this time. Don't worry. I'll be very careful. I'm not going to let anything keep us from our well-deserved retirement." I kissed him quickly and started out the porch door.

"Take your gun."

I stopped. "I'd rather not."

"I'd rather you did."

I didn't argue. I knew that tone of voice. I reached into the wicker basket near the door, the one that held my garden gloves and my revolver. I tucked the small Smith and Wesson into the specially designed pocket in my denim skirt and left.

I walked onto the deck then down the steps leading onto the stone path, which in turn led down the hill to the lake. The lawn on either side of the path was starting to green but it was still early in May and often cool overnight. The morning sun was beginning to banish those white spots of frost on the lawn. I tugged my blue sweater to cover my red-striped knit top, fighting the chill.

Dina trotted ahead of me, staying close as per her training. She wouldn't dash away unless I gave her permission to do so. Not only was she a marvelous pet, but she truly was a good guard dog and had been trained as such.

Our house sat on a hill on our small island, several acres large. We had built it so either a deck or a porch was on all sides of the house. This gave us a view of the entire expanse of Flamingo Lake. It was so named because of its odd shape, with one big fat bay where our island sat, two long narrow channels on the south end, and a single undulating channel at the north end. I've seen the lake from the air when we came in by plane and it does appear somewhat like a big bird, if you squint hard enough.

Flamingo Lodge was situated on the south end of the lake. It was small, catering mainly to fishermen who could afford the stiff price Mike Butterfield, our manager, charged for a week of getting-away-from-it-all. At peak season, twenty guests could stay in the ten rooms in the big log cabin. The place was booked years in advance because Butterfield provided amazing amenities, including gourmet meals that he cooked himself. His wife, an Ojibwa native, was also an exceptional cook and her brothers were guides to the best fishing spots on the lake. Mike's two sons were attending college in the Twin Cities, majoring in Hospitality Management. They planned to return here and take over the business when Mike retired.

The guests at the lodge had strict orders not to bother us on the island, and usually they obeyed. Of course, it helped that we had a motorized dock that was kept raised most of the time. There was a thirty-foot drop-off all around the island except for one small beach area on the south side. Anyone who tried to dock there had to work a boat through large rocks that could tear out the bottom. Often the only sign we saw of the guests were the boats puttering past on their way to the prime fishing spots at the north end of the lake.

Dina and I stopped by the steps and I tapped in the security code for the dock. With a faint clink of meshing metal below us, the walkway inched downward. It was an ingenuous system, a combination of gangplank like those used on cruise ships with a simple winch and pulley. The base was sunk into the bedrock of the island and the gangplank swung out over the water. Mike's launch was equipped with a platform where the gangplank was secured.

When we first built the house, we had a conventional dock to make it easy to unload building materials and supplies. But once construction was completed, we destroyed the old dock and installed this simple gangplank system.

"Let's go, pup." I gestured and Dina went ahead of me, pausing now and again to sniff at something in the vegetation on either side of the wide wooden steps.

Despite what I said earlier, I was still nervous. It's not everyone who can run away from their past, but we did it, making new lives for ourselves here in the Boundary Waters Canoe Area Wilderness, or BWCAW as locals called it. We were on the border between Minnesota and Canada and surrounded by forest, lakes, and wildlife. The nearest town, population one thousand, was about six miles away and the only way to the lake was via a twisting paved road through dense pine woods, unmarked and unmapped. Lodge visitors and delivery people knew the way but otherwise we stayed private.

Until now, of course. I watched the boat approach from the middle of the steps, a mix of apprehension and excitement making me shift nervously from foot to foot. Dina looked at me over her shoulder as though to say, *Enough already. I have this handled.* I leaned over to touch her head and her butt quivered in appreciation.

Mike slid the boat into position and soon he hopped out, the boat swaying with the movement. He's a big man, so he displaces a lot of water. He helped a woman out of the boat and they walked along the dock to the stairs, the woman ahead of him.

I came down a couple of steps to meet them. "How do you do, Miss Lewis," I said, extending my hand.

The woman facing me appeared like any typical newsgirl with long blonde hair tied back in a ponytail, blue eyes, a flawless complexion, and a slender, athletic figure. I knew quite a lot about Carol Lewis because when she requested the interview, I had Chessy research her for me. It was exactly the sort of job Chessy loved. She was my private detective for twenty years and she had amazing contacts scattered throughout Minnesota and beyond. I also guessed that Chessy had a special interest in this woman given our convoluted past.

Carol Lewis was twenty-seven, an ex-cop and new to journalism after a stint in print journalism in Chicago. She was dating a professional football player, had a dog named Dodo, and lived in a trendy loft in St. Paul in a part of town I used to know well. She was tall, almost as tall as Mike, who was six-foot. I silently applauded Lewis' apparel of jeans, sneakers, and a loose summer-weight sweater. It struck the right note of casual professionalism and practical wearability for someone visiting a lake-front home.

"Thank you for meeting me, Mrs. Hatterley. I appreciate you taking the time." She shook my hand then released it to steady the heavy messenger bag slung over one shoulder.

"Your letter was clever. It intrigued me." I saw

Mike watching us with his usual hawk-eyed gaze. "We'll call you when Miss Lewis is ready to return to the lodge."

"Sounds good." He ambled back to the launch, pausing once to wave at the house.

Miss Lewis looked at the hill above us. "Is your husband at home?"

I went up the steps and she followed, Dina scampering ahead of us. "He's busy right now. I'm afraid only I'm available to chat." I walked to the grouping of wooden chairs painted red in the grove of trees on the hill below the house.

She fell into step beside me. "You two have been together a long time."

Well, that wasn't a secret. Anyone who knew anything about us knew our history, but I didn't mind reiterating it. "Yes, we have. We met in college, in the late 60s. We were both teenage prodigies. He was sixteen and I was fourteen when we met. We both attended M.I.T., majoring in Applied Mathematics." I smiled faintly. "We had our picture taken for *Time Magazine*, as I recall."

"Then your husband murdered a man." Lewis paused as if she expected me to contradict her.

"He wasn't my husband at the time. And he was convicted of murdering someone," I corrected. "Convicted on largely circumstantial evidence. But please. If we're going to talk over old history, why don't we get comfortable?" I moved to one of the Adirondack chairs facing the lake. Trees would shade the chairs in the afternoon, but now they sat in the May sunlight, a gentle breeze drifting over us when we settled down in the seats. The sunlight was welcome. The ice had gone out on the lake only two weeks earlier, an annual rite of spring in the North.

"I'm curious. What led you to us?" I crossed my ankles on the wooden footstool in front of me and draped my denim skirt over my calves, making sure my gun remained securely in place.

"The senator's papers were recently transferred to the University of Minnesota." The girl sat after a quick glance at the seat, probably confirming it wasn't used as a bird roost. I once again applauded her intelligence regarding outdoor living. "I was doing a retrospective about her and I decided to go through some of her correspondence."

I smoothed out a wrinkle in my skirt. "That wasn't what I meant. How did you find us?" I waved a hand at the pristine wilderness around us. "We aren't exactly in the mainstream."

"You were hard to locate," she admitted. "There were no phone records, no utility records, no deeds or property transactions."

I glanced at the wind turbine in the distance, not far from the lodge. A smaller version sat behind our house and we also had solar panels as backup. "We're off the grid here. Our own well, our own power supply. And as for phones . . ." I pulled my cell phone out of my pocket and held it up for her to see. "We're not completely out of touch with the world."

She frowned. "I couldn't find any record of a mobile account."

I tucked the phone back out of sight. "Don't forget. My husband and I either designed or assisted in the design of most mobile computing technology. It's rather easy to modify and mix signals. Almost as easy as it is to manage other electronic records."

Understanding slowly dawned in her baby blue eyes. "You hacked the system," she said with a grin.

I lifted one shoulder in a negligent shrug. "Somewhat. We're still very active in certain computer forums and on various social media sites. And my husband is an avid video game player and is quite well known in those circles. While we're unknown, we're just not known as us, so to speak." I let my hand drop over the side of my chair to touch Dina's head where she sat next to me. "You said something about Senator Hart's papers. What did you see that led you to us?"

Lewis leaned near me, her ponytail swinging with the movement. "There's been a lot of speculation about why the senator abandoned her run for the Presidency. She was popular with Republican voters, she had an excellent record in the senate, and she appeared to be well liked by many people. Granted, that was a decade or two before women became a mainstay in political office, but she had the funding and the backing. Why did she drop out of the race decades ago?" Lewis shifted position in the chair so she could face me.

I shifted my attention to the trees in front of the house. He stood on the deck, watching us. Lewis couldn't see him from her vantage point, but I had a clear view of him. "Are you asking me for my opinion? She was wounded when someone shot her in Rice Park. Isn't that reason enough? Or perhaps she didn't want to undergo the rigors of a bid for the Presidency. Perhaps she didn't want to subject her family to such an experience." I was hard-pressed to say that with a straight face. Senator Roberta "Ruby" Hart would have sacrificed her children to Satan for a chance at the Oval

Office.

"You owned a house in Richmond that burned down. For a short while it was thought you died in the fire, but it happens that the man who died in the fire was an employee of Senator Hart's. I remembered seeing your name in association with your software company, so I did some research." Carol kept her eyes fixed on me, a tactic which I suppose was meant to make me self-conscious if I decided to try to evade any questions. What she didn't know was that I had no qualms about spinning a whopping big lie and throwing it right in her face.

"And what did your research reveal?" I tilted my head to the sunlight.

"It didn't make sense. What connection could there be between someone like you—a liberal woman who ran a cutting-edge software company—and a woman like her? She was conservative, somewhat reactionary in her viewpoints. She was opposed to the social platforms you supported. Why would you two be associated in any way?"

"Perhaps it was coincidence," I pointed out.

Lewis shook her head. "I don't think so."

"What then?" I prompted.

"I did some more research about you. Your name was linked with Senator Hart's in a roundabout way. Then six months later, you married your husband, the charges against him were expunged, he was awarded a million-dollar settlement from the state, and the senator abruptly retired, essentially going into seclusion. Her records were sealed for twenty years and recently released to the University." Lewis leaned on the arm of her chair, staring eagerly at me. "What happened, Mrs.

Hatterley?"

Logic warred with common sense and caution. Lewis appeared so young, so eager. I leaned my right elbow on the arm of my chair and propped my head against my hand. That allowed me to hear the tiny radio in my ear more clearly. "I don't know," I said for the benefit of my husband who watched us from the house. "How much should I tell you?"

He laughed softly. "Go ahead. It's a good test. Tell her everything. We've got eyes and ears all around the island. If she's the advance guard, we'll know it soon."

"Please," Lewis said, unmindful of this one-sided conversation. "I admit, I want a good news story, but I'm also curious." She smiled, the picture of innocence.

"Well, I suppose you're right," I murmured. "What can it hurt to tell?"

He laughed again. "I have you covered."

I straightened and smoothed down my skirt. "Please. Call me Alice." I glanced at the deck behind us and waved. He waved back and disappeared into the house. From there he'd probably go to the cupola where he had a clear view of the area. That's where most of his guns were stored.

"Madison and I were together when we were in college, but we were so young then. I was sixteen and he was barely eighteen when we became involved. I suppose you could say our story started then, but I think it really started when we met again, years later," I said.

Chapter Two

In 1998, a ghost walked into a gymnasium to stand in front of me. "Hello, Alice."

I stood, not sure my wobbling legs would support me. I was seated at the intake area, a series of four six-foot long tables forming a simple barrier at the entrance into the gym. Military veterans had to stop at one of our tables so we could gather some preliminary information and give them the questionnaire everyone filled out. We were in the last day of a three-day Stand Down and new arrivals kept trickling in, attesting to how many homeless vets needed help in Minneapolis/St. Paul.

"Where have you been, Madison? I've been searching for you for years." I said the first thing that popped into my head, probably because it was true.

"Your hair isn't blonde and curly anymore." He tilted his head as he regarded me. "When did it change to brown?"

I self-consciously touched my light brown hair, cut into a simple bob that brushed my chin. "In my twenties. I colored it blonde for a while but then I got tired of coloring and curling."

"Oh." He smiled faintly.

I barely recognized him. I'd been seeking him for five years, my search beginning a few years before I sold my company in California and moved back to Richmond, Minnesota, a small town south of the Twin

Cities. The detectives I hired couldn't turn up a recent trace of him, but six months ago we got a lead that he was in the Twin Cities, living among the other nameless, homeless people who eked out a living on the streets.

He didn't appear at any of the homeless shelters during the brutal winter and I gave up hope that he was still in the area. I volunteered for this May Stand Down event held in Bloomington, centrally located south of St. Paul and Minneapolis. I envisioned what I'd do if he appeared, somewhat careworn and tired. We would sit down and talk, I would give him the money I set aside for him then I'd put my guilt behind me and get on with my life.

I didn't envision this skinny, bearded, tangle-haired man whose dark blue eyes peered so intently into mine. His pale blue shirt sleeves were rolled up and tattoos snaked up his arms, flowers and animals and colored patterns that seemed to writhe in the glaring overhead lights. He wore baggy and dirty jeans, ratty looking sneakers and carried a grimy knapsack that bulged with God knew what.

"Any problem, Alice?" Theo Gliriday moved closer to me behind the tables separating us from the vets entering this high school gym. Theo and I were co-coordinators for this Stand Down event in St. Paul. We'd worked together at other Stand Down events and at the Christ Church Kitchen on Dodgson Street, serving free meals.

"No problem." I gestured to Madison, pointing him to a spot on my left where other tables were located, forming the side of the small square that enclosed Theo and me inside. "Come over here. Let me get you logged in." I stepped over boxes of brochures and handouts to the IBM-PC and pulled out the metal folding chair in front of it.

"You should fill out an intake card. That way we can keep track of how many come for funding." I was talking to distract myself while I typed his name with trembling fingers. *Madison A. Hatterley.*

"I go by Asa now."

He must have slipped between the tables because he now peered over my shoulder. I forgot how quiet he could be. Madison moved with all the grace of a dancer, light and lithe on his feet. Then what he said sank in. "You don't use Madison anymore?"

"No. I use Asa." He surveyed the tables set up in the gym. "I like that song. I used to listen to it a lot."

I focused on the faint background music coming through the sound system on the stage on my left. *Riders on the Storm.* We played what these vets expected to hear. The Doors, Jimi Hendrix, Eric Clapton, Credence—the soundtrack of the 60s and the 70s, the soundtrack of a generation.

His gaze scanned over the computer. I had set up this database, syncing it with government sources which were notoriously outdated and inaccurate. Several of the fields in his record were outlined in pale red. "You designed this, didn't you?" He leaned over to stare closer at the screen.

"Yes, I did. How did you know?"

He tapped the monitor, showing me a glimpse of more tattoos on the underside of his right arm. "It's how the fields are arranged on the screen. You always did like to have things in a certain order. And the red outline is the color you'd use." He straightened, frowning. "That data is wrong."

I was aware of Theo, who had taken my place at the table closest to me, putting him conveniently near if needed. I confess I was glad to have him there, even though Theo was small, slender, and somewhat timid. Madison—no, Asa—was not what I expected and I wasn't sure if I knew how to handle him anymore.

"Much of the information we get from Washington is wrong." I turned my attention back to the PC. "I decided it's better to have my own files and do a comparison to what we got from the government."

"Where do you store it? It takes too long to do comparisons on a PC. What do you have for the workhorse?"

"I have access to an IBM server. I'll upload it tonight and run the algorithm then." I was typing as I talked, sorting through the information on my screen.

"That's right. You own a software company, don't you?" He stood very close to me, and for all his bedraggled appearance, he didn't smell too bad, just a bit musty and sweaty.

"I used to own the company. I sold it." I tapped the screen. "What should I correct?"

"You gained weight. You used to be thin."

"I also used to be sixteen," I said, turning back to the screen. "Now I'm forty-five and fat."

"You're not fat. You're just not thin. I like your hair that way. It's better with your face than the curly style. Your face is round and your eyes are so big. Your hair is better short because it's easier to pay attention to your eyes. They're so dark brown."

Trust Madison to analyze my mature appearance. It had taken me a long time to get past the blonde and curly stage of my life and accept my plainer self. He did it in a matter of seconds.

"He's a real charmer, isn't he?" Theo muttered behind us.

I glanced over my shoulder. He watched us with undisguised suspicion, his gaze fixed on Asa, who still stood close to me, his gaze fixed on the monitor. "Theo, this is Madison—Asa—Hatterley. He always tells the truth. Hence his comment about my weight." I looked up at Madison. "This is Theo Gliriday. He coordinated this event."

Madison stuck out a somewhat clean hand. "Thank you. If you would advertise this at the underpass at 7th and Ramsey, you'd get more men to come in. There are ten Viet vets who regularly flop there, plus four from Desert Storm, and two from Bosnia."

"Madison counts things," I said before Theo could reply. "He's good with numbers." That was an understatement, but there was no need to go into that.

"It's Asa. I don't use Madison anymore." He stood with his hand outstretched, his arm trembling slightly.

"Okay," Theo said doubtfully, cautiously shaking Madison—no, Asa's—hand. "I'll make sure to send some folks out there to see if anybody needs help. Thanks." Theo glanced at me. "Sounds like you two have some catching up to do. I'll have Chessy fill in for you." He waved to the slender woman working with another volunteer, handing out bottles of water and the small plastic bags of freebies for the vets. "If you need anything, just holler." Theo meandered away but didn't go far. Most of the vets who came to these events were grateful and calm, but there had been outbursts now and again.

"Did I hurt your feelings?" Asa dug his hands into his jeans pockets and hunched his shoulders. I recognized that pose. He was withdrawing, 'fading' as we used to call it. He would block out the world and go into his Special Place whenever something upset him.

"You didn't hurt my feelings," I said. "The truth sometimes isn't pleasant, but that doesn't mean it shouldn't be told."

"You're wrong. Sometimes people should lie." He stared at the PC. "That's a good song, too. We used to dance to that song, didn't we?"

A Whiter Shade of Pale. "Yes, we did." I pointed to the folding chair next to the table. "Sit down, Asa. Let's talk."

"Everything okay, buddy?" someone called.

The voice came from the intake tables on my right. A massive black man stared over Theo's head, glaring at me. He looked like an ex-football player, with bulging biceps straining his Grateful Dead T-shirt, a beefy neck, and thighs as big as my waist that strained his blue jeans. His shiny bald head added to his tough-guy appearance.

"I'm fine," Asa said, sitting down next to me. "This won't take long."

The big man grabbed the registration form from Theo and bent over the table to write. Catherine Chessy approached him on his left, holding out the plastic bag full of samples—soap, shampoo, shaving cream, mouth wash, and a toothbrush, nail file, disposable razor, and comb. Contact information was printed on stickers pasted to the outside of the bag. "Move out of the way, okay? You can sit over there to fill it out." She pointed to the bleachers where other vets were laboriously filling out the short questionnaire.

The man straightened, staring down at her. Cat was in her twenties, slender and tall, but she was dwarfed by him. That didn't bother her in the least. She tucked her long strawberry-blonde hair behind her ears and tried to move past him to the next man in line. When the big man didn't budge, she shoved the plastic bag into his hand and smiled at him. "Please?"

He snatched the registration form off the table and stalked to the bleachers. The big man hunkered down over the form like it was the final exam for law school. Chessy handed a card and bag to the next man in line.

"Who's that?" I turned back to the computer.

"Butterfly. He's a friend of mine."

"Butterfly?"

"Mike Butterfield. Butterfly is his nickname."

"Odd nickname for such a big guy. Where'd you meet him?"

"In prison."

I nearly knocked the keyboard off the table. "What?"

"Isn't that in my records?" He scooted his chair closer to me and reached for the keyboard.

"Wait a minute." I raised my elbow to keep him away but he ended up putting his arm around me and leaning closer. "What are you doing?"

"Don't update it," he whispered.

"What?" One red-outlined field blinked at me. *Last known address.* "Why not? I'm supposed to. That way we can actually have some reasonably correct records."

"Don't. I don't want them to know where I am."

"Who?"

"The government. Her people."

His breath was warm and smelled faintly of onions. "What are you talking about?"

"We need to talk someplace where they won't see us. I need your help, Alice. That's the reason I finally came to talk to you."

"What?"

"I've seen you other times. I wasn't sure I could trust you, though. Then when you sold your company, I decided I could."

I turned my head. His face was inches from mine, his thick long hair loose and hanging down around his shoulders. There were streaks of gray in the dark brown and hints of gray in his thick beard. It hid the oval shape of his face and distracted from his high cheekbones. He was only forty-eight but his hair, grimy clothes, and beard made him appear twenty years older. "You've been watching me?"

"Of course. I knew you were trying to find me. The people you sent weren't very good. That's why I followed you here. I thought you'd move here. You always liked it better than in the big cities out west." He surveyed the gym, eyes flickering over the tables that had been set up with volunteers from different housing organizations, medical groups, and job corps people there to hand out information.

"You followed me here? When?"

"Two years ago. Right after you moved here. I moved here, too." His eyes seemed to drill into mine. He always focused intently, his attention single-minded and direct. I first met him when I was fifteen and he was seventeen, but I always thought I was the grown-up because he often acted so childlike. It wasn't until later that I realized he had a form of Asperger's Syndrome. I

19

was simply a child genius. Madison was borderline autistic and a child genius.

Asa. His name is Asa now. He's not the teenager you knew. This is someone new.

"You were here? You knew I hired private detectives?" I had assumed the 'private' in 'private detective' meant that they worked somewhat covertly, but apparently I was mistaken. "Why didn't you contact me if you knew I wanted to see you?"

"I told you. I wasn't sure I could trust you. You did a lot of work for the government. But once you sold your company, I thought you might be okay again. This is a good song, too."

Heart of Gold. I kept my temper with difficulty. It never did any good to get mad at him. If I did, he'd get more withdrawn. "I sold the company three years ago," I said softly.

He nodded. "I know. I waited until I could be sure."

I longed to grab him by the shoulders and shake him. I'd been searching for him for five years and now he was telling me he was here all along, standing in the shadows and watching. "Damn it, Madison, you know you can trust me. I've spent a lot of time and money searching for you. Why the hell didn't you get in touch with me?"

"My name is Asa. Forget about Madison." He drew away from me and his lips, partially hidden by his beard, flattened into a straight line. "People change. I wasn't sure about you."

"Yeah. No kidding." I glared at the computer monitor, the gray words on the black background imprinting on my brain. *Age, birthdate, birthplace, terms of service, branch of service.* It was like a foreign language. Nothing made sense.

"The government put me in prison. I had to be sure you weren't working for them." That was as close to an apology as I'd get from him. He never apologized. Never said he was sorry. Never expressed regret. *Why should I?* he asked once when I challenged him about that. *I'm not wrong. You're expecting an unrealistic reaction.*

I scrolled through the information, flipping to the next screen. *Avenal State Prison, Avenal, California.* "What were you doing in California?"

"It's a long story." He stood. "Come on."

"I can't leave. I'm volunteering here." I noticed all the empty spots on his record. "We need to update this."

"You don't understand. It might be dangerous. We need to leave before anyone sees me. I took a big chance coming here but I had to see you."

"I wanted to see you, too." I took a deep, steadying breath. "I owe you, Madison—Asa. I took your idea and I built a software company on it. I owe you a lot."

He regarded me, dark eyebrows drawn together in confusion. "What idea?"

"Your search algorithm. I took it and I built an interface around it. Didn't you recognize it? When the first browsers came out, they used your heuristics."

"Browsers?"

"You know. Computers connected to the World Wide Web. They use browsers to access different web sites like Alta Vista and Yahoo."

"Oh. That."

"It's the next big thing, Asa." I stood, too, and

turned so my back was to Theo, hopefully giving Asa and me some privacy. "There's a lot of money in browsers, and I'm getting a piece of it. I owe you because it was your idea."

"But you did something with it, so you don't owe me anything."

"We need to go." The big black man—Butterfly—had come around the tables and now faced us, peering over the computer. "I don't like this. There're too many people here."

"I know." Asa's gaze bounced from me to the computer then back to me. "Don't put anything in there about me. Pretend I didn't come here. I'll get in touch with you later."

"Wait, no." I put a hand on his arm when he tried to walk away. "Asa, don't go. You don't understand. I have money set aside for you in an account. I need to give you the information about it. There's no reason for you to be homeless anymore. You can buy a house or get an apartment and—"

"Don't you get it?" He shook off my hand and moved to join his friend, pushing against the computer table, which wobbled with his action. My box of disks tipped over and disks spilled out. Asa gathered them into a small stack. "I can't buy a house or rent an apartment or do anything normal. If I do, they'll find me. I have to stay homeless."

"Who will find you? I don't understand."

"I'll get in touch," he said over his shoulder. He and his friend walked around the tables, heading for the exit.

I tried to slip past the computer table, too, to follow him, but the hem of my yellow Stand Down T-shirt

22

snagged on the box of diskettes perched on the edge of the table. By the time I righted it and them, Asa and Mr. Butterfield were halfway to the door.

"Did you fill out your form?" Chessy stepped in front of the two men, effectively blocking their exit.

"We're not filling out any forms," the black man snapped. "Step aside."

"We're here to help," Chessy insisted. "You don't have to fill out everything. Give us what information you want to share. Oh, wait. You left your bag on the bleacher. Here, take another one. And take one for your friend." She pushed two plastic bags at the black man and he automatically took them from her.

I reached them, dodging around two other vets to do so. "Asa, what's going on?" I stopped in front of him, joining Chessy to block them. "We only want to help."

"You can't help me here. I came here to talk to you, but there's too many of them around." Asa tried to step around me but I grabbed his arm again.

"Too many of who? Who are you talking about? What happened?" I pulled him closer to me. "Why were you in prison?"

Chessy distracted Asa's big companion, tugging him to the intake table where we had brochures laid out. "Here, take some information with you even if you won't stay." She thrust several different flyers into his hands, now full of samples and paperwork.

Asa gazed down at the floor, at the wall, to the left, to the right—anywhere but at me. "They said I killed somebody," he muttered.

"What? That's ridiculous. You wouldn't kill anybody." I put both hands on his biceps and shook him. "Asa, look at me. Don't pull your tricks on me. Tell me what happened."

"I don't know what happened." He stared down, his hair hiding his face. If this had been any other man, I would have said he was checking out my boobs. But this was Madison—Asa. Boobs weren't high on his list of Noticeable Items.

"Okay, that's fine." I had a lot of experience dealing with his fugues. We had once been best friends, our friendship born out of our shared misery at being the youngest PhD candidates ever at M.I.T. I knew Asa could be infuriatingly obtuse unless he was questioned in exactly the right way. "Tell me what you know, then."

"We gotta go, man." Mr. Butterfield said. "Come on." He dropped the bags and the paperwork on the table, some of the samples scattering onto the floor.

"You stay out of this," I snapped, my hands still on Asa's arms. "Tell me."

"They trained me to kill people when I was in the Marines." Asa twisted his neck, still focusing anywhere but at me.

"The Marines?" I almost choked. "I thought you got drafted into the Army. How the hell did you end up in the Marines?"

"I was drafted to the Army, but they found out I could shoot so they sent me to the Marine school for snipers."

I gaped at him, my mind trying to wrap itself around the idea of this socially inept math genius as a sniper. Holy shit in a bucket, what a mismatch that was.

"I was really good at it, so I did it a lot. When I got out, I couldn't get a job. That's when I think I was hired to kill somebody." Asa raised his head then and stared me straight in the eyes. "I'm not sure. That's why I needed to see you. I need you to get into my head and figure out what I did."

"Oh, crap." I knew exactly what he meant. It all started to make sense to me now. He used to have blackouts where he didn't remember what he did. I knew how to question him to find out the details. But murder?

Impossible. This was Madison, or Asa, or whatever name he went by. I knew him. There was no way he was a killer. Okay, yes, he'd been a soldier, but a killer? I pushed speculation off to the side for the moment. "You went to prison, though? They convicted you?"

"That's where I met Butterfly. He didn't think I should have been convicted. I got out four years ago." His dark blue eyes were haunted. "I didn't mean to kill anybody, but I think I did."

Movement in the middle of the gym caught my attention. Vets were gathered around all of the tables except for the one on the end, near the rear exit. The two young men who manned that table—a job coalition from the southern suburbs—were moving around the card tables where they had their brochures laid out. Vets moved out of the way of the two men when they hurried across the gym.

They were too intent on me. Or on Asa. "Go," I said, releasing him. "I'll meet you at your lucky spot. Eight o'clock tonight."

"You will?"

I turned to Asa's friend. "Get him out of here."

The big man saw the two men walking toward us. "Let's go," he said, grabbing Asa by the arm.

"Stand fast," I said to Chessy while I moved into place, blocking the exit with my body so Asa and his friend could leave.

"You got it, sister." Chessy angled her body, effectively covering the space on my right. "Can I help you?" She grabbed the nearest man and jerked him to a halt, tugging on his blue cardigan sweater. "We can't allow you to leave. If those vets wanted to talk to you, they would have done so here."

"Let me go. I want to talk to them." The man tried to shake her off, but she held him firmly.

"We don't allow the vets to be harassed by the vendors. I'm sorry, sir, but you need to wait here." The man tried again to free himself but Cat clung to him like her namesake, dragging him to a stop.

I feinted around the other man, dodging him to block his exit. "You can't go," I said. "There are people lined up at your table." I pointed and the man turned. His left foot landed squarely on a sampler tube of toothpaste and white goo squirted out.

I rammed my shoulder into him, and his feet slid on the toothpaste then kicked up. He landed on the floor with a crashing thud. I landed on top of him, piling into his chest. "Oh, I'm sorry," I babbled, digging my elbows into his stomach. I pretended to roll off of him and managed to land a knee on his groin, which made him sit up with an audible groan. "Oh, God, I'm so sorry. I'm such a klutz, I'm so sorry."

"What's going on?" Theo bustled over to join us, glaring at the two men. "You guys aren't supposed to leave your table. It's in the rules." He brandished a pamphlet, thrusting it at the man tangling with Chessy. The man grabbed for her and staggered back, hitting his

26

head on the wall with a resounding clunking sound.

I was pretty sure we didn't have any such rules brochure, but I followed Theo's lead. "That's one of the stipulations for having a table," I said, glaring at the man who struggled underneath me. "You get back there right now or I'll report you."

The man thrust me away with one sweep of his arm. I landed on my butt near the bleachers when the man jumped to his feet. He wedged himself between Chessy and his partner. She staggered back, tripping and falling. Theo steadied her then reached a hand to me to help me to my feet.

"You made a big mistake messing with us," the man I tussled with muttered while he helped his partner stand upright.

Chessy grabbed him by the shirt collar and hauled him around to face her. "No, you made a big mistake messing with me. Don't fuck with us unless you have either a warrant or some pretty damn big guns, you hear me?" She pushed him and he stumbled to the exit, glaring back at us over his shoulder. His partner followed, eyeing Theo balefully when Theo brandished the pamphlet at him.

Chessy turned to me. "What's going on, girl? Why's the CIA after you?"

Grace Slick started to sing *White Rabbit* in the background. I knew exactly how she felt.

Chapter Three

"CIA?" I brushed off my jeans, using that action to hide my face. "Why would the CIA be here? You're crazy." I smiled shakily at Theo. "And what was that about a rule booklet?"

Theo showed me the brochure he was clutching. *STD: Signs and Symptoms* brochure. "We should have a rules pamphlet."

"I'll get right on that," I said.

"Good."

"I was joking, Theo."

"I'm not."

Chessy stared at me, arms crossed over her yellow Stand Down T-shirt. "They were CIA. They weren't Fibs. Those dolts can't find their ass with both hands in a closet with a light on. For some reason the CIA was here pretending to be helpful. Why?"

Theo dropped the brochure back onto the table and shooed us back into place. "Ladies, we have people waiting to come in. Let's talk about this later, okay?"

I nodded gratefully. "Sure thing." No way in hell would I discuss the possibility of the CIA chasing me with Cat Chessy, the Queen of Government Conspiracies. She was sure that Monica Lewinsky was a puppet for Republican insiders; that Timothy McVeigh was acting as a covert agent for factions within the government when he blew up the Federal

Building in Oklahoma City; and that the so-called El Nino effect was really the result of secret meteorological testing. No day could pass without a news story being called into question.

"I'm checking out their table," Cat declared, staring at the now-empty canvas cubicle.

"Clean up that junk on the floor first, would you?" Theo pointed to the squished toothpaste and other tubes that burst open during our melee. "I don't want anybody slipping and falling."

"I'll handle it." Chessy stalked to the end of the gym and the locker rooms where we stored our purses and jackets and where janitorial supplies were located. She paused by the vacant table and grabbed a brochure.

"What was that all about, Alice?" Theo asked, thrusting an intake questionnaire and plastic bag at the man in front of the table. "Fill this out and come back," he snapped, keeping his attention focused on me.

The poor man grabbed the form and scurried away, undoubtedly sure he was the cause of Theo's temper. "Asa Hatterley and I are old friends," I said in a low voice. "We went to school together. He was drafted and I lost track of him."

"I heard you guys talking. He was in prison, right?" Theo snatched a completed intake form from another veteran and skimmed it quickly. "Second table on the left, over there." He tossed the form into one of our sorting boxes and waved in the general direction of the gym. "Alice, I appreciate the fact the guy is an old friend, but you need to be careful. You know as well as I do that some vets don't adjust well to civilian life."

"I know. Don't worry, Theo. I'm sure—" I handed a questionnaire to the next man in line. "Fill this out, please, and bring it back. Then we'll be able to direct you to the right spot."

"I have trouble with forms," the man whispered. Like so many of the vets here, he was dressed in shabby clothes and his matted black hair and dirty hands told me he'd been living on the street far too long. He shuffled in place, staring at the floor.

"I'll help you." I was happy to escape Theo's grilling. "Come on, we'll sit over here. I'll ask you some questions and I'll fill in the form for you." I grabbed a clipboard and led the way to the bleachers, gesturing to the man to sit. "Now then, what's your name?"

He settled near me but not close, for which I was thankful. I suspected he'd be pungent. "Leo Griffin," he said in a hoarse voice.

"Okay, Leo. Maybe you can answer a couple of questions for me. What was your branch of service?"

"Eighty-Second," he muttered. "Out of Fort Bragg."

I wrote *82nd Airborne*. I'd read enough intake sheets to understand his cryptic comment. "What were your dates of service?"

"I know that guy you were talking to." He turned toward the exit doorway. "The one with the big black guy."

"Really?" I tapped the clipboard with my pencil. "Your dates of service?"

"March 1969 to April 1973. I'm sure I know him."

I nodded while I wrote down his information. Most vets were pathetically anxious to find familiar faces among the other vets who showed up. I doubted he knew either Asa or Mr. Butterfield. "What brings you to Minnesota? Are you staying with friends or family?"

He swung back around, still hunching over with his head bowed and his eyes focused on the wood of the bleachers where we sat. "I been traveling around. I heard this might be a good spot to be for a while."

"Where are you staying?"

He picked at a tear on the leg of his jeans with broken, claw-like fingernails. His fingers were long and slender with red, ragged cuticles. He was a short man and somewhat squat, although his loose, faded Hawaiian shirt and baggy jeans hid his physique quite effectively. "Been hanging out at the Mission over on 83rd. Where do you live? You live around here?"

I ignored his question and made a mental note to check with Pastor Ludwig at the Mission. "What brings you here today, Leo? Do you need specific services?"

"Where's that guy from? He's from around here, isn't he? I'm sure I served with him."

"I doubt that. He was Marines. You were Airborne." I noticed Theo gesturing me to the tables where four veterans were lined up. "I'm sorry, I have to go. Do the best you can with this form and turn it in to us. There are several groups here today to help you. Feel free to wander around and talk to anyone. And make sure to get a bag before you leave. There's useful stuff in them, like shampoo and things, with all kinds of contact information for shelters and government agencies."

I stood but Leo grabbed my hand, yanking me back down to the bleachers. "Don't go. I can't fill out that form. I'm no good at shit like that. I'm sure I know that guy. He was buddies with a friend of mine. Where's he living? Maybe I can track down my buddy."

I wiggled my hand out of his surprisingly strong

grip. "We don't give out information about the people who come here." I thrust the clipboard at him, pushing it against his chest and circumventing another grab for me. "Fill this out and Theo will talk to you in a few minutes." I got away while he was fumbling with the clipboard.

"Did that guy grab you? What was that all about?" Chessy asked when I joined her and Theo. She had a plastic bucket and a rag and was busily swabbing the floor, pushing the rag around with her foot while she greeted incoming visitors.

"Nothing. Just the usual. Too much stress, not enough good food, and probably a little bit of alcohol abuse tossed in." I turned to the next man in line and handed him the intake form and small bag of freebies.

"I checked that table. I took some of their business cards. I'm going to call and find out if they're legit or not." Chessy dragged one of the tables forward slightly to partially cover the dampness. "That's good enough."

"Of course they're legit." I glanced at a form a vet handed me and skimmed the information. "Why don't you start with table three?" I suggested. "They can put you in touch with social services." The man nodded and ambled away.

"What do you mean, of course they're legit? How do we know?" She held up a pasteboard business card. "Anybody can have a few business cards printed. I'm calling. There's a pay phone in the lobby. You got a quarter?"

"I have a mobile phone." I reached for my denim book bag, tucked under the table.

"Are you crazy? Everybody knows the government monitors the calls made on those phones. They can't monitor every pay phone, though."

I didn't bother to argue. Instead, I dug in my pocket and pulled out a handful of change. "Here. Get me a can of pop while you're at it."

"I'm on it." She picked through the coins and grabbed a few quarters then headed for the exit, matching pace with a couple of vets who were leaving.

Chessy soon returned and reported that the phone number on the business card went to an answering service. She was told the volunteers had been called away on urgent business and the social services group would pick up their materials from the Vets Administration office if one of us could pack them for them. "They're phonies, I'm sure of it," she said. "Urgent business, my ass."

"Maybe they are, but there's no way for us to find out who they are," I pointed out.

"I'll find out," she said. "I've got an idea on how to track them down."

I didn't ask for details. Chessy was taking Criminal Justice classes part-time at the University and fancied herself a budding detective. If she said she'd find out, she probably would. She was learning quite a few surprisingly useful tactics in her college classes.

We were kept busy for the rest of the afternoon with answering questions and helping the volunteers who manned the information tables. I also taught a brief seminar about job hunting and one introducing the vets to basic computer use, an essential tool if they were going to produce a resume. Most of them had never even seen a personal computer, much less used a keyboard, but I felt we needed to try at least.

The last attendee left at six that night. This was the

final day so everything had to be taken down, boxed up, and loaded into the panel van we borrowed from the Vets Administration.

"How do you know that guy? The one from earlier?" Chessy asked while we put away our materials. "The one who's being chased by the CIA."

"It's a long story." I sat down at the computer and began backing up my data, using a new box of 3.5 inch floppies I purchased for this event.

"We have time," Theo said. "Talk."

I considered a simple lie, but I'm not very good at that, so I settled on an abbreviated form of the truth. "When I knew him, his name was Madison. He grew up in St. Paul. I grew up in Richmond. We were both sort of advanced, academically."

"Advanced how?" Cat briskly sorted brochures to put them in their proper boxes.

This was the tricky part. It was always hard to talk about my academic past without sounding like I was bragging or blowing it out of proportion. "We both tested out of high school when we were about eleven or twelve years old."

"What?" Theo stared at me, unsorted intake forms in his hand. "Tested out?"

I nodded, focusing on the computer screen. "My parents were on the faculty at the University of Minnesota. They knew a child prodigy when they saw one. I was reading by the time I was three and could speak four languages by the time I was four. When I was five, I was reading at a college level." *Although I could barely understand the moral and ethical concepts I was reading,* I thought, remembering my confusion about Dostoevsky and Hawthorne.

I no longer was bitter about my unconventional upbringing. My academically astute parents viewed their three children more as science experiments than progeny and we were treated accordingly. My two sisters excelled in their chosen fields—medicine and clinical psychology—just as I excelled in math and computer science.

"What happened?" Cat tucked stacks of brochures into a cardboard box, ready to use at our next event in the fall.

"Madison's parents didn't know what to do with him. His father was a factory worker and his mother—" I hesitated, not sure how to describe his mother. "She was a flower child, I guess you could say." A drug-addled, irresponsible child-mother who hated her drunken husband and her odd child, blaming both of them for her squalid lifestyle. "Anyway, I went to M.I.T. when I was a kid."

"How old?" Theo still stared at me. I could see him out of the corner of my eye while I removed one diskette and inserted another. The computer churned, making clunking noises when data was transferred to the diskette.

"Almost thirteen. I finished my second PhD when I was nineteen. I was at M.I.T. for a year when Madison was admitted. He was sixteen. I was fourteen. Unbeknownst to anyone, he'd been taking college level courses under a different name, so while he was in junior high school, he had enough credits for a B.S. degree."

"Why'd he do that?" Cat hefted the box onto the dolly. "Why not go to college?"

"He didn't know he could. He didn't have a lot of

supervision." That was an understatement. His father spent most nights after work drinking at a bar and his mother spent most of her time finding different men to sleep with. "Besides, Madison—Asa—he's not very social. He was probably more comfortable taking correspondence courses than sitting in a class. He probably never even considered the idea of going to a campus."

"I'm surprised his parents didn't notice," Theo said, his lips thinned in disapproval. "Wouldn't they notice if he's acing all his classes?"

I swapped out the full diskette for an empty one. "His parents weren't really there, if you know what I mean. And they didn't have any money for school anyway. Madison paid for the classes by gambling."

"Gambling?" Theo stopped any pretense of working and now focused solely on me. "What kind of gambling?"

"He bankrolled an adult to play in backroom bar poker games for him. He was too young to play, but he got this guy to play for him."

"How did that work?" Chessy asked. "Most bars won't let a little kid into a backroom poker game."

"They will if the guy says it's his kid and he doesn't have a wife to take care of the kid. They were like real Oliver and Fagin characters, but Asa was Fagin."

Chessy and Theo regarded me blankly then Chessy nodded. "Oh, you mean like the movie, *Oliver*. My mom loves that movie. It's got a lot of singing and dancing. She likes that kind of thing."

"Close enough," I said. "Asa and this guy played the backroom circuit. They worked out a system where Asa would sit next to the guy and watch what hands were dealt. Then he'd signal the guy what to do. Asa had a real knack for poker."

"It's not always that easy," Chessy said.

"My first PhD was in Human Cognition. I was interested in artificial intelligence and I had to take a lot of cognition and psych courses." I noticed Chessy's puzzled frown so I hurried on. "Anyway, the way he described it to me, it's like when Asa played poker, he was able to immediately analyze each opponent's mannerisms and risk-taking behavior. Based on that and his ability to memorize cards, he could accurately predict what most opponents would bet about eighty-percent of the time."

"Poker, huh?" Chessy began filling another box with more brochures and office supplies. "It's hard sometimes to figure out somebody's tell."

A *tell* was that unique signature that everyone had, the little twitch or tic or nervous gesture that signaled stress or excitement. "That's the really interesting thing about him," I said. "Madison doesn't have a tell."

"Everybody has a tell," Cat declared.

"He doesn't. Trust me. Play poker with him sometime and you'll see." I inserted a new diskette into the drive and continued copying files.

"Okay, so he lied and got a college degree. How did he get to M.I.T.?" Theo resumed sorting through intake forms. I was relieved. This was the tricky part and I didn't want too much attention on me while I skirted around the truth.

"It came out that he had gamed the system and that pissed off a lot of University people. It made the U look bad that some kid could ace their courses. But then they tested him and found out he was off the charts. M.I.T.

contacted my parents, they arranged for him to come with them when they visited me, so he could see the campus. And before you know it, he was on campus, working on a double Master's in Cognitive Science and Mathematics. That's when I met him."

There was no need to talk about my childish infatuation with a senior college boy in my M.I.T. degree program who tried to take advantage of a sixteen-year-old graduate student. No need to mention how Madison intervened and saved me from gang rape. No reason to describe how socially isolated we were and how lonely, a thousand miles from home with no one our age to talk to.

Except each other. Our friendship evolved into a love affair, two kids exploring their sexuality. It wasn't only the physical attraction. It was all the intellectual stimulation from our classes, from the challenges of finally being able to compete among our peers even though those peers were a decade older than us.

"Okay, you guys went to college together. What happened then?" Cat asked, ever practical. "How did he end up in prison?"

"I don't know. He graduated a year ahead of me and he was drafted right away."

"That's stupid," Theo said. "The guy's a genius. Why would they draft him?"

"I don't know. The chairman of his department protested like crazy, but he was drafted anyway. He wasn't any good at correspondence, and I only saw him once, when he graduated from Basic Training. He told me he was going into a special school. Then—I never heard from him again."

"Didn't you try to find out what happened?"

"Of course. I contacted his parents, but they were divorced and—" How to explain all the efforts I made as a twenty-year-old newly graduated student juggling a research grant, a new job at a new University, a new town, and a new life. "You need to understand. He wasn't very good at—" I threw up my hands. "Never mind." I powered down the computer then began dismantling it, rolling up cords and cables.

"It seems weird to me. Why would the government draft somebody who's a genius?" Theo tucked the intake forms into a manila folder. "And what's all that about prison? How does somebody who graduates from M.I.T. end up in prison?"

"I don't know and that's what has me worried. Madison—Asa—was not at all socially competent and it's really possible somebody took advantage of him. I need to find out what happened to him and why he's so worried now that people are after him." I loaded the heavy monitor into the padded box then put the CPU into its box, stacking both of them on the dolly I appropriated for use.

"He's got a reason to be worried," Cat said, stacking the last of her boxes on the dolly. "Somebody is after him. I'm telling you, those are government agents of some kind. Why the hell are they interested in him?"

"If people really are after him, then you need to keep away," Theo said. "I don't always agree with Chessy about all those so-called conspiracies, but sometimes she might be right. If the government is after him, who knows what might happen?"

"I won't know until I get his story." I put all the rolled-up cables into the shoebox I brought, tucking the box next to the computer. Then I lined up my disks, the 3.5-inch ones going into my shoulder bag and the other 5.25 ones going into the box to be dropped at the Vets Administration office on Monday.

As I did, I spied another one on the table with a label I didn't recognize. I used yellow labels for all of my diskettes but this one had a red label. When I examined it, I recognized it was a high-density zip disk. I never carried those with me because I didn't have a portable zip drive.

I slipped it into my bag along with the other ones. It was probably a spare that I tossed in at some point. I helped haul boxes out to the van which took several trips. I slipped into the restroom and swapped my Stand Down T-shirt for a blue-and-white striped knit top. Finally, at seven o'clock, everything was wrapped up.

"You want to grab a bite to eat?" Theo asked. He and Chessy were getting into the van, which they'd return to the Vets Administration.

"No, I'm beat. I think I'll go home. I'll talk to you guys later." I headed for my car, parked not far from the van in the parking lot.

"If you need anything, you call me," Chessy said. "I mean it."

I waved acknowledgement and went to my burgundy Ford Escort. The car was warm from its day in the sun despite the slightly opened windows. I had an hour before I had to meet Asa, if indeed he'd show up. I had enough time to grab a hamburger somewhere then drive to Asa's "lucky spot," the bar near the airport where he'd made much of his gambling money.

The place changed hands over the years and now was an upscale 'bistro,' catering to young professionals.

Asa would probably be turned away at the door, but if I went there I knew he'd find a way to get in touch with me.

I put my denim bag on the passenger seat and drove out of the parking lot, getting on the frontage road that paralleled busy Interstate 494, the main artery around the Twin Cities. As I did my bag sagged open and I glimpsed the odd diskette on top of the others inside. On impulse I changed direction, making a quick right turn at the stop light and getting onto the Interstate. Traffic was relatively light, but there was still a bottleneck at certain spots that had me zipping in and out of clogged lines of cars.

I reached the exit before the airport and drove up the off-ramp, barely beating the light to make a right, then racing south on residential streets until I reached a small strip mall. I parked in front of the computer store, grabbed my bag, and went inside.

Hacker's Haven was a mixture of Radio Shack and Blockbuster Video, with a few computers on display, a small shelf of mobile phones, racks of video game disks, and a large array of game consoles. Shelving at the back of the store held assorted computer peripherals, cables, wiring, electronic parts, and miscellanea.

Manny "The Mouse" Fury waved at me from the checkout counter. Like his name, he was a small, mouse-like youth with a thatch of brown hair, a straggly beard, and an equally scrawny body. What he lacked in physical appearance, he made up for in computer expertise. The Mouse was a gifted hacker whose hobby was dismantling old computers to create new ones.

"What's happening, Aly?" He was ringing up a sale

for a young boy who appeared to be buying a video game if the gory cover on the disk case was any indicator.

"Not much. I was wondering if you have a zip drive I can use. I've got a disk I want to check."

"Sure, no problem. Hang on a second." He finished ringing up the sale and handed the plastic bag to the kid. "Remember what I said, right?"

The kid nodded. "Got it." He left hurriedly, shooting me a suspicious glance as he went.

"Did you sell him a war game?" I asked.

"Hey. The kid said he was 18. He can buy a game rated M." Mouse shrugged his thin shoulders. "Just because the government has decided to label stuff, doesn't mean I have to enforce it."

I didn't argue with him. Mouse was opposed to the new video game rating system and he'd expound on his dislike at the drop of a hat. I avoided the subject as much as possible. I fumbled in my book bag and found the red-labeled disk. "Can I check this on your drive?"

"Use the machine in the back." He jerked a thumb over his shoulder. "You know where it is. Don't let anybody know I let you use it."

"My lips are sealed." The back-room machines were all the high-power ones and weren't really available to the public. I had helped Mouse customize a couple of them, though, so I had a few privileges the regular customers didn't have.

I edged my way through the metal shelving units at the back of the store and opened the white door leading to an equally crowded back room. Two desktop computers sat on one desk, one with the casing off and the insides exposed. That desk and another one were littered with computer parts, papers, and copies of *Byte* and *Computerworld.* I took the chair at the intact computer and tapped the keyboard. The screen cleared and the Windows desktop screen appeared.

I inserted the zip disk into the external drive and clicked the icon to give me a directory listing. The drive churned and clunked then a list of files appeared on the screen. I stared at the information scrolling past. I paused the display and double-clicked on a file which appeared to be an image.

"Holy crap," I muttered.

The photograph was grainy but clear enough to see presidential candidate Ruby Hart, naked on a beach with two young men stroking her body.

Chapter Four

I recognized her, of course. Anybody would. She was the most well-known public figure in America. A woman who was making a serious bid for the Presidency. This was a younger version of her, but her flame-red hair, high cheekbones, and big green eyes were unmistakable. The young version had curly, tumbling hair, exaggerated red lips, and heavy makeup, but she was still Roberta "Ruby" Hart, Senator from Minnesota and one of the Republican Party's darlings.

Naked, on a beach, with two young men doing God knows what to her. With her husband nowhere in sight.

I clicked on another picture, which was even more explicit. She was on her hands and knees and one young man was behind her and she was kneeling over the other man below her and her mouth—

"Holy crap," I muttered. Hart had a reputation as a straight-laced, Christian, upright lady with an adoring, albeit older, husband, a lovely daughter, a handsome son, and a constituency that would not approve of group sex.

I closed the pictures and scanned the list of files. Most were image files, but there were ten or twelve documents and a spreadsheet or two. I opened one of those and found page after page of dates, numbers, and initials that made no sense to me. I closed that file and opened another one. This was more current, apparently.

It, too, had dates, numbers, and initials, but the dates were more recent.

I sat back in the rickety office chair and stared at the screen. Where did the disk come from? I kept the computer table very tidy at the event because the equipment was loaned to us from the Vets Administration. I didn't want anything happening to their IBM-PC. Neither Theo nor Chessy used the computer. It was better to have only one person responsible for the data entry to minimize errors.

I ejected the disk and dropped it back into my bag. The only other person who was near that table was Asa. It had to be him. Where did he get pornographic pictures of one of the most powerful women in American politics?

There was one place to get the answer. I left the back room and went into the store, where Manny was talking to an elderly lady who regarded a mobile phone with an expression of dubious curiosity. "Talk to you later," I said while I passed.

"Good seeing you again. Stop by when you can stay and I'll show you some new software I'm developing. Cutting edge stuff."

Knowing Manny that could mean an incredibly delicate hack into a government database or a new software game featuring unicorns and fairies. I waved good-bye, hopped in my car, and headed east toward the airport.

Asa must have slipped the disk in with the others when he was sitting at the table. Did he know those men were after him? Is that why he handed off the disk to me? He said he'd been following me, had followed me to Richmond. He knew I'd be at the Stand Down event and he brought the disk, knowing I'd be able to read what was on it.

What happened to him from the time he graduated until now? War, prison, homelessness. None of that made sense. Asa was one of the most brilliant people I knew, and I knew more than my fair share. He could be making a killing on computer innovations, dot-com companies, or any of the new technology hitting the market.

Instead he was being chased, living on the streets, and meeting me clandestinely. None of this added up. I was a mathematician and that bugged the crap out of me.

I pulled into the strip mall in East Bloomington, one of many dotting the main highway leading to the airport. The Tee Time Bar and Grill occupied one corner of the mall next to a ladies' clothing store. I found a parking spot not far from the entrance and slung my denim bag over one shoulder before locking the car and going to the front door. The boxes of diskettes made the soft-sided bag bulge, but I wouldn't leave valuable data lying in my car.

I took a second inside the front foyer to let my eyes get accustomed to the murky darkness. The transition from sunset to smoky bar took some adjusting. The eating part of the place was on my right and the bar was on my left. A low wall separated the two areas, so smoke from the bar seeped into the restaurant.

I took a step to my left and scanned the rectangular bar surrounded by small round tables. A handful of people sat on bar stools and three of the tables were occupied. I didn't see anyone who looked like Asa. I went back to the foyer and the hostess, a tiny woman in an equally tiny black miniskirt and towering high heels, approached me.

"Are you Alice?" she asked.

"Yes, I am."

"Follow me, please. Your party is waiting." She sashayed off into the restaurant, moving confidently on those impossible stilettos. I tried to figure out how she kept her miniscule skirt from riding up while maintaining her balance. It was a feat I know I couldn't have managed.

We went through a dimly lit room filled with diners, through a doorway, and into another room that was half full. She wove her way around the tables and through another archway into a smaller room with six or seven tables, three of which were occupied. A bank of windows were near the parking lot, the glass darkened, probably for privacy.

The hostess gestured into the room then left. I stopped, uncertain where to go until I saw the big black man at a table facing the doorway. I would not have recognized him except for his surprising size. He wore a dark green dress shirt rolled up at the sleeves and a tie that was loosened around his neck. Despite his size and physical presence, he seemed like a busy executive who stopped by for a drink after work.

A man sat opposite him, his back to the door. It wasn't until I neared them that I recognized Asa. His shabby clothes were gone, replaced by dark trousers and a stylish pressed blue dress shirt and a sedate blue-striped tie. He stood when I reached the table and smiled at me. His beard was trimmed closely to his chin, highlighting his high cheekbones. Straggly, matted hair was replaced by trimmed and clean dark brown hair swept back from his face with a hint of curl. All trace of the dispossessed homeless person was gone. In his place was a sophisticated urbanite, a hip man with striking good looks and excellent taste in clothing.

"I didn't recognize you." I took the chair he pulled out for me. "This afternoon or right now. I don't understand. Where did you get those clothes? Where do you live?"

He put his hand over mine where it rested on the table. His nails were manicured and appeared better than mine with my rough cuticles and short-cut nails. His were neatly trimmed and buffed. "Did you bring it?"

"The disk?" I reached for my bag, which I'd set on the floor, but he squeezed my hand.

"No. Not here." He ran his fingers over mine, touching the small bones gently. "I ordered a drink for you. I thought you might be past the Tequila Sunrise phase, so I ordered white wine." He smiled at me, his eyes intent on mine. "It's good to see you, Alice. You don't know how much I've missed you."

I pulled my hand away from his. "You missed me so much you moved here and never got in touch with me?" I kept my voice low with difficulty. I searched for him for years and he was a few steps behind me. "What's going on? I saw what was on that disk."

Asa leaned back in his chair and smiled triumphantly at Butterfield. "I told you she'd read it. I told you."

The black man scowled at me. "The less you know the better it is for you."

"It's a little bit late for that," I snapped.

Asa leaned to one side when a waitress appeared and set a lazy Susan of appetizers on the table. "Thank you," he said, smiling at her. "Bring us another round of drinks, would you?"

The girl nodded, her gaze lingering on his face. "Be right back." She hurried away, casting one look back over her shoulder at him.

I knew why. This suave, confident man was the epitome of a successful businessman with a hint of dangerousness about him. He was sexy and sweet, all at the same time. What happened to him in a few short hours to transform him?

Asa handed me one of the small plates the waitress set down. "When I was drafted, they did a series of medical and psychological tests on me." He handed a plate to Butterfield and gestured to the platter of appetizers. "Dig in."

"Asperger's Syndrome?" I asked.

He nodded. "I was lucky. One of the psychologists was involved with experimental treatment of high-functioning autistics. They came up with a treatment plan that helped me."

Butterfield glared at Asa. "It helped you right into prison."

I sipped the wine sitting next to my right hand. It was crisp and perfectly chilled. Not the house wine, that's for sure. "Back up," I said. "What happened when you were drafted? I wrote to you and I contacted your parents. It's like you fell off the face of the earth."

His mouth twisted up in a wry smile. "My parents divorced. Dad died in a car accident, driving drunk. Mom is someplace in Vegas. The last I heard she was dealing blackjack at a third-rate casino off the Strip.

They didn't really care what happened to me. Once all the publicity about their child genius wore off and they found out they couldn't exploit me, they lost interest." He spoke without bitterness, but I heard a hint of remorse in his factual voice.

"My parents are gone, too. Dad got cancer and Mom remarried and moved to Oregon. She had a heart attack a year ago." I put a couple of celery sticks, chicken wings, and mozzarella sticks on my plate and dolloped sour cream next to them. "What happened in the Marines?"

"I was drafted," Asa said, sipping a tall glass of dark beer. "But it wasn't completely legit. Somebody gave it some help. I didn't find out until later that it was rigged. The military wanted me, you see."

"They wanted your brain," Butterfield muttered. "Figured they could put it to good use."

Asa nodded. "You remember what it was like on campus, Alice. Government recruiters were everywhere. And every time they approached me, I turned them down. Well, they figured a way they could get me without needing my consent." He regarded me steadily. "The same way they got you."

"They never got me," I said. "I never worked for the government."

"What about the grant you had at Carnegie-Mellon? What about the D.O.D. contract work you did at the Supercomputer Center? What about all those government contracts you had for your company?"

"That's different." How did he know about the grants? The contracts? I sipped more wine, wondering how much of my past was private and how much was known.

"You worked for the government. So did I. My work was a little more straightforward." He fell silent when the waitress returned with our drinks.

"Anything else I can get for you?" She stood close to Asa's left arm. Her skirt wasn't as short as the hostess' skirt, but it still showed a lot of her long, slender legs.

"Not right now." Asa raised his eyes to her, one hand sliding against the side of his beer glass in a caressing, sensual fashion. "Thank you."

She smiled and backed away, almost falling over a chair while she moved. He turned to me when she was gone. "As I said, I was medicated when I got into the service. And they taught me biofeedback and some other tricks to help manage my symptoms. Then they found out I was excellent at two things: strategy and marksmanship."

"Guns? You?"

He plucked an onion ring from the tray and put it on his plate. "It's all concentration. Shooting is just…" His eyes lost focus and I could tell he was deep in a memory. "It's Zen."

I nodded doubtfully. "What about the strategy part?"

"Ah, now that was interesting. It was jungles and guerrilla warfare and trying to anticipate what an unconventional enemy will do. Computers weren't around, at least not where I could use one. But I really didn't need one."

"I don't get that." Butterfield set his empty beer glass aside and reloaded his plate with wings, cheese sticks, and onion rings. "I've seen how you do that stuff, you know, count cards and calculate stuff in your head.

How's that work?"

"You know about the cards?" I asked.

"Sure. That's why Skinny there survived prison." He gestured at Asa with a chicken bone. "Otherwise he woulda died."

I turned to Asa. "Would you please tell me what happened to you?"

"Okay. The short version. I went to the Marines. They trained me to be a sharpshooter. I got out after four years and I drifted. I didn't know what to do with myself. Remember I said they medicated me? Well, I didn't know it, but some of the medication was—" He turned his face away, his eyes once again distant.

I waited for him to speak but he seemed lost in thought. I tapped my empty wine glass but he apparently didn't hear me.

"Hey, man." Butterfield spoke sharply, snapping his fingers once. "Chill. Get frosty. Remember your hook."

Asa blinked and seemed to return to reality. "Yeah. Thanks. Some of the medication was experimental. I got prescriptions after I left the service, but I think they messed me up. That's when I killed that man."

"What man?"

"Harry March."

I switched my empty glass for the new glass of wine, giving myself a chance to digest that information. "I don't remember it."

"It was 1976. He was killed walking to his car in Los Angeles. He made movies and was going to the movie studio."

Where was I in '76? I graduated in '71 at the age of 19, got a research job at Carnegie Mellon, worked there for a few years then worked at the Supercomputer Center. In '76 I was still in Pittsburgh, embroiled in a love affair that went nowhere and in a dead-end job that bored the crap out of me. "I don't think I read about it," I said. "Why was his death important?"

"Because he once dated a girl named Roberta Hart who wanted to become president someday. And he had pornographic movies of her and he was going to take them public unless he was paid a lot of money."

"Holy crap," I breathed.

"In the late 1960s she ran away from home, when she was a teenager in California. She hooked up with Harry March, who was a pimp and a porno kingpin. She made a series of pornographic films with him, then her father split them up. From what I could find out, he had her kidnapped."

"Yeah, a real Patti Hearst job," Butterfield said.

Asa nodded. "The old man claimed she'd been brainwashed by March. Her father threatened to press charges unless Roberta returned home. She refused. He didn't really have a leg to stand on because she was twenty at the time and no one could prove March had been with her when she was a teenager. Her father had her kidnapped and hospitalized. By the time she got out of the hospital, she was once again Daddy's little girl." He smiled lopsidedly.

"Did he know about the films?"

"If not then, he did later. Fast forward to 1976. Roberta is now married with two adorable children. Her husband, Redmond King, is a bigwig in the banking industry and he fully supports his lovely wife in her political aspirations. Her father decides it's time for her to start making her move in the Party. Through a series of really astute political maneuvers, she and her husband move to Minnesota, supposedly for his job promotion."

"And she decides to run for state representative," I said. "I remember that. My mother was upset because they weren't real Minnesotans. She wanted to vote for Hart because she was a woman and a young up-and-comer, but Hart was a Republican and my mother never voted Republican. She and my father argued a lot about voting for someone because of gender."

Asa toyed with the onion ring on his plate. I realized he hadn't eaten anything. He still appeared calm and confident, but I sensed a growing tension about him, like a spring being wound tightly. "There she is, starting off in politics and the Republican Party is grooming her for a high-level position. They needed a viable woman candidate."

"But in her past there were pornographic films standing between her and her ambitions. How did you get involved in all this?"

"Her father knew my commanding officer. I stayed in touch with my C.O. when I got out of the service." He stared into space again. Butterfield frowned and began to speak then Asa shook his head and said, "I was directionless. My C.O. knew that." He faced me. "I think they changed my medication so I would kill him. But I'm not sure. The drugs they gave me were intense. I don't know what really happened. What do you think, Alice? Am I a murderer?"

I searched his eyes, seeking some trace of the boy I used to know. He was gone. Madison was in the past. This was Asa. "I don't know," I whispered.

"Hell, no, you're no murderer," Butterfield stated.

"I know murderers and you ain't one."

I was happy he broke the solemn moment. "How do you fit into this?"

He shot me a gap-toothed smile. "Me and Skinny Boy met in prison. He was about to get his ass—" He stopped suddenly and his skin darkened. "About to get his ass whooped. I broke up the fight and helped him out."

There was an incredible wealth of untold stories in those few simple words. Asa concentrated on his food but I saw his hands tremble slightly when he dipped a celery stick into a glob of sour cream. "How long were you in prison?"

"I was in for thirty for aggravated b-and-e," Butterfield said. "Gated out after fifteen for doing clean time. Skinny and me, we made a killing inside."

"What? Killing?"

"We ran a card shark con," Asa clarified quickly. "Butterfly protected me and I counted the cards."

"But isn't that illegal in prisons?" I looked from one man to the other. "I didn't think gambling was allowed."

Both regarded me with innocent expressions. "Yes, ma'am, it is," Butterfield said. "We didn't play for money. Not money on the inside. We played for money on the outside."

I shook my head. "What?"

"There's a limited amount of reward to playing in prison," Asa said. "We had to be careful. If we were too successful, we'd be killed. Since both of us were short-timers, we played for a few favors in prison—better food or private showers or nicer clothes. But we also played for money on the outside."

"A con would give us a chit that we took to his homeboys. They had to honor it or he was dead meat." Butterfield's eyes widened and he set down his beer glass. "I'm sorry. That was nasty, wasn't it? I'm not much used to talking to ladies."

"That's fine." I waved away his momentary indiscretion. "How did you end up in prison, Asa? How did they catch you?"

Asa swirled the last of his beer and drained it. "I'm not quite clear on that."

"Medication," I said. "They drugged you."

"They did something to me. I'm not sure what. I was found not far from the place he died. My fingerprints were on the gun. I was a sharpshooter. It was a tricky and dangerous shot, one that I could easily make but one that would be hard for a regular shooter."

"You ever see him shoot?" Butterfield asked. "He's crazy good."

"I was given a public defender and two months later I was in a prison in California. I got twenty years. I was lucky I didn't get life, but the lawyer managed to get me diminished capacity and threw in all my military service, so I got a lot of sympathy."

"And that's where we met," Butterfield said. "You want that last chicken wing?"

I shook my head. "Please, take it. What did you do when you got out?" I eyed his clothing then Butterfield's. He was dressed as sharply as Asa. "How did you do this? The clothes and the haircut and everything?"

"Anything is easy if you have money."

"But—"

Asa nudged his plate away. "You know how easy it

is to hack a database. When I got out of prison I decided M.A. Hatteras had to become homeless. But that's not a fun way to live."

Butterfield snorted. "No shit."

"That's when I created Mason Dias, a.k.a., The Mad Hatter, owner of the Hacker's Haven chain of computer stores."

"You're the Hatter?" The Mad Hatter was a legend in the hacker community, a computer programmer so gifted he once broke into the FBI's computer system and sent the Director a private email telling him exactly how the break-in was done, chiding him for lax security. "But I've seen pictures of the Hatter. That's not you." The Hatter was a short bespectacled man with thinning blond hair and a paunchy gut.

Asa grinned. "It's easy to hire an actor to play a part."

"Mason Dias." My mind clicked into overdrive, rearranging letters. "One letter less," I murmured. Asa grinned and nodded.

"What?" Butterfield asked. "What's that mean?"

"It's the only test I ever flunked," Asa said.

"We were in an artificial intelligence course," I said to Butterfield. "Each person in the class created an artificial persona and programmed it for daily interactions. The assignments built on each other throughout the whole semester until our personas were interacting with each other and reacting to each other."

He nodded doubtfully. "Okay. I kinda understand."

"Our final was to have our individual personas avoid each other throughout a simulated day and do so in such a way that it didn't draw attention." That was a vast over-simplification and didn't come close to describing the hours of work that went into the programming. I slaved on that program for days, tweaking and refining and trying to anticipate any possible permutation.

Asa didn't. He spent at least a day thinking about it, reading through assorted textbooks. Then he vanished into the library where I found him, sitting in the middle of the Social Sciences section, an area we seldom visited. When I asked what he was doing with a pile of baby books around him, he said "research."

"When it came time for the test, we all launched our programs as part of the master program the instructor had devised," Asa said. "At the end of an hour, the instructor calculated how many times each persona had interacted with another one. I had zero interactions."

"You cheated," I said, struggling not to laugh. "I thought the teacher was going to have a stroke. He couldn't figure out how you did it." I turned to Butterfield. "Given the parameters of the test, there wasn't any way anyone could avoid another person totally."

Butterfield frowned at Asa, obviously struggling with the concepts. "How'd you do it?"

Asa shrugged. "I changed my name. Each persona had our names."

"And the instructor considered that," I pointed out. "He ran an algorithm to see if anyone had created an anagram of their name. A rearrangement of the letters in a name," I said to Butterfield, who appeared confused. "Asa did create an anagram, but he left out one letter, so the instructor's program failed to find it."

Butterfield looked from me to Asa, his face

squinched with thought. "You couldn't throw in a ringer, could you? I mean, this program would figure you were a whole new person. Wouldn't that send up an alert?'

Asa nodded. "I changed his program."

"Huh?"

"Asa's program went in, sought out the professor's program, and changed it allow a ringer, as you put it." Suddenly all the pieces began falling into place. "That's what you did," I whispered. "You launched a program to allow the creation of a new person."

He smiled. "My stay in prison taught me a lot of things. One of which is that it's very important to have the right persona, whether you're inside or out."

"So you created the Mad Hatter." I smiled at Butterfield, who appeared bemused by this conversation. "The Hatter is a legend in computer circles. He's a hermit, like Howard Hughes was. The Hatter made a fortune on a new computer keyboard design. He's got a chain of computer stores that are the coolest thing around. Rumor has it he owns major shares in companies like Google and Silicon Graphics and a lot of shares in Apple and Microsoft."

"What's a google?" Butterfield asked.

Asa grinned. "I'm betting it's money in the bank." He glanced over his shoulder.

As though called by telepathy, the waitress appeared and set the small serving folder on the table. "I hope everything was satisfactory," she said with a dimpled smile.

"Perfect. Thanks." He smiled in return and picked up the faux leather folder, opening it to examine the bill.

She moved away. I intercepted her speculative look. "I believe you've caught the attention of our server," I said.

"What?" He glanced at me then returned to examining the bill. "That's not important."

"Not important? Most men would be flattered to be the subject of female attention."

He took a slender wallet out of his back pocket and pulled out two twenties. "Her attention isn't important to me. I love you."

He said it so matter-of-factly that I wasn't sure I heard it. "What?"

"I love you." He tucked the bills into the faux leather binder and set it next to his plate. "I've always loved you. You're the only woman I'll ever love." He picked up his beer and finished it in one long swallow.

Chapter Five

I stared at him then at Butterfield, who shrugged, massive shoulders rising and falling. I turned back to Asa. "That was years ago. You can't still love me."

Asa set the glass down. "Of course I do."

"Haven't you met any other women since we were involved? Haven't you had other relationships?" I was stalling for time, struggling to figure out what to say.

"Why is that relevant? Do you think I'd compare you to them? Is there some standard of love that I'm supposed to measure my love against?" His navy eyes were wide and guileless. The questions were legitimate, at least to his way of thinking.

That was the key. I had to remember. Asa was not like other people. His reasoning was straightforward and logical if it were a perfect world. Unfortunately, we didn't live in such a place. I had no response for his declaration. I couldn't claim to still love him. He had been my first love, but he wasn't my last one.

"What does it matter?" Butterfield said suddenly. "The big point is that you found each other again and she can help us figure out what happened to you to land you in prison."

I let my shoulders drop, realizing I was hunching as if to dodge a blow. "Why do you care what happened years ago? You served your time and you're free now. Apparently you have more than enough money to live the way you want to live. What can I do to help you?"

Asa glanced at Butterfield and a silent message of some sort passed between the two men. "Someone is after Madison Hatterley," Asa said. "You saw it today at the school. It's not the first time Madison has been a target."

He spoke of himself like he was talking about a stranger. I suppose in some ways, Madison Hatterley, homeless person, was a stranger to The Mad Hatter. I think in the old days he often was able to step away from involvement and view himself and his actions dispassionately. That's why he was such an exceptional A.I. programmer. Asa saw human actions in terms of cause and effect and seldom factored in the randomness of emotion.

"When did it start? Is that why you became homeless in the first place? Was somebody after you?"

Asa smiled impishly. "I became homeless because I was a mess. Now I'm occasionally homeless, when it suits my purposes." He glanced at a large, expensive-looking watch on his wrist. "Speaking of which, let's continue this talk at home. I'm sure you have more questions."

"Home? Where's that?"

"We have a building in the Minneapolis Warehouse District, not far from the river."

"We?"

Butterfield pushed back his chair. "Skinny has the third floor, I got the second. Ain't nobody bothering him unless they go through me first."

I leaned over to pick up my bag from the floor. When I did, my view through the window shifted and I noticed a car in the parking lot behind my car. Two men were in the front seat, barely visible in the pool of light cast by the old-fashioned T-arm lamps scattered throughout the lot. The window to the restaurant was almost opaque, but I could see the parking lot clearly. "I think someone is watching my car."

"I know they are," Asa said. "I'm counting on it. You'll ride with me. Give Butterfly your keys. He'll take care of your car."

"But how—?"

Butterfly held out a hand the size of a catcher's mitt. "We do this kind of shit all the time. Take a chill pill, I got this."

I reluctantly dropped the keys in his palm. "Won't they watch my house, too?"

"Perhaps." Asa stood. "If they do, we'll use it to our advantage. Ready to go?"

I got up and followed him out of the small room, into the larger room then to the main restaurant, threading our way between the tables. Before we got to the front entrance, Asa took a right turn and went into the bar. I hesitated when Butterfly left through the front door.

"This way, Alice." Asa gestured from the bar.

I entered the room and followed him past the bar and the half-dozen patrons seated there. Asa waved to the bartender, a swarthy man mixing a cocktail. The man nodded an acknowledgement but otherwise paid no attention to us.

Asa took my hand and led me through a swinging door at the back of the bar. "I own the restaurant," he said. "Through a series of dummy corporations. I made sure there was a private entrance." We walked down a short narrow hallway to another door and emerged into a small lot, gated on two sides and with a brick wall making up the third side of the private parking area. A sleek dark green BMW coupe sat near the door.

Asa opened the passenger door for me and I slipped into luxury. The seats were as soft as glove leather and the dash had inlaid bits of wood. The entertainment system embedded in the dash was state of the art. He got into the driver's seat and pressed a button on a small remote box near the gear shift. The gate in front of us began to swing open.

"Won't Mr. Butterfield be noticed when he drives away in my car?" I asked. "Will he be followed?"

"Your car will be followed but he won't be driving it. He's walking out of the restaurant with a woman who looks something like you, especially because she's wearing a hooded jacket and the parking lot is mostly dark. There's going to be an accident in the parking lot. The car behind yours will be hit. The two men won't be able to get away for some time. During the distraction, the woman will get into your car and drive to a store near your home. She'll leave your car there, change clothes, and Butterfly will pick her up and take her back to her apartment."

He drove out of the private lot, making an immediate left turn onto a frontage road. I turned in the seat in time to hear a crashing noise behind us. I caught a glimpse of Butterfield leaving the restaurant, a short woman next to him. Then Asa turned the corner and the restaurant was gone from sight.

"You'll drop me at the store and I'll get my car. Nobody will know where I've been." I regarded him in dusky twilight. He drove with single-minded concentration, shifting the car smoothly and keeping his gaze swinging right then left to assess traffic. "They won't know I saw you."

"That's the plan." He glanced at me. "Sometimes the simple plans are the best ones." He made a left turn at the traffic light, squeaking through while the light turned red, then he made a series of turns that had me lost. I'm sure it lost anyone attempting to follow us, too.

I sat back on the luxurious seat and started mentally tallying my list of questions. At the top of the list were the files on the zip disk. "How did you get the pictures of Ruby Hart?"

"I have the original tapes. From the movies. I made the stills from those."

"How did you get them?"

"I'm hoping you can help me figure that out."

"Me? How would I know anything about it?" I stared at him when his silhouette was highlighted then fell into shadows when we drove past street lights.

"You understand about people. Maybe you can tell me why someone would send me a box full of porno movies and old letters."

"Someone sent them to you?"

He nodded. "I received a box shipped to my old home address, the one the military had on file. I set it up long ago so anything sent to that address would be forwarded to a mailbox store. They contacted me when a package arrived."

"When did you get it?"

"A few months ago. I read through what was in there and that's when I realized who Harry March was and what he had to do with Roberta Hart." Asa slowed the car and made a right turn into an open space at the bottom of a three-story brick building on a corner of a city block. The bottom story of the building was painted white but the upper stories were dark brick with white trim around the five sets of windows on the street. The neighborhood was obviously industrial but lacked the grit and dirt I associated with commercial areas.

"Who sent it to you?" Other buildings on the street were a mix of brightly lit and all dark. Then I lost sight of them when we went downward into a drive barely wide enough for a large car and about twice as tall as a car. A wooden swing arm blocked any further movement down a slight incline.

"I have no idea who sent it or why." He took a card out of his shirt pocket and inserted it into a card reader. The swing arm lifted and we drove forward to a large steel door.

"Where are we?"

"Loft district." Asa flipped the card over and inserted it into a different reader and the door opened inward. "Most of the buildings around here are used by artists and sculptors. There's a coffee shop on the ground floor of this building. Butterfly has the second floor. I have the top one."

He drove forward into a small parking garage with space for about six cars while the metal doors closed after us. The walls were concrete blocks painted white and the beige floor gleamed, like polished linoleum. Overhead lighting was soft and highlighted each individual parking space. A black pickup truck and a boxy blue Jeep were parked next to each other near a red metal door.

Asa drove into a parking space across from the Jeep and turned off the car. I got out and went with him to the red metal door. He touched a button next to the door and it slid open, revealing a small elevator with an old-fashioned brass number panel and round raised buttons.

He inserted a key into the panel, turned it then pressed "3". The elevator chugged upward. "When I bought the building I kept as much of the old architecture as possible," he said, nodding at the polished wood paneling and the crown molding carved with leaves and flowers. "They had good workmanship. They took pride in what they did."

The car lurched to a stop and the doors opened into a small foyer. Straight ahead was a kitchen on my right and a laundry area on the left. A kitchen island with a sink separated that space from the living room. A small rectangular dining room table with four chairs was in front of the island, dark brown placemats on the surface. Everything was neutral-colored: birch wood cabinets, gleaming white appliances and sink, brown and white tile floor, and a white backsplash of subway tile made the kitchen feel large and airy.

I walked forward and saw a black metal spiral staircase leading downward on my left. I went into the living room, which had light-colored wood floors, recessed lighting, and exposed brickwork on the exterior walls. Floor-to-ceiling windows let in moonlight which lit the entire space with a soft glow. Walls on the left and right each had one doorway. Otherwise it was all open space with the kitchen, dining area, and living room all flowing into each other.

Asa touched a control panel on the wall and lights came on near the grouping of chairs in the middle of the room. Music began to play softly in the background. I recognized Eric Clapton's recent blues album.

"Do you want a glass of wine?" Asa went to the fridge.

"Yes, thanks." I took in the tasteful, simple home. The colors were all muted beiges and browns with occasional color coming from the red brick of the wall, a beautiful area rug of golds and burgundy, large framed photographs, the pillows, and an afghan tossed over the back of a brown couch.

"White wine or red?"

"Whatever you have opened." I turned to survey the room. "I guess you don't need the money I saved for you. I kept a thirty-percent share of the royalties I get."

"My investments have done well." He poured a dark red wine into a tall wine glass. "Perhaps you could donate it to the Vets Administration or another vets' charity."

I went to the couch but stopped when a large cat uncurled itself from the end cushion and stretched. It took me a second to decipher its appearance. The fur was a mix of black, yellow, and orange in a disorienting splatter-like pattern, or rather, lack of pattern. When it regarded me through sleepy golden eyes, I couldn't discern the shape of its face because of the paint-like effect.

"That's Duchess," Asa said from behind me. "She lives here or downstairs, in Butterfly's apartment. He rescued her when she was a kitten. She's missing a leg."

Sure enough, the cat jumped down and loped across the room to us minus her front left leg. The cat ignored me and made a beeline for Asa, who stood at the kitchen island. He shook a treat out of a jar and held it out to the small cat. The animal nipped it daintily out of his fingers then rubbed against him.

I added the cat to my growing list of shocks. When we were younger, Asa hated cats. He claimed they were too unpredictable to be acceptable pets. I went to one of the large windows to study the quiet street. "You never used to like cats."

"I never really understood them."

I smiled at the cars below me. "You think you understand them now?"

"They're random. It's the randomness that makes them interesting. Do you want some chips or anything to go with the wine?"

"What I want are answers." I turned.

He stared at me over the island, a bottle of beer in one hand. "About what?"

I raised my hands. "Everything."

He joined me in the living room where I was staring at an enormous photograph of the motherboard of a computer. The intricate detail of the circuitry and the brilliant colors of the sheathing made it seem like a close-up of some foreign city.

"Start from the beginning," I said, taking the wine from him and going to the couch to sit. "What happened in the Marines?"

"You don't need details," he said with a wry grimace. "I was lucky. I was shifted around a lot and for a while I was stationed in the Middle East. I learned two great lessons from my time in the service. How to shoot and how to manage my disease."

I sipped the wine, a smooth Cabernet with a silky texture. "You said they gave you medication. Are you still taking it?"

He settled on the couch opposite me. The cat jumped up next to him and pressed against his leg, fitting her body to his thigh. "When I got out of the Marines, I wasn't sure what to do with myself. I was able to get the prescriptions filled, but I didn't like how it made me feel. I tried to wean myself off them. When I went to prison, I had to go cold turkey. I was dependent on the drugs. But while I was in the Marines they also taught me discipline and focus and how to monitor myself. I learned about biofeedback and meditation. I found ways to handle it without the drugs. Sometimes I get off track, but I just need to focus and relax."

"Chill," I murmured. "Get frosty."

"You saw that. Butterfly knows when I need a reminder." He sipped his beer then set the bottle down on a glass and wood coffee table between the two couches. "It's like what you used to do. You could always tell when I was getting anxious. All you had to do was look at me in that certain way and I knew I had to refocus. You managed my disease long before I even knew I had it. That's why I need you now. Nothing I'm doing is working."

"What do you mean?"

"I can't get a handle on why someone is after me after all this time. I need you to figure it out. Your mind works in a different way than mine."

I smiled. "Anyone's mind works in a different way than yours. I'm not special."

"But you know me," he insisted. "They say I killed a man but I'm not sure I did it. I was messed up with drugs, but I don't think I did it. Why would someone pin a murder on me?"

"Let's back up a minute." I kicked off my sandals and drew my feet up on the couch next to me. The dark fabric was slightly nubby but still soft and comfortable. "Tell me what happened with the shooting."

Asa ran his left hand over the cat's body. She angled herself so she was pressed more firmly against him, her purr so loud I could hear it. "I have the trial transcripts. I'd like you to read them first, before I tell you what I remember."

"You're assuming I'll help you."

He tilted his head to one side. "You're curled up on my couch and you're making yourself at home. That's not the body language of someone who's going to reject me."

"Don't get smug. I'm thinking about it." I sipped my wine, going through my mental checklist of questions. "How did you do it?"

"Do what?"

"This." I gestured around the beautiful apartment. "Don't tell me about the Mad Hatter. The government has to be on to you. It's impossible to be completely hidden from them. Who are you really hiding from?"

For the first time he appeared less than confident. "It's a long story."

"I've got all night," I snapped. "Tell me."

His mouth quirked up in a smile. "All night? That sounds promising."

"Asa." I leveled a glare at him.

"Okay. I confess." He raised his head and regarded me. "I work for the FBI in a new task force they're starting. It's all about cyber crime. They've asked me to consult."

"Consult?"

"In a manner of speaking. They're trying to stay in front of hackers. They're worried about data breaches at defense installations and key embassies."

"And you hacked their communications system so it makes sense they'd have you help them." I nodded, my mind clicking through different scenarios. "They let you alone if you help them. Quid pro quo." I didn't wait for his answer, but continued, thinking out loud. "That means it's not the government who's after you. It's someone else. Someone who has to do with the shooting? But why? That was a long time ago."

"Who would send me that box full of damning evidence about Roberta Hart?" Asa picked up his beer and took a long swallow.

"A political rival," I said. "That's easy."

"Not so easy. How would her rivals get access to that material? As far as I know, no one knows about that unsavory time in her past."

"Nothing is really secret in the world anymore. Now that computers have become a part of daily life, it's so much easier to dig around and find information. What I can't figure out is why they haven't killed you."

Asa sat back on the couch, pressing his shoulders against the cushion. "What?"

"It makes sense. Whoever sent you that box must know you won't go to the media. They sent it to you to keep it safe. If Hart's people know you have it, why haven't they come after you?"

"Maybe that's who chased me today."

I shook my head. "Too amateurish."

"Why won't I go to the media?"

"Because you're the Mad Hatter, a reclusive millionaire."

"They don't know I'm the Hatter."

"Are you sure?" I stood up to pace, my usual mode

of deep thinking. "There's a common denominator here."

"Roberta Hart."

I shook my head. "Not only her. It's the government."

"I don't understand."

"She's a United States Senator now. She's part of the government infrastructure. You're part of the government infrastructure."

He propped his right ankle on his left knee and jiggled his foot. "I'm not part of the government."

"Of course you are. You're paid a fee, aren't you?" I didn't wait for his reply. I paced around the couch, staring at the wood floor. "If you're paid a fee, there's a record. If there's a record, someone can find the record. What committees does she serve on?" When he didn't answer, I stopped in front of him.

Asa stared at me, his bottle of beer partially lifted. "I never thought of that."

"She may have clearance for all kinds of data. But she wouldn't send you damning information about herself. It has to be someone else who wants to see her exposed. So to speak." I smiled faintly.

A shrill buzzing came from my denim bag, which I'd set on a barstool at the kitchen island. I fumbled it open and pulled out my mobile phone. "This is Alice."

"Hey, this is Chessy. Can you talk?"

I turned my back on Asa for privacy then realized it was both rude and futile given the openness of his apartment. I went back to the couch. "I thought you didn't trust mobile phones."

"I'm using a scrambler. They won't be able to listen in."

"What? Where did you get that?"

"At Radio Shack. They have everything."

"Radio Shack?" I doubted they sold a scrambler for mobile phones, but if it kept her happy, so be it.

"Listen, I got some intel about those jerks at the school today."

Asa watched me, frowning slightly. I moved the phone to one side. "My private detective is reporting in," I explained.

Chessy laughed. "I like the sound of that. Private detective. Do you think I can get a P.I. license without police experience? I'm taking Administration of Justice classes to get into law enforcement, but maybe I don't need it. Maybe I should be a P.I. instead."

"Chessy, why did you call me?"

There was a sharp crackling sound then she said, "Those guys. Okay. I went to the office where they said they worked."

"The job place?"

"Job place, my ass. There wasn't any office. I drove all around the block but all that was there was a strip mall with a bar, a barber, a clothing store, a shoe store. There wasn't anything like an office there. When I called the number again, the woman told me they were hired to answer phones and that's all they knew. They wouldn't tell me who paid them. Who signed them up for the Stand Down?"

The phone sitting on the end table near Asa's couch rang with two sharp buzzes. The cat jumped down and ran past me into the kitchen, obviously startled by the noise.

"What do you mean?" I asked Chessy while Asa answered his phone.

"You and Theo set up the vendors, right? Did Theo sign them up? Who cleared them to have a booth?"

"Theo didn't set them up. It's all set up by the Vets Administration. They choose the people who have booths there." I looked at Asa. He was speaking into the phone, his voice low. "It's the government again," I told him.

He nodded but I could tell he was focusing on whoever was speaking to him.

"Is someone with you?" Chessy asked. "Where are you? I tried calling your house but nobody answered."

"I'm not at home. I'm with a friend."

Asa smiled at me. "That's unfortunate," he said into his phone. "I'm not surprised, though. I'm sure she'll understand."

I pulled my phone aside. "What will I understand?"

He held up a hand for quiet. "Okay. Thanks." He hung up and stood, picking up my wine glass.

"No more for me," I said around my phone.

"There's a little bit left in the bottle. Finish it for me." He disappeared into the kitchen.

"Are you with that guy?" Chessy demanded. "Are you sure that's smart? Where are you? Are you sure you're safe?"

"Of course I am." Now I did wish I had some privacy. Chessy's questions were hitting a bit too close to home for comfort. I was in an apartment with a man I probably didn't know well at all. I had no idea where we were and he was a self-confessed murderer.

What the hell was I thinking?

"It's almost ten o'clock. When are you going home? I want you to call me as soon as you get home, you hear me?" Chessy sounded like a scolding parent. I could imagine her tucking her long red-blonde hair behind her ears while she readied herself for a fight. "Where are you now?"

I glanced around the room but there were no clocks visible. "I'm in south Minneapolis," I said. "I'll be home in an hour or so."

"You call me as soon as you get there."

"I'll call you in the morning," I said, overriding her protest. "It's late and I'm tired."

"First thing in the morning, you promise?"

"Of course. Thanks for calling, Chessy." I touched the *Off* button before she could continue to berate me.

"What did she have to report?" Asa came back to join me on the couch. He handed me the wine and reached over to pick up his bottle of beer.

I tucked my phone into my back pocket and took a sip. "Those guys who were chasing you at the school lied about who they were affiliated with. They gave a false address."

"It sounds like she cares a great deal about you. Are you good friends?"

"We met when I moved back to Minnesota. We both volunteered at several events and get together now and then for a movie." I sipped some more wine. "Yes, she's a good friend, I guess. I never thought of it that way. Who were you talking to? What will I understand?"

"That was Butterfly. He was reporting in, too."

"Was there a problem with my car?"

"No, he couldn't leave it where we planned. It's farther away."

"I should be going. It's getting late. I can't believe how fast time has gone."

"There's nothing like talking a conspiracy to make the hours fly. What did you mean about the government is involved again?"

"You should talk to Chessy about conspiracies. Anyway, the Vets Administration set up the vendors at the event today."

"Another government agency." He drained his bottle of beer and set the empty on the coffee table. "The Vets is a pretty low-key agency. If someone wanted access to their files, it would probably be easy."

I finished my glass of wine and leaned forward to set it on the table next to Asa's empty bottle. "It's probably not the most secure government department," I agreed. "And now I really should go. You've given me a lot to think about."

"I'll drive you to your car," he said, standing.

I got up, too. The room spun crazily then everything went black.

Chapter Six

The room was dark except for faint rectangles of light. Windows. I turned over and after a second I saw a gleam of pale yellow in the distance. I focused on it as hard as I could and finally decided it was a doorway.

At the same moment I realized I had to go to the bathroom. I raised my head and touched the bed around me. Unfamiliar bed, unfamiliar room, but familiar feeling of needing to pee. I fumbled my way out of the linens covering me and managed to sit up on the side of the bed.

I wore a long T-shirt, my panties, and nothing else.

Somewhere in the haze of my mind I knew this should be alarming, but I was too focused on getting to the bathroom to care at the moment. I lurched to my feet and took four staggering steps until I clung to the doorway lintel. I pushed open the door and entered a tiled bathroom dimly lit by soft wall sconces. Everything was in neutral tones. Beige towels, dark brown bathtub and shower, white sinks, pale yellow walls.

This wasn't my bathroom. Mine was pastel green and pale purple. Mine had a separate little room for the toilet. This one had a low divider. I didn't care. All I cared about was that the toilet was there and I reached it in time.

I ran some water over my hands then found my

way back to the bed where I collapsed.

When I awoke again the rectangles of light were brighter. Off-white linen roman shades covered three tall windows on my left. I propped myself up on pillows to peer around me. I was in a square room in a double bed with a plain wooden headboard. My coverings were dark brown and the sheets were pale beige. A beige upholstered chair was in the corner opposite me. My clothes were neatly folded on its cushion.

I pushed back the covers and looked down at my loose T-shirt, khaki brown with *Hacker Haven* printed above a picture of the HH logo—a stick figure of a running man with lightning bolts zapping him on the butt.

I did not own a T-shirt like that.

I stood, my bare feet touching a hard wood floor. I walked to the dresser against the wall to the right of the bed. It was made of pale wood, long and sleek with nine drawers and no discernable hardware. Another upholstered chair sat between the dresser and a closed door. A fluffy, pale yellow bathrobe lay on the chair. In the middle of the dresser was a black tray with a crystal goblet and a big bottle of Perrier water in a small ice bucket. The ice was still in tiny cubes. It hadn't melted.

I opened the bottle and poured water into the glass. A note on the tray sat upright on the folds of the stiff paper.

I'll explain

It was written in Asa's distinctive angular handwriting. Next to the tray was a black binder notebook, thick with pages. I opened it. *State of California vs. Madison A. Hatterley.* The trial transcript.

I sipped the water, letting anger wash through me. He drugged me. Asa drugged me, dumped me in here, changed my clothes, and—

My hands trembled so bad I spilled water when I set the goblet down. Did he rape me? I forced myself to catalog my body. There was no telltale stickiness between my legs. No pain, no stiffness, no soreness. It had been years since my last affair but I remembered the aftermath of sex. There was none of that here.

And this was Asa. I drew in a steadying breath, then another, then another. I wasn't raped. I was being treated like a guest at some kind of spa resort. I finished the glass of water, picked up the bathrobe, and went into the bathroom.

I took my time, luxuriating in the warm water, running through last night's conversation in my head. By the time I finished, I had a good idea what to say. I blew my hair dry with the dryer I found in the linen closet then examined myself in the bathroom mirror. I didn't wear much makeup but it felt odd without at least a touch of mascara and blusher.

I pulled on my clothing and sandals then settled down to read. It didn't take long. The legalese was dense and hard to decipher, but within an hour I had digested most of the text. I carried the book with me and opened the door.

I was steps away from the kitchen island and the small dining table in front of it. Asa and Butterfield sat there, plates of food in front of them, each man with a magazine folded on the table next to their left hand.

Asa wore faded blue jeans and a tucked-in dark blue work shirt. His neatly trimmed beard showed streaks of gray in the sunlight streaming through the skylights above the table. He pulled off his horn-rimmed glasses and looked up at me. "I can explain."

Butterfield sat opposite him with his back to my bedroom door. His dark blue T-shirt stretched taut against his back when he twisted in his chair to peer at me, hunching his right shoulder slightly.

I moved past the two men to the kitchen and the coffee pot sitting on the island. Asa watched me warily, turning in his chair to do so.

"Despite your best efforts, I assume my car was followed last night," I said. "Mr. Butterfield probably drove past my house in a different vehicle and thought the house was being watched. Therefore, you thought the best course of action was for me to stay here." I set the notebook on the edge of the counter and opened a cupboard near the stove. As I suspected, it contained the mugs. I pulled out a brown one with the Hacker's Haven logo on it. "You thought I wouldn't believe you and I would insist on leaving. If I left, you would be compromised. Therefore, you had to make me stay." I poured a mug of coffee, went to the fridge, and found the cream container.

I poured the cream into my mug, tilting my head to listen to the faint music playing overhead. "That's Neil Young singing. I don't recognize the song." I sipped the coffee then added another dollop of cream, stirring it with a spoon I found in a drawer. "You gave me enough of a drug to make me sleep, not enough to cause any residual side effects. Probably something from the benzodiazepine class. Maybe Valium or Xanax, both of which you have been prescribed in the past."

"It's Neil Young's album from last year." Asa

picked up a piece of bacon from his plate and snapped off a bite. "It's a new drug called Ambien."

I regarded him over the rim of the mug. "You are just as arrogant and just as overly confident as you ever were."

Butterfield gaped at me, a piece of toast in his hand, forgotten. I smiled at him. "He keeps forgetting that I'm as smart as he is."

"I didn't forget." Asa smiled faintly. "I've always said it's better to ask for forgiveness than permission."

I flung the coffee spoon at him, narrowly missing his head when he ducked. It clattered along the floor and disappeared under the couch. "Wrong."

"We were doing what we thought was—"

I fixed Butterfield with a quelling glare. "I appreciate that, Mr. Butterfield. But it was still stupid and ill-advised." I eyed the plate in front of him. "I'm hungry."

He sprang to his feet so fast I almost laughed. "You have a seat there and I'll get your breakfast for you. Relax. Have a seat. Go on there." He gestured frantically to the other empty chair, to the right of his chair. The fourth chair, on his left, was occupied by the cat, Duchess, who did not appear like she'd be amenable to moving.

Butterfield bustled into the kitchen while I sat, coffee mug in hand. Asa unfolded his magazine and set it next to his spoon, lined up to his placemat. *Byte.* I glanced at Butterfield's magazine. I couldn't see any identifying information but given the brightly colored photographs of men in football uniforms, I assumed it was *Sports Illustrated* or another periodical of that ilk.

"How did you know I didn't have some lonely pet

at home, waiting for me to return?" I asked Asa.

"I've done my research. You have your lights on a timer in the living room, your neighbors are elderly and go to sleep early, and you have no pets." He sipped his coffee from a mug similar to mine. "It seems like a charming house, by the way. Very cozy."

"It is. I'm happy with it." I regarded the plate of food Butterfield set in front of me. Scrambled eggs, bacon, sausage, and a flaky biscuit. The food steamed and the plate was warm, kept so in the oven no doubt.

Butterfield sat again and broke off a smidgen of bacon for the cat, who took it with a delicate nip. "It looks kinda small, maybe."

I shook out my napkin. "It suits my purpose. Let's see. Obviously, you've had a good opportunity to prowl around my neighborhood. Garbage truck?" I took a bite of scrambled eggs. They were delicious, very moist with a hint of rosemary. "No, maybe a repair truck of some kind? We've had a lot of cable television issues lately." I turned to Asa.

He smiled across the table at Butterfield. "You owe me ten dollars."

The big black man pulled a wallet out of his back pocket and extracted a bill. "She's a good guesser." He dropped the bill on the lazy Susan in the middle of the table and spun it to face Asa.

"I don't guess," I said. "I evaluate. For example, Asa was unsure about my reaction to his deception. That's why he's sitting where he is today. Normally he sits facing the kitchen with his back to the living room, but today he sat where he is because he wanted to see my face as soon as I left the bedroom." I cut up the sausage link as I spoke and took a bite. "Correct?"

Butterfield narrowed his eyes. "How'd you know that?"

"The placemat where he's sitting is uncreased. There are no crumbs near it. At my place setting, though, are a few breadcrumbs and a slight discoloration where a glass sat. Obviously someone uses this seat often. There was no reason for you to change seats. My feelings are irrelevant to you. Therefore, Asa must have chosen to change his seat."

"I told you," Asa said, sipping his coffee.

Butterfield finished the last bite of scrambled eggs on his plate and pushed it to one side. "You guys make me tired. You're thinking all the time."

I grinned at his rueful announcement. "It's a habit," I assured him. "We don't do it consciously. I suppose it's like you."

"Huh?"

"You're always assessing a situation to see if there is danger nearby. Possibly a byproduct of being in prison or perhaps a less than happy childhood." I smiled sympathetically at his stunned look. "A talent like that is as useful as excessive thinking, believe me. It's probably more useful, actually."

"That's why we make such a good team," Butterfield said, nodding to Asa, who watched us with a bemused smile. "He's brains and I'm brawn."

"Indeed." I glimpsed the cat, sitting across from me, her face barely visible above the edge of the table before ducking out of sight again. "I assume you want to find out who those men were at the event yesterday," I said to Asa. "Will you use me for bait?"

He frowned. "That's not quite the word I was thinking of."

"It seems appropriate to me." I buttered the biscuit and sampled it. "Very good. Your creation, I assume?" I said to Butterfield.

"Now how did you know Skinny didn't make the biscuits?" the big man asked.

"Good biscuits require a careful touch or the dough will be overworked and they come out tough. Asa doesn't have that kind of patience."

Asa grinned. "I told you."

Butterfield sighed, pulled out his wallet, and put another bill on the lazy Susan. "I should know better than to gamble with you."

"It isn't gambling with him. It's a science. He only bets on sure things." I turned to Asa. "Right? You're betting I'll help you because you think you know me. You think I still care for you and you think I'll want to help."

"It's not a sure thing. It's more of a hope." He got up and went to the kitchen. His white sneakers squeaked loudly on the tile floor when he turned the corner of the kitchen island. "I know you don't love me, but I hope there is some residual feeling that would encourage you to help me."

I couldn't see his face clearly because his head was lowered. His eyelashes, long and dark, were shadows on his pale skin. His hair was curlier today, unruly where it brushed his ears and the collar of his shirt. "I haven't seen you for decades," I said. "It's unrealistic to expect me to still love you."

He raised his head, his dark eyes wide and focused on me. "It was unrealistic for us to fall in love in the first place."

Butterfield's gaze went from me to Asa then back

to Asa. "Hey, man. Relax. Come on. This isn't how it's supposed to go down. Chill."

"It's okay," I said softly. "This had to be said. No, it wasn't unrealistic. We were both teenagers and we were scared and alone. We turned to each other."

"It was more than that," Asa said. "Far more."

"That's not important now." Butterfield appeared and sounded desperate, a man who was seeing carefully laid plans derail. "What's important is who's after you and why."

"You're right. That is important." I turned to Asa. "I read the transcript."

"What?" He blinked and I thought I saw his memories evaporating.

"The transcript of your trial."

"All of it?" Butterfield asked, disbelief evident in his voice.

I nodded. "I think I have the salient details in mind. There are a few I'll want to check once you tell me what happened." I peered around the dining area. "You don't have any clocks. What time is it? I left my watch in the bathroom."

"A little after eight-thirty," Butterfield said. "He doesn't like clocks."

"I don't need clocks," Asa corrected. "I don't make appointments that require a set time for attendance. I had enough of that in college, the service, and prison."

Butterfield grimaced. "Yeah, no shit about that."

"I need to call Chessy. Otherwise she'll have the police out searching for me." I folded my napkin and set it next to the plate. "What was in the box?"

Both men stared at me. "What box?" Asa asked.

"The one you got. You said you got a box with

porno movies and old letters. What else was in the box?"

Asa smiled. "You see how her mind works?" he said to Butterfield.

The black man nodded. "Yeah. It jumps all over."

"Not at all. Alice always kept a checklist in her mind of details she needed to know. I remember that from school." Asa leaned against the counter. "You always knew when something was incomplete. You kept a tally of all the parts that were needed to solve a problem and if you didn't have all the parts, you made a point of trying to find them."

"I'm organized," I said. "It makes sense that we should focus on what was in that box. It appears that most of your troubles began when you received the box."

"Not really," Asa said. "That's one reason I set up the Mad Hatter persona. I thought M.A. Hatterley was being followed."

"But it's escalated since then, right?"

He nodded.

"What was in the box besides the movies? Do you have it here? Can I see it?"

Asa straightened. "It's in secure storage. I made copies of enough of it so I could prove I had the contents if needed. There was a scrapbook of Roberta Hart's, maybe from high school. Several letters from an apparent pen pal in Europe. A jigsaw puzzle."

"Jigsaw puzzle?"

Butterfield snorted. "More like two or three. All messed up. It's like somebody dumped a couple of puzzles into one box. There wasn't a picture or nothing to tell what it was."

"And you couldn't solve it?" I asked Asa. "He was the jigsaw king when we were in college. We used to have contests to see who could put them together fastest. He always won."

"Butterfly is right. The puzzle didn't make any sense. The shapes didn't match."

"Forget the shapes. The colors were all wrong," Butterfield said.

I smiled. That was an old argument I had with Asa. He sorted pieces by shape then by color. I always sorted by color then shape. "That's odd. Why send you a jigsaw puzzle?"

"Why send me anything? The only connection I have to Roberta Hart is the fact I killed her ex-lover."

"You were convicted of killing him," I corrected. "Who would send it to you and why would they send it? What would they hope you could do with the information inside?" I nudged the questions to one side to join the others that were unanswered. "First things first. I need to call Chessy."

"Is that the blonde chick?" Butterfield picked up his plate and mine and went to the kitchen, nudging Asa to one side so he could reach the sink.

"Yes. She was concerned that I was with you." I took my dirty silverware and coffee mug to the kitchen island and handed them across to Butterfield. "And it turns out she was right."

Asa glared at me over the countertop. "You weren't harmed."

"I was shanghaied." I spied my bag on the coffee table where I left it the night before. I sank down onto the couch and pulled out my phone.

"We need to draw out the men who are watching

your house," Asa said. "Can you trust her? Would she help us? Are you sure she's a friend?"

"Of course I'm sure. How could she help?"

"Have her meet us at your car. You take me into your house. I can hide in your car. She'll take Butterfly. When the men watching see him, they'll make their move. But I'll already be inside and in place."

I tried to visualize what would happen but there were too many variables. "Are the men watching my house the same ones who tried to get you at the school?"

Asa nodded. "Probably. Or part of the same group."

"FBI? CIA?" I fumbled with my phone, trying to remember how to retrieve the phone number Chessy used the day before.

Dishes crashed into the sink. I twisted on the couch cushion in time to see Butterfield staring at me. "What? Feds?" He stared at Asa, who was inserting a key into the lock of a top kitchen cupboard near the door. "Man, when you said you were consulting for the cops, I figured it was, like, the local fuzz would call you up now and then and ask a couple of questions about computer software or something. You're working for the Feds? I mean, like, really working for the Feds?"

"I doubt if it's the FBI," Asa said, pulling open the cupboard. "If anything, it's CIA or a subgroup." He reached into the cupboard and pulled out a wooden box, setting it on the kitchen counter. "You want yours?" he asked Butterfield.

"Shit, yeah. Throw in an Uzi while you're at it. Shit," Butterfield mumbled, picking broken dishes out of the sink. "The damn Feds. Shit."

I gave up on understanding their conversation and returned my attention to my phone. I finally retrieved Chessy's number and managed to place the call.

"Where the hell have you been?" she demanded as soon as I identified myself. "It's almost nine o'clock. What happened? Are you okay?"

"I'm fine." I hesitated, not sure if I should involve her in Asa's troubles. He was watching me from the kitchen, where he and Butterfield were consulting about several rectangular boxes on the counters. "I may need to ask a favor."

"I did some more checking," she said, talking over my words. "I called a guy I know who knows a guy in the local Vets Administration office. He made a few calls, did some gossiping—you know how that goes. Anyway, he said that there was a fuss at the offices this week because somebody high up asked a favor and had some people reassigned there temporarily. Like, very temporarily."

"Really? Do you think those were the guys at the school yesterday?"

"It has to be, right? We need to talk to that guy you were with, you know, the one with the big black dude. Find out what he knows. Did he tell you anything last night? Does he have any idea why somebody is after him?"

"No, he doesn't. I think he's—"

"Okay, here's what we need to do. You get in touch with him and we'll meet him. Wait. That won't work. He's homeless, right? Damn. How can you find him again?"

I considered the kitchen, where Asa had his back to me. "I think I can find him."

"Great, okay. You and I meet with him and find out what he knows. He must have some idea why these guys are after him."

"I don't think he does."

"We'll figure it out," she said.

"Why would you help?" I kept my voice low. "You don't know him."

"He's a friend of yours, right? And besides, this is my first case. It's good practice. Here's what we'll do. I'll—"

"Hold on." I pressed the phone against my thigh while I walked to the kitchen. "Chessy is on the phone and she wants to help. Where's my—holy crap, Asa. What's that?" I gaped at the big black gun he held.

"It's a Luger." He reached into a rectangular box and pulled out another gun. "This is a Smith and Wesson."

"Those are guns," I said, my voice breaking into a squeak. "Guns," I repeated.

"Of course they are. Did she say she'd help us?" He nodded to the phone, which I still had pressed against my leg.

"I'm not going to ask her to help if guns are involved."

Butterfield held up a similar gun. "There will be guns," he said solemnly. "Ain't no way we're going anywhere unarmed."

There were so many things wrong with what he said I wasn't sure where to start.

"Is she going to help us? Can she meet us at the car?"

"Where is my car?" I'd forgotten completely about it.

"Lexington and 94th, in the Walmart parking lot," Butterfield said. "Have her meet us there in an hour." He turned back to Asa and they conferred again, probably about more firepower. Good Lord, for all I knew, he had grenades in that box of his.

"Chessy, meet me at the Walmart on Lexington in Bloomington," I said into the phone. "We'll be there at ten o'clock."

"We? Are you with him? Wait a minute. Are you still with him? Alice, do you—"

I pressed the *End* button. "I have to insist, Asa. No guns."

He smiled.

****

An hour later I unlocked my car in the Walmart parking lot. It was positioned near the grocery side entrance, not far from the frontage road. I glanced around nervously, but the Saturday morning shoppers were uninterested in me and Asa.

"Where is she?" Asa shifted the gray knapsack he brought from his right shoulder to his left one. "Is she usually punctual?"

"Odd talk coming from a man who doesn't have any clocks in his house and doesn't wear a watch. It's not ten yet. She'll be here." I gazed two parking slots to my left, where Butterfield sat in the blue Jeep, which Asa used to drive us here. The big man had that relaxed and slightly bored appearance like any other suburban husband waiting for his wife to finish shopping.

A yellow VW Beetle careened into the parking lot, whipping past my car and stopping opposite it. Chessy jumped out of the car and strode to me. Her blonde hair was bundled back into a ponytail. That and her denim shorts, T-shirt, and white Keds made her seem like a refugee from a beach party. I suppose that was fitting since she grew up in California and moved to the Midwest a few years earlier.

"Where is he? This is crazy, you know that, Alice? It's crazy. This guy is indigent. He's homeless and—" Chessy stopped so suddenly I thought she'd tip over, her eyes fixed on Asa. "Is that him?"

"Catherine Chessy, this is Asa Hatterley," I said. "Asa, this is Chessy. She's a very good friend of mine and I trust that you will not get her into any kind of trouble."

Asa held out his hand. "I'll do my best."

"You clean up good," she said, shaking his hand. "Let's talk. Who are those guys who chased you yesterday? I'm thinking they're Feds, right?" She pulled a battered red spiral notepad from her back pocket and flipped it open. "I talked to one of my professors and he gave me a few good ideas on how to do some research. I think if we—"

"Miss Chessy, my colleague and I have a plan," Asa said, touching her arm and steering her toward the blue Jeep. Butterfield got out when Asa and Chessy approached. I hurried forward and reached them in time to hear Asa say, "provide backup for our operation. It's critical you and Mike leave five minutes after us so you arrive close to when we arrive."

"Chessy, you don't have to do this," I said, interposing myself between her and the two men. "It might be dangerous and I don't want to do anything to jeopardize you."

She jammed the notepad back into her pocket and pulled me to one side, away from the Jeep. "I'm happy to help. Is this on the up and up? You think somebody is watching your place? Is this guy in trouble?"

"Asa was convicted of killing a man but he doesn't think he did it. It's complicated," I said when I saw her startled look. "The man who was killed had compromising pictures of Senator Roberta Hart."

"Ruby Hart? That stuck-up beauty queen?"

I nodded. "He received some letters and pictures of her when she was younger. They were, well, very explicit."

"Who sent them?"

"We're not sure. But we think they belonged to the guy who was killed."

"Wow," she breathed. "What's he going to do? Expose her? Give it all to the media?"

"He can't. Who would believe him? A convicted killer trying to smear a beloved public figure." I took a deep breath. "I believe him. Someone is after him and we need to find out why."

Chessy nodded thoughtfully, then turned back to face Asa. "Why go through all this? Why not face those guys and see what they want?"

"That's what we're doing. I want to make sure I have them in a place I can control so I can get the answers I need."

I knew what he was saying. He spent seventeen years in jail for a crime he didn't remember committing. "Do they have the answers?" I asked.

"If they don't, they know who does. It's the only way," he said. "For the first time they've come out in the open."

"Because you came out in the open to find me," I said. "I was the bait."

"No." He stepped closer to me and put his hands on my upper arms, holding me solidly in place. "You were the reason I came out of hiding. And because I did, they showed up. You were never the bait, Alice. I had to see you again. I had to talk to you. You'll be able to help me figure out what happened."

I stared into his dark blue eyes, so intent on me. "Okay," I said. "Let's go find out."

Chapter Seven

"They'll see you," I said to Asa, who lay on the back seat of my car, a gray stadium blanket draped over him and his knapsack in the foot well near him. Sunlight from the trees overhead flickered with shadows while we drove through Richmond, a little town south of the Twin Cities.

"They don't expect to see me so they won't see me. Quit worrying."

Quit worrying, he said. I had a man hidden in the back seat of my car. He was carrying at least one gun. I watched him put it into a holster under his denim suit jacket, nestled next to his arm pit. Government agents were after him. He drugged me the night before. He was convicted of killing a man.

Good God, I must be crazy.

I gripped the steering wheel harder, trying to stop my trembling. The past twenty-four hours was like a trip down the proverbial rabbit hole, where my entire world was turned upside down. I'd gone from being a respectable, approaching-middle-age, retired woman with a comfortable income to an accomplice to a recluse involved in a potential blackmailing scheme.

That was the conclusion I'd come to when I thought about the contents of that mysterious box sent to Asa—or so he said. Did I have any proof that someone sent it to him? Could I believe him? Why should I believe him? This had to be about blackmail. Roberta "Ruby" Hart was daughter to a wealthy man and married to an even wealthier one. She could pay any amount to keep that porn information a secret.

But why would Asa blackmail her? He had enough money. Was he an accomplice to someone else? Not Mr. Butterfield. He appeared to be a harmless individual, an odd thing to think about a man so obviously tough. Perhaps harmless was the wrong term. Extortion required planning and organization, two talents I doubted Mr. Butterfield possessed.

"You're worrying again." Asa's voice was soft and humor-filled.

"Consider this from my point of view," I said.

"Consider it from mine," he replied.

That gave me pause. His point of view was hard to know simply because of his illness but if I considered the bare facts of the matter, it was appalling. Drugged, unsure of his own past, hiding from an unknown foe—

And in love with a woman he really didn't know. Asa loved me as a girl. He didn't know the woman I became. He was in love with the past, not the present. I was sure he'd come to realize that, but what effect would it have on him when he did?

That conundrum occupied me until I reached my suburban street. "We're almost there," I said. "Just another block."

"Do you see any strangers? Anyone you don't recognize?"

"I don't know everybody on the street. I've only lived here a year." My house was the third of four on the left side of Queen's Court, a small street tucked between two bigger streets that carried most of the traffic in this neighborhood. A ravine and stream separated our homes on Queen's Court from the homes on larger King Street, which was above us at the top of the ravine. Our lot sizes were generous, about an acre each. Consequently, I didn't have a lot of near-neighbor interaction.

"Any construction going on? Repairs? Landscaping?"

I checked the rear-view mirror but couldn't catch a glimpse of Asa. His blanket blended in with the gray of the car upholstery. "Nothing unusual. The people across the street are having their garage re-roofed and those guys are here today." I had a sudden thought and almost slammed on the brakes while I considered it. "Hey. You said last night my house was being watched. How did you know? I'm sure if a couple of guys were lurking in a car, it would be noticeable."

"I didn't say that. You did."

"What?"

"You assumed that's why I knocked you out and kept you at my house."

"Well?" I demanded.

He laughed softly. "Butterfly did a drive-by and said he saw people watching your house. That doesn't necessarily mean somebody was doing a stake-out in a car. It might have been somebody walking a dog, or people sitting on a porch or somebody taking a stroll."

"That doesn't mean my house is being watched. Maybe somebody was out walking their dog."

"Maybe. But I trust his instincts. He's good at this kind of stuff."

"What kind of stuff is that?" I turned into my driveway and touched the garage door remote control button clipped to the passenger visor. The garage occupied the southwest corner of my house and the master bedroom occupied the northwest corner, with the rest of the house between the two.

"Let's call it hide and seek. A grown-up version."

I pulled forward into my two-car garage and shut off the motor then tapped the remote again to close the door. "Now what?"

"Now I go into the house while you go outside and get your mail. Butterfly and your friend will be here in a few minutes. When they show up that's when the agents will arrive."

"You're sure?"

He sat up and pushed the blanket to one side. "They'll be moving in when Butterfly arrives. Seeing him will disorient them. They're not expecting him. I'm counting on surprise."

"Where will you be?"

Asa opened the car door and slid out. "Better you don't know. Take your time getting the mail." He sent to the door leading to my house.

"Wait a minute. What if I have a security alarm?"

"You don't. You don't even lock this door." He disappeared inside before I could ask him how he knew that.

I left via the outside door on the left side of the garage and walked down my short drive to the mailbox on the street. I retrieved my morning newspaper and yesterday's mail then came back to the garage, sorting through the letters while I went. It felt as if every person outside was watching me—Mrs. Lewis next door, who was watering her petunias. The construction guys across the street. The boy on the bicycle riding past.

Were they all spies? All spying on me? My pace quickened while I envisaged those prying eyes. I entered the short hallway with my laundry room on the right and went into the dining nook to set down the newspaper and small stack of mail. There was no sign of Asa. He was either in my bedroom or had taken refuge in my guest bedroom on the northeast corner of the house or my office on the southeast corner.

My doorbell rang. I whirled, narrowly avoiding a vase sitting on a corner table. I went through the living room to the front door, peeking out the spyhole to my covered front porch. Two men in business suits stood outside. They reminded me of Mormons—clean cut, bland, unremarkable, and calm. One might have been as young as any Mormon recruiter while the other, the dark-haired one, appeared in his thirties.

I pulled open the door. "Sorry. We don't allow solicitation in this neighborhood and that includes religious proselytization as well."

The older man smiled. "I think you know we're not with a church. Can we come in?"

"Not unless you show me some identification." I stood in the center of the doorway, trying to block it with my presence. They were both several inches taller than me and probably far more muscular, but I wasn't going to let them in without a fight, if need be.

Chessy's yellow VW pulled into my driveway with a screech of tires. One of the men turned to watch while Chessy got out of the vehicle. It took longer for Butterfield to unhinge himself from the front passenger seat and stand. The suit-man's eyes widened when he got sight of Butterfield's bulk.

The other man, the taller and I think older one continued watching me. He had thinning brown hair and light blue eyes and the sort of face I couldn't describe. He'd be a perfect criminal because his features were so nondescript no one could remember him.

"Problem, Alice?" Butterfield hurried to the wide concrete steps at my porch.

"These gentlemen would like to come into my house but they refuse to show identification," I said, crossing my arms.

"We didn't refuse," the older man said. He began to push his coat to one side.

"Hold on," Butterfield said, sidestepping the other man to move in front of me. "You got anything to show her, you show me first."

"Yeah," Chessy said, pushing between the two men to stand next to Butterfield. "You want in, you gotta go through us."

The older man held up his hands. "No need to be hostile."

The other one, the younger one, moved to the left to ease his way around Chessy. "Stay right there," she snapped, turning to face him.

He stopped. "No need to be upset. We merely want to talk to Miss Little. Why don't you let her decide who she talks to?"

"Because you guys sound like government goons to me." Chessy took a step toward the two agents. She was Beach Girl Barbie staring down Businessman Ken. "Where'd you come from, anyway? Who do you have spying for you?" Her gaze bouncing from house to house on my street. "How many are working for you?"

"Perhaps we can go inside," the older one said.

"No need to have a disagreement in front of the neighbors. Am I right, Miss Little?"

I considered refusing him but decided a confrontation was what Asa needed. "Come in," I said, stepping back and going into the living room. Chessy followed, glancing over her shoulder at the two men.

Butterfield stepped to one side and the two men filed into the room. Butterfield closed the door and stood with his arms crossed, a large Buddha-like sentinel guarding my home. Chessy moved to stand in the entryway to the dining room, which also effectively blocked access to my office and the guest bedroom. She took up a pose that mimicked Butterfield's, alternately glaring at one man then the other.

"My name is Charles Dodge," the older man said. "My colleague is Robert White."

"Identification?" I asked.

"I believe Mr. Hatterley can vouch for us." Dodge's gaze took in my living room, going past Chessy to the hallway. "You have an attractive home. I'm a fan of Mission-style furniture myself. They go well with the Craftsman layout of your home. The colors and patterns are rather unique."

I doubted he was there to admire my oak-framed couch and loveseat with two matching armchairs. "I'm a fan of Frank Lloyd Wright. I bumped the colors up a notch. Why are you here? What do you want?"

"I want to talk to you about your problem. Come out, Mr. Hatterley," he said loudly, turning to the left and short hall leading to my bedroom.

Asa stepped out of the kitchen behind me, gun raised. "I should have known," he muttered.

I backed up and stumbled against my coffee table.

My kitchen wasn't really large enough to hide someone. The room was open on two sides, one to the living room and one to the dining room, and the part that wasn't open had appliances or cabinets. What did he do, blend into the walls? "Asa, what's going on? Do you know them?"

"Of course he does." Dodge didn't appear at all concerned that a man was approaching him with a gun aimed at his head. "I hired him to help us track down hackers and other cyber criminals."

I looked from Dodge to Asa then back to Dodge. "I thought you guys were software people. Software people don't spy on people and carry guns."

Dodge smiled briefly. "Some of us do. Besides, hunting hackers isn't our only job."

Asa took two more steps forward until he was a few feet away, his sneakered feet noiseless on my hardwood floors. He held the weapon with both hands, the butt of the gun cradled in his left hand, his right hand holding it aimed at Dodge. I couldn't detect any noticeable tremor or movement. It was like the gun was part of his arm. No, more like he and the gun were rooted in the earth. Asa's concentration was totally on Dodge to the exclusion of everything else.

Butterfield moved closer to White. "Why don't you take a seat?" he suggested, putting a hand on the young agent's shoulder and pushing downward.

White dropped into my gold-and-red armchair with a thump. He tried to stand but Butterfield stared down at him, standing so near the agent couldn't move.

Dodge regarded me. "I apologize, Miss Little. You should not be involved in this."

"Collateral damage?" I demanded. "Isn't that what

government types always call it when innocent civilians get messed up because of what you do?"

He raised one dark eyebrow. "That's more a military term, but yes, that is what it's called when unforeseen consequences arise out of an action." His gaze swung to Asa. "Rather like what happened when you killed Harry March."

Asa's attention didn't waver. "I'm not certain I did."

"The court thought otherwise."

"Courts have been wrong before." Asa took another step forward.

"What do you know about the killing?" I asked, desperate to diffuse the tension choking the room.

"It was a difficult shot," Dodge said, his eyes fixed on Asa. "Not impossible but difficult. You were seen near there and the weapon was one you trained on. The bullet came from a rooftop with a low iron railing along the edge. Your fingerprints were found on the railing. Why were you in California? Why were you in Burbank that day?"

"What?" Asa snapped.

"Burbank. Why were you there?"

Asa's eyes narrowed in thought.

"You told me you were meeting somebody," Butterfield said. "One of your old service buddies was gonna set you up with a job."

Asa nodded uncertainly. "I don't remember. I got discharged out of the Marines in Colorado. I played cards for a while in Vegas then I went to L.A. I'm not sure why."

Dodge smiled. "Exactly. There was no reason for you to be there except someone you know suggested you join him there."

"You're saying he was set up." I edged my way around the sofa to stand next to Asa on his left. "We know that. Tell us something we don't know."

"We know why Harry March was killed. He knew too much about Roberta Hart. What we don't know is exactly what he knew about her. We don't know who set you up to kill him. And we don't know why someone wants you to reopen all of this again."

"Reopen?" Chessy asked.

"For some reason, Roberta Hart's people are interested in Madison Hatterley."

Asa lowered the gun slightly. "The guys at the Stand Down event."

"Among other things."

Asa stilled. "Computer searches? Government databases?" His eyes narrowed in thought. "Public databases, too, probably. Damn. I should have set up a monitor."

"A what?" Chessy asked.

"A monitor," I said. "If somebody searches for specific things, you can set a program so you'll get notified. It's like a flag that gets raised if somebody searches for you."

"Maybe *you* can set a program," she muttered. Butterfield nodded agreement.

Dodge smiled. "Precisely. The men who chased you work for Roberta Hart."

"Wait a minute," I said. "How did you know about that? How did you know about that little run-in at the Stand Down?"

Dodge glanced at me. "Please, Miss Little. Give us some credit. We had people there."

"What? Who?"

He didn't answer but returned his attention to Asa. I glanced over my shoulder at Chessy, who shrugged. Government agents were interested in Asa. Asa was trying to find me. I was at Stand Down events. It was either Theo or Chessy. Not Chessy. She didn't have the temperament to work for a large bureaucracy. Of course, she might be a consummate actress, but I doubted it. It took two seconds to evaluate all possible candidates. "Theo," I said in disbelief. "Seriously? Theo?"

Dodge's head jerked. "They were right. You are as smart as him."

"She's often smarter." Asa pushed his jacket to one side and holstered his gun. "What do you want from us?"

"I want you to contact Roberta Hart and pretend to blackmail her." Dodge spoke to me.

"Why would she believe that?" I tried hard to appear innocent. "Does she have some reason to be concerned about blackmail?"

Dodge just stared at me, his face expressionless.

"Why me? Why not Asa?" Even as I spoke, I knew the answer. "She probably followed the trial when he was arrested. She had an interest in the case. She might recognize him."

Dodge nodded. "Like he said. Often smarter. Besides, we think she might be expecting the blackmailer to be a woman."

"Why?" Chessy skirted Asa and me, going to stand next to Butterfield. "Why a woman?"

White shot her an irritated glare. "That's privileged information."

Little pieces of data clicked into place. "She's

already being blackmailed or at least you think she is. And you think it's a woman. That means you're recording her calls and you heard something suspicious. That means you had her under surveillance. That means that you knew there was something in her past that might merit blackmail."

Dodge stared at me, his pale blue eyes flat and emotionless. "Good guessing, Miss Little. And that's all it is."

My living room phone rang. Dodge whirled but couldn't see it. I walked to the end table and picked up the receiver of my Alice in Wonderland phone, purchased at Disneyland a year earlier. The base was shaped like lush vegetation with a statue of the Caterpillar holding the receiver next to a mushroom that flipped open to reveal the push button numbers. "Hello?"

"Miss Little, this is Roberta Hart. We need to meet so we can talk."

I stared at the phone base. "I beg your pardon?"

"Don't play games. We need to talk."

I stared at Asa, my eyes so wide it hurt. "It's her," I whispered. "Hart."

"How did she get your phone number? What does she want?" Chessy asked.

Dodge grabbed the phone and covered the mouthpiece with his hand. "Tell her you'll call her back. Tell her you aren't private."

I nodded. Made sense to me. I needed time to gather my scattered senses, if nothing else. He handed me the phone and I said, "I have people here with me and I'm busy. Give me your number and I'll call—"

"Are you insane? I'll call you. Thirty minutes.

Don't think you can intimidate me. It won't work." Her voice was low and I heard other voices in the background, but her meaning came through loud and clear. "Thirty minutes." The phone went dead in my hand.

I hung up the receiver. "She said she wants to meet with me. Why?"

Dodge gestured to White. "Get the equipment, now. We need to get set up."

"Equipment?" I watched as White dashed for my front door.

"A wiretap," Dodge said, picking up my phone base.

"That's illegal," Chessy pointed out.

"So is blackmail." He pulled a small screwdriver out of his inside coat pocket and bent over the phone.

"Be careful," Asa said. "The newer phones can be tricky. Those Disney models use a different kind of base."

"Trust him to know about phone structure and wire taps," I muttered.

Chessy tugged on my arm, pulling me into relative privacy near my front door and away from Asa and Dodge. "I'm not sure if you should go along with this," she whispered. "These guys are pros. I think it might be dangerous."

Butterfield joined us. "I don't think you got much choice. They're gonna do it whether you want it or not."

"I'm a citizen," I said. "They can't just come in here and—"

"They can and they did," Asa said from across the room where he and Dodge inspected my phone.

I broke away from Chessy and Butterfield to

confront the two men. "You weren't surprised," I said to Dodge.

"What?" He glanced at me then continued unscrewing something on my phone.

"You weren't surprised she called me. Why?"

He removed a metal disc from my phone. "As I said, we've been keeping an eye on Senator Hart. She's on several very sensitive Senate committees and because of that, she's under careful scrutiny." He glanced at Asa. "I told you we weren't only after a few hackers."

Asa nodded. "You knew that I got information about her. You know someone sent me something."

"We suspected. There are a lot of coincidences happening right now." Dodge peered into the insides of my phone while he spoke. "Miss Little moved to town. Mr. Hatterley followed her. Roberta Hart returned to town when Congress recessed and she received an unusual phone call from a woman that upset her a great deal. She also set up a committee to explore her options for the future but one of the people on her exploratory committee is a man with suspected ties to the criminal underworld."

"The presidency?" I asked.

"If that bitch gets elected, I'm moving to Canada," Chessy said.

"If she gets elected, I'm going with you," Butterfield muttered.

"As I said—too many coincidences. It doesn't all add up, but there's something not right and somehow I think you're all in the middle of it." Dodge stepped to one side when his partner came back into the house carrying a black duffel bag.

I tugged on Asa's jacket. "Give it to them. Let them handle it."

Asa stared at Dodge, who returned the look without flinching. "Okay," Asa finally said. "I have it stored somewhere secure. I'll give it to you later."

"Good." Dodge walked over to stand in front of me. "Miss Little, please. Try to relax. I know you're not a blackmailer."

"I didn't know anything about any of this until a day ago. I wasn't even sure if Madison—Asa—was still alive."

Dodge nodded sympathetically. "I believe you."

"Well, isn't that relief," I muttered. "So glad you believe me. What government department are you in? I never did see any identification."

"I thought we decided I didn't need to show you any because Madison vouched for us."

"You decided that. I didn't." I sorted through the list of questions in my head, wondering which he might answer. "What committees does she serve on? You said she was on some Senate committees."

Dodge stilled. It was odd to notice it because he was preternaturally calm but he seemed to freeze momentarily. "That's a matter of public record."

I nodded, already moving to the next in my list of questions. She must be on a sensitive foreign relations committee for some federal agency to be interested in her. I'd find out about that later at the library. "You didn't ask what kind of extortion material Asa received."

"That's irrelevant, really."

"No, it isn't. There's personally embarrassing things, there are youthful indiscretions, and there are really stupid mistakes." His eyes narrowed when I said *youthful indiscretion.* "Any of those might derail a political career. Are any of them worth committing murder?"

"We'll be late," White muttered from across the room. "This is taking too long."

Asa peered over White's shoulder while he fiddled with my phone. "If you'd let me do it, I know some shortcuts."

Dodge shook his head. "Thanks for volunteering, but we have time." He turned back to me. "I meant what I said. I didn't want to involve you." He glanced at Chessy, who now perched on the edge of one of my living room armchairs, Butterfield next to her. "Any of you."

I barely heard him. One of those checklist items in my head was clamoring for attention. The box of evidence sent to Asa. He said there were things in that box that made him understand how Harry March and Roberta Fox were connected.

What things? Letters? Photos? I needed to see what was in that box of damning evidence. This truly was a jigsaw puzzle and I knew I was missing some key pieces.

"Done," White said, straightening. He bumped into Asa, who stepped back.

"Okay, here's how we need to handle this," Dodge said to me. "When she calls, the tape recording automatically starts."

"Where is it?" I asked.

"Right here." White tapped the black duffel with his foot. "It's a wireless signal."

"We'll want a copy of that," Asa said, peering over

him at the bag.

White nudged it further away from him. "Of course."

Which meant never, I suppose. "What am I supposed to say to her? I'm not a blackmailer and she thinks I am. Should I go along with it?"

Dodge nodded. "Absolutely. Tell her you want to meet her. We need to know what she's willing to do to keep that information a secret."

"What do you mean?" I glanced at Asa, who walked back to the kitchen, his hands dug into his jacket pockets.

"She's willing to deal with a blackmailer or a supposed one," Dodge said when I began to protest. "How much is she willing to pay?"

"In other words, how important is the damning evidence," Asa said from the kitchen. "Do you have any juice, Alice?"

"In the fridge. Will you arrest her?" I asked Dodge. "Blackmail is illegal."

He stood. "That depends on what happens when you meet with her."

"It might be dangerous." Butterfield still stood near the front door, arms crossed on his massive chest.

"If you want my help, then it's my project," Asa said from the kitchen. "I run it."

"We run it," I corrected.

"We?" Dodge eyed me doubtfully.

Chessy stepped forward. "Yeah. Us. You got a problem with that?"

Butterfield stared down at her. "Chill, Blondie."

She straightened. "Who are you—"

I glared at both of them. "Chill. Both of you. It's

112

our operation. We decide how it should be done."

Dodge kept his eyes on Asa, who leaned in the kitchen doorway, my orange juice carafe in one hand. "As long as you keep us in the loop on what's going on, I don't see that as a problem."

"That's crazy," White said. "You can't let civilians handle this."

Dodge turned to regard the younger man. "We'll discuss it later."

The phone rang.

Chapter Eight

"Agree to meet her in a public location," Dodge said. "Tomorrow, no earlier."

I nodded and picked up the phone. "Hello?"

"Let's get down to business. You need to meet me in two hours at this address. 734 North Portland—"

"I won't meet you today and I won't meet you at a private address." Hart's preemptory way of talking was not only annoying, it was insulting. "You'll meet me tomorrow at noon at the Edina Country Club in the dining room."

Asa grinned, holding up the orange juice container in a mock toast. "Touché."

"That's impossible," she snapped.

"Which is impossible? The time or the place?"

"Both."

"Take it or leave it. You're the one who wants to meet, not me." I waited, receiver pressed hard against my ear. I kept my gaze on Asa, trying to ignore Dodge, who watched me with hawk-like fascination. "How did you get my name and phone number?"

Dodge shook his head, frowning at me. "Stick to the script," he whispered.

"Screw you," I said, my hand over the receiver. "Well?" I demanded into the phone.

"The postcard."

"What postcard?"

"Don't play games with me. I received a postcard made from a photo that has—" She hesitated. "It has special meaning to me. Your name and phone number were on the card."

"When did you get it?" Dodge reached for the phone but I twisted, eluding him. I walked as far from the base as the springy cord would let me go.

"Yesterday. Why? Are you worried the postal service is lax in their duties? I can't be seen meeting with you at the country club. Be reasonable."

"Why not? I'm a relatively wealthy woman who might want to contribute to your campaign. Why shouldn't you be seen meeting with me?"

This was met by dense silence. The previous background chatter was gone. I had an impression of a small room where sound wouldn't travel far. Either that or her mouth was very close to the phone receiver. "Two o'clock. Meet me in the lounge. It's a private club. Use my name to be admitted."

"I have a membership," I said with great satisfaction. "I'll see you then." I hung up before she could sputter out a reply.

"You have a membership at Edina CC?" Chessy asked. "Really?"

I nodded. "It comes in handy when you're doing business. Besides, it's a tax write-off." I handed the phone to White. "Take off the bug thing."

Dodge shook his head. "She may call again. It stays on."

"Now wait a minute. I didn't agree to be under surveillance forever."

"It won't be forever. It's just for a few days until we find out what's going on."

"Obviously something illegal is happening." Asa walked into the room, a glass of orange juice in hand. "Why don't you arrest her?"

"We can't arrest her on suspicion. We need proof." White picked up the canvas bag and headed for the door.

"The American justice system at work," Asa said.

White stopped and turned. "If you've got a problem with it, you can always leave the country."

"Actually, I can't. I'm a convicted felon." Asa drained the orange juice and set the glass on the kitchen counter before coming into the living room again. "Even if I could get a passport, few countries would welcome me."

White opened his mouth to speak but closed it again when Dodge faced Asa. "It's possible your conviction might be overturned."

"Ah. You mean if I help you, you'll help me?" Asa sank down on my couch, the picture of relaxation. "Sorry. I don't believe you. I have a few issues with trust when it comes to our government."

Dodge stared down at him for a long second. "You went to prison once, Madison. It can happen again."

I stepped in front of Dodge, forcing him to take a step backwards. "This time he has me to help." I pushed one finger into Dodge's chest. "It won't happen again."

He leaned forward slightly but I didn't budge. My finger dug into his pectoral muscle. "We'll see, Miss Little." He edged back, away from me. "We won't be far."

"How far is not far?"

"We'll be in touch beforehand," Dodge said over his shoulder. White was already pulling my front door open. "Don't worry. We'll have it under control."

"Yeah, right," Butterfield muttered. "If we're not careful, that crazy-ass bitch will frame us all for murder."

"Let's see her try," Chessy snapped.

Dodge smiled briefly. "We have a lot invested in this operation, Mr. Butterfield. We're not going to waste this opportunity." He left, pulling the door closed behind him.

"Now what the hell does that mean?" Butterfield turned to Asa.

Asa jumped to his feet and ducked into the hall leading to my bedroom. A second later he returned with the knapsack he brought. He sat back down and undid the clasp on the bag, pulling out the smallest computer I'd ever seen.

"What's that?" I asked, watching him open it.

It booted immediately with no visible disk slots. "It's a prototype," he said. "I built it."

The machine was only a foot square. "What kind of chip does it use?" I peered at the backlit green screen. "How do you cool it?"

"Cool it?" Butterfield said. "How do you type on it? It's too small."

Asa fitted his fingers to the miniature keyboard. "You get used to it. Chips are getting smaller. I'm using a beta version in this. It doesn't require cooling the way the older chips did."

"That solves the weight problem," I said. "Portability at a price."

"Do you know what they're talking about?" Chessy asked Butterfield.

He shook his head. "Something about computers, I

think."

Asa inserted a small black rectangle into a slot on the back of the computer. "What's that?" I bent over to peer at the device.

"It's a new kind of storage unit. I'm helping test it."

I reached my hand out to touch it but Asa slapped it away. "Stop it. Quit being so nosy."

"Nosy? You're in my house, you helped those guys bug my phone, I'm acting like a blackmailer because you—"

He held up a hand. "Wait a minute." He typed furiously, eyes intent on his screen. "Okay. Go ahead."

"What?"

"They left a directional mike in the phone. I disabled it." He got up and put the small computer on the end table next to my phone. "All they'll get is music now."

"How?" I walked around the computer, trying to see any cables or wires. "It's not hooked to the phone. How does it work?"

"New technology. Wireless transfer. I'm working with some people on a standardized protocol."

Chessy threw her hands in the air. "What the hell is going on?"

Asa rummaged in his knapsack again. "When they put a wiretap on Alice's phone line they also put a microphone in the phone which is supposed to transmit anything we say in this room. I set my computer to intercept the signal and transmit music. By the time they figure it out, we'll have a chance to talk and decide on our next move." He pulled out a black device like a price scanner used at a supermarket. "I'll check the rest of the house and make sure they didn't put other mikes around."

"How would they do that?"

He flipped a switch on the device then shot me a disbelieving glance. "You don't have a security system and—"

"Yeah, yeah, I know. I don't lock my door." I dropped down on the couch. "Go ahead. Debug my house."

Asa grinned. "Yeah. I like that. Debugging." He headed for my bedroom.

Butterfield hurried after him, giving my phone on the end table a wide berth. "I'll go help," he muttered. "Maybe he'll need some backup."

Chessy sat next to me. "This is getting crazy."

"I'm sorry. I didn't mean to get you involved." I flopped back, struggling to remember why I did involve her. Maybe I didn't. Maybe Asa did. I shook my head. It didn't matter now. "I can't believe Theo is working for these guys."

Chessy leaned forward, hands clasped between her knees. Her long blonde ponytail bobbed as she spoke. "I always wondered about him. I don't know. He always seemed too nosy, too willing to help."

I had never noticed anything of the kind, but she was probably right. "This still doesn't add up."

"What doesn't?"

"Any of it. Why did someone send Asa that box of stuff? Who sent it? What did they hope to gain?" Asa reappeared and headed for the kitchen. "Where is that box? I'd like to see what's in it before you give it to the Feds."

"Sure." Asa handed the black bug-thing to Butterfield, who took it gingerly, holding it away from his body as if it might explode. Asa reached into my kitchen and grabbed my fold-up stepstool from its spot near the fridge, positioning it in the hallway.

"What are you doing?" I asked when he climbed up.

"Getting the box." He reached to the ceiling and pulled down the small white strap that held my attic steps in place. Tugging gently, he lowered the stairs while backing down the stepstool. As the stairs descended he moved the stepstool to one side so he could get onto the interior ladder.

"You hid it in my house?" I demanded, jumping to my feet.

He was halfway up the steps. "It seemed the safest place."

"Damn it, you have no right to barge into my house and hide stuff in my attic." I stood at the foot of the wooden stairs, glaring up at him while he vanished.

A scraping and thumping sound was all I got for reply. I turned on Butterfield. "Did you know about this?"

He backed away from me, bumping into the kitchen doorframe. "I do what I'm told, you know? He's the brains, I'm the brawn."

Chessy stomped to a spot in front of him. "Just because he tells you what to do doesn't mean you have to do it. Don't you have any decency? Honestly, you can't just go breaking into somebody's house and stuff junk in their attic."

"We didn't have to break in. She didn't have the door locked." Butterfield smiled apologetically at me. "You need to lock that outside garage door and this inside door, too."

"Can you give me a hand here? We all know Alice needs a security system and she needs to lock her doors." Asa peered down at us from the hole in my ceiling.

"I didn't think I needed a security system until you re-entered my life," I snapped, heading for the ladder.

"Not you. Butterfly. This box is awkward." Asa gestured to the big man. "Get up here."

Butterfield jammed the bug-finder into Chessy's hands and scrambled up the ladder. After a few minutes of grunting and maneuvering, a large white cardboard box sat on the coffee table in front of my couch.

Asa scrambled down the ladder just as I was reaching for the lid. "Don't touch it," he said, shoving me aside.

"Hey!"

He gently lifted the lid, slipping his right hand underneath it while he moved it. "I set up a couple of booby traps. Let me disable them first."

"What if I got up in the attic and found it?" I demanded. "What would happen?"

He removed the lid, revealing a mouse trap sitting on a heavy cardboard tray covering the entire inside of the box. Around the trap was a perimeter of double-sided tape which Asa carefully avoided. As he moved the tray, the trap snapped, the vicious sound making me jump.

"Good heavens. I could have lost a finger."

"You never go in your attic," he said imperturbably. "Your digits are safe."

"But what if I had a roofer come out or the electrician or—"

Asa turned and put his hands on my shoulders. "I

would never hurt you. I knew this was temporary and I knew it was safe." He kissed me quickly, a fast brushing of his lips against mine then he turned back to the box.

"That doesn't make it right." I wasn't about to be diverted by that kiss. "Who sent Hart the postcard?"

"What postcard?"

"She told me she got a postcard made from a photograph she recognized. It had my name and phone number on the card."

Asa lifted out the cardboard liner and set it aside on one of my armchairs. "I didn't send it to her."

"Whoever sent you this box sent her the postcard. I wonder what the picture was." Something else from the conversation with Hart niggled at the back of my mind but I couldn't dredge it up to the surface.

"What is all this stuff?" Chessy put the bug-finder on the coffee table and knelt next to it to peer into the white box.

"Clues," Butterfield said. "I guess," he amended when all of us stared at him.

I joined Chessy, sitting opposite her on the couch. "It's a storage box," I said.

"No, it's a paper box. The kind that reams of paper come in. I see them in the copy room at the school." Chessy reached inside and lifted out a brown shoebox held shut with a rubber band. "What is all this stuff?"

"Someone sent this to Asa and we're not sure who or why." I pulled out another shoebox, this one bigger than the one Chessy held. I opened it cautiously. Inside was a stack of air mail letters of varying sizes, all in their envelopes and all with foreign stamps. The paper was flimsy and fragile, but the ink was still dark on the address section.

Roberta Hart, Placerville, California

I stared at the smeared postage cancellation mark in the upper right corner. "This is from the 60s. She must have been in high school." I leafed through the letters in the box. There was a mix of letters on the blue air mail stationery and others on regular paper, along with a few birthday cards and one Thank You card.

I carefully opened one air mail envelope and pulled out the flimsy sheet of paper. I used to have a pen pal in Scotland and I remembered how fragile the paper was, almost cloth-like in flexibility and so easily torn. I smoothed open the sheet on my coffee table.

Cherie: Il semble depuis toujours que je t'ai vu. Est-ce seulement un été?

"My French is rusty," I muttered. "Let's see, it's something like 'it feels like a year since…*que je t' ai vu*…since I saw you or was able to see you. Has it only been a summer? I think that's what it says."

Chessy opened the brown shoebox. "Look at this. A bunch of flowers and junk." She held the opened box out so I could see inside.

"Corsages. You know, from Prom and special dances." I touched one dried rose, still surprisingly intact. The ribbons around the flower were faded to a dark gray and a faint cream color. "Of course, I didn't go to Prom. I was too young."

"What?" Chessy frowned at me. "Oh, yeah. You were like a child genius or something, right?"

I nodded. "I was ten or eleven when I was a senior in high school. I couldn't stay out past eight o'clock at night much less go to a dance with the big kids." I saw Asa watching me, smiling. "I didn't go to dances in college either, but I had a corsage or two for Homecoming and a couple of other holidays. Let's see, what was that one? Oh, yeah. Pi Day, in March."

Asa laughed. "It seemed appropriate that a math major should celebrate Pi Day."

"What's Pie Day?" Butterfield asked.

"March 15," I said. "315. It's the first three numbers for pi."

"What pie?" He looked from me to Asa. "I don't get it."

"It's an inside joke," I said hastily when Asa started to explain.

"I didn't go to Prom, either," Chessy said, re-lidding the box and setting it to one side. "The foster parents I had in high school didn't believe in that kind of stuff."

"What kind of stuff?" I pulled out another letter from the box on my lap.

"Anything fun. They were really religious. I couldn't do anything the other kids did. Besides, there wasn't any money for a prom dress or anything like that."

Her voice was dispassionate but I heard an undercurrent of bitterness. I glanced at her then at Asa, who had resumed his inspection of my house. He was on the other side of the living room, running the black box near my bookcase.

He looked over his shoulder and our eyes met. I recognized Chessy's tone of voice. I heard a similar tone in Asa's voice when we were younger, whenever he talked about his parents. Asa recognized it, too. "They sound like hard asses," he said.

Chessy shrugged and reached into the big white

box again. "They had firm ideas on how to raise good Christian kids and we had to toe the line or else. They were professional foster parents and they had plenty of practice."

"What do you mean?" I asked, opening the letter in my hand.

Butterfield reached into the white box, his hand colliding with Chessy's. He jerked back like he'd been burned. "Yeah, I know about those kinds of parents. Had a lot of them in the projects. Each kid means money in the bank."

"Yep," Chessy said. "I was with that family for six years. Longest I was ever with one family. Couldn't wait to get out of that house." She delved into the box and pulled out a small plastic case. "A bunch of photographs. Are these all hers? How did somebody get these?"

Butterfield pulled a videocassette out of the box. The cover was a garish yellow with a buxom, half-clothed woman seated on a porch swing between two men. They each had a hand on one of her breasts and one of her thighs, effectively making her appear like she was a wishbone in some erotic tug of war.

"Is that one of them?" I held out my hand. "One of her movies?"

Butterfield hesitated then gave it to me. The woman on the cover was young, plump, and voluptuous. "That's not Ruby Hart." I handed the tape to Chessy to examine.

"It's not her on the cover but it's her in the movie," Asa said from the kitchen, where he was examining my kitchen cupboards.

"You watched this?" I examined the title. "*Sexy

Sorority Slaves?"

Butterfield reached into the box again and pulled out another shoebox. "Research, you know. Had to figure out why somebody sent it to him."

"Yeah, right." I set the tape to one side. "What's that?"

"It's that jigsaw puzzle I told you about," he said, shaking the box so I heard the soft shuffle of pieces.

"I still say it's one puzzle," Asa said from the dining room.

"It can't be one puzzle," Butterfield said, setting the shoebox next to me on the couch. "There're too many colors and too many flat sides."

"You tried to put it together?"

Asa poked his head around the dining room wall and stared at me.

"Okay, stupid question." If there was a jigsaw puzzle, Asa would try to solve it. I opened the box and sighed when I saw the jumble of pieces. "Maybe I'll give it a try." I set it back on the couch and delved into the big box again, pulling out a scrapbook. "I still don't get it. If all this stuff belonged to Roberta Hart, how did someone get their hands on it?"

"Maybe that guy she lived with," Chessy said. "Maybe he had it."

Asa stopped in the hallway leading to the office. "What guy?"

"You said she lived with a guy, right? Maybe he had it." Chessy pulled another videocassette out of the box, this one with a woman on the cover hiding coquettishly behind a miniscule beach towel with sand and sea around her.

"I didn't say that." Asa remained standing in the

hall, staring at Chessy.

"Well, somebody did." She stood to peer into the box. "There're five or six videos in here. Are they all porn?"

"Even if she lived with someone, why would she take all this with her when she left home?" I sank back on the couch, scrapbook on my lap.

"I'm betting she didn't take all this," Butterfield said, leaning in the kitchen doorway and watching us. "I'll bet she took some of it. The rest of it belonged to that dude."

"What dude?" Chessy asked.

"That Harry guy." Butterfield moved out of the kitchen to join Asa, still standing in the hall. "You don't figure they bugged the whole house, do you?"

Asa considered it, frowning. "What?"

"The house, man. They didn't bug it, did they?" Butterfield repeated.

Asa shook his head. "I don't know." He went into the spare bedroom, Butterfield following.

"Did you sleep with him last night?" Chessy asked, glancing over her shoulder.

"Not your business." I opened the scrapbook. The first page was a color glossy school picture of a group of students standing in front of a trophy case. The three boys and three girls were posed with one large trophy was between them, obviously the focus of the picture. From their clothing I'd guess mid-1960s. The girls all had bouffant hairdos and wore navy blue skirts and white shirts. The boys were clean-cut, wearing white shirts and dark slacks. *Placerville French Team Takes State* read a newspaper clipping on the same page.

"You shouldn't get tangled up with him," Chessy

said. "He's trouble."

A black-and-white version of the glossy picture accompanied the newspaper article. "I am tangled up with him," I said, staring at the yellowed picture. The caption underneath had a list of names. I spied *Roberta Hart* next to *Juan Santiago.*

"Then don't get tangled further."

I turned the page in the scrapbook. "I want to help him figure out what happened." More newspaper clippings. A certificate for *Société Honoraire de Français.* A flyer for *Fly Me to the Moon Prom.* Pictures of couples on a dance floor in what appeared to be a high school gym. There wasn't a caption for this one and the picture was so faded I couldn't tell the details.

"That's probably not safe."

"Of course it is. You heard him. Asa would never do anything to hurt me." I leafed through the book. Invitations to parties, more pictures, a report card here and there. It was an encapsulated history of one girl's journey through high school.

"Hey, Alice, I know you think you can trust him, but can you?"

The back of the scrapbook was jammed with papers and pictures. Roberta ran out of pages before she ran out of memorabilia. I set the book down and began sorting through the papers. "Of course I can trust him. You need to understand. Asa and I went through a lot together when we were younger. No matter what has gone on between now and then, I know I can still trust him."

"How do you know?"

I looked up, startled by the insistent sound in

Chessy's voice. She sat on the floor opposite, her gaze fixed on me. Her long neck, high cheekbones, and full lips were more suited to a model than to a woman pursuing a career in law enforcement. Add in the blonde hair and her long, slender figure, and she could have probably made a good living on the runway in this year's fashion show.

"Why are you worried?" I asked.

"Crap, who wouldn't be worried? This guy isn't exactly acting like a rational person."

"I'm not a rational person," Asa said from the doorway.

Chessy turned at his voice, overbalancing and falling into the coffee table. The stack of videocassettes tumbled to the floor, clattering on the hardwood. "That's what I mean," she said. "You're not a normal person."

"I said I wasn't rational. I didn't say I wasn't normal." He'd removed his jacket and when he moved into the room I could clearly see his gun, strapped into the holster under his left arm. He sat in the armchair near the computer. Butterfield followed him, standing near my fireplace.

"Asa," I said warningly. "This isn't a logic argument. She has legitimate worries."

"But you don't have worries," Chessy said. "I don't get it."

I stared at the papers I still held. Old report cards, a letter, an invitation to a party, some photographs. This was Roberta Hart's past. I raised my head to regard Asa, who was such a large part of my past. My trust had its basis in that past but also in several very simple facts. "You need to understand. Asa has a mental illness that makes it impossible for him to lie."

Chessy's eyes opened wide. "What? That's crazy."

"No, it isn't. Think about it. Lying requires a certain kind of imagination mixed with ego. The reason most people lie is because of ego." I looked at Asa. "Are you the smartest person in this room?"

"About what?"

"By any measurement of intelligence, are you the smartest?"

"Probably," he said. "You might have me beat in some areas. Butterfly has me beat in others and I daresay your friend has me beat as well."

I turned to Chessy. "There is no hint of ego in that answer. It's simple fact."

"Okay, he doesn't lie about his I.Q. That doesn't mean he won't lie about other stuff."

"Lying is counterproductive," Asa said. "It takes too much effort to remember a lie. It's much easier to tell the truth." His mouth moved in a faint smile. "Alice taught me when it was polite to tell the truth and when I should avoid it. She never taught me how to lie."

Chessy stared at him, her body so tense I saw her tremble. "Why are you stalking Alice?"

"He's not stalking me," I said. "He's a friend and he came to me for help."

"I love her," Asa said. "I wanted to see her again. I know she can help me find out what happened."

"You say you love her, but you don't act like it. You hid from her until it suited your purpose to finally talk to her. If you loved her, you would have contacted her years ago, when you knew she was searching for you."

"I was in no condition to contact her," he said

quietly. "I had to get my life in order before I could see her again."

"Would you quit talking like I'm not here in the room?" I stood, the forgotten papers on my lap fluttering to the floor. "Chessy, I appreciate your concern, but please believe me when I say I trust him."

I saw anger, fear, and uncertainty in her pale green eyes. Then she turned to Asa. "Don't you think it's time to figure out if you're a murderer or not?" Chessy's voice was hushed as if she was afraid to raise the question.

I held myself still, waiting to see what Asa would say. He straightened in the chair. "I suppose I've been avoiding it. You're right. I do need to know."

"You think Alice can figure it out? How?"

"Are you sure?" I asked Asa. "It's been a long time. It may not work anymore."

"What might not work?" Butterfield demanded.

I held up a hand. "It's best not to talk about it. I'll do it and we'll see what we find out." I turned to Asa. "Let's see if you killed him or not."

Chapter Nine

"Let's get comfortable." I walked to my Bose stereo in the built-in bookcase near the fireplace and slipped in my six-disc CD magazine, a collection of music from the 60s and 70s. Stevie Winwood started to sing *Arc of a Diver*. I led the way to my couch, picking up the dropped papers and tossing them on the coffee table next to the white box.

I sat and as I expected, Asa sat next to me on my left, taking the spot he used to take years earlier. Our shoulders touched and his right arm was warm against mine. His gun was out of my line of sight, but I sensed its presence like a weight dragging against him.

"When we were young, Asa had blackouts," I said to Chessy, who sat in one of my armchairs opposite us. "Partly as a result of his illness and partly from the drugs they gave him to keep him calm." I took Asa's right hand in my left and rested it, palm up, on my palm. "We found out that I could talk him through the blackouts and help him remember what happened."

"She hypnotizes me," Asa said softly.

"It's the ultimate form of trust," I said. "He trusts me to do this. I trust him to do the right thing for me."

She nodded grudgingly. "I've never known that kind of trust. I didn't know it existed."

"It does." Butterfield's voice was hushed and respectful. He had taken up position by the front door, like a bouncer at a bar ready to keep out anybody not wanted. "Doesn't happen often in the world but sometimes it does." His eyes were fixed on Asa as he spoke.

Asa smiled. "Yes, it sometimes does." His fingers, lying on my hand, twitched.

"Should I take notes?" Chessy reached into her back pocket and pulled out the battered red memo book. "In case there're things we need to check on?"

"Good idea," Butterfield said, admiration evident in his voice.

She blushed, cheeks turning a dark pink. "I'm training to be a private detective. You need to think about shit like that. Do you have a pen somewhere?"

I gestured at the end table where the computer sat. "Bottom drawer." I turned back to Asa and flexed my fingers. "You remember how this goes. Close your eyes." I turned slightly closer to him and ran my right index finger over each of his fingers while I spoke. "Relax your mind. Allow it all to go. You know I'm here. You know I'll protect you."

Butterfield's eyes opened wide. I shook my head. *Don't speak*, I mouthed.

"I know what you're afraid of," I whispered. "You're afraid if you relax, it won't come back. You think you must control your mind in order to be smart, in order to be you. But you don't have to. I'll make sure you come back. Relax with me for a few minutes."

I watched Asa's face, waiting for the telltale softening of his jaw, that faint appearance of sagging in his taut shoulders. "Relax," I murmured, stroking his fingers. "I'm here. I'll bring you back. I always have."

It took longer than it used to. Before, I could

hypnotize him immediately. But it had been so long and he was out of practice with trust. Finally, after five minutes of gentle coaxing, I knew he was under. I began with a few basic exercises to help him relax further.

"What did you do at noon on Tuesday of this week?" I needed to be specific with him. My questions had to be targeted and detailed. Asa remembered facts, not emotions or concepts. "Where did you have lunch?"

"Egg salad," he said immediately. "Schultz's deli on Thirty-Second."

I glanced at Butterfield. He nodded, his head bobbing like Jesus on a dashboard.

I tried a few more questions from earlier in the year then I said, "Let's step back further, Madison. Do you remember moving to Minnesota?"

"Found out where Alice was so we moved. Easy to do."

"Easy to move or easy to find her?"

He smiled faintly. "I always knew where she was. I tried not to pay attention to her. But then I knew I needed her. That made it all easy after that."

I frowned. The words made no sense. I glanced at Butterfield, but he shrugged, big shoulders shifting up and down.

"What about the Marines?" I thought it would be best to skip prison completely and I knew I was right when I saw him tremble. "What is it?" I asked, stroking his hand.

"Don't want to remember the Marines," he muttered.

"Okay," I said. "Do you remember college?"

"Hated college. Loved Alice." He smiled dreamily.

134

I smiled, too. "Alice loved you, too." I stroked his hand, reliving that heady euphoria of love and lust and loyalty. "What classes did you take in college?"

"Quantum physics. Advanced Mathematical Theory." He rattled off a few more class titles then said, "When I graduated, I lost Alice."

I froze. "What do you mean?"

"College was a special place where we could be together. But when I left, I knew I'd lose her. I was right, too." He sounded so sad.

I gently stroked his hand. "You were too young to stay together."

"I know. I wish I'd found her sooner now that I'm older. But I suppose it had to happen like this."

"Like what?"

"I had to find out how much I needed her. I need her as much as I love her. I didn't know that before, but I do now."

Surprise knocked the breath out of me. I gaped at him but he didn't see me. He stared straight ahead, his eyes locked on a private vision. "Why do you need her?" I asked.

"To find out what happened on that day. That's one thing."

I wasn't sure I wanted to know what other thing he might need me for. I decided to skirt the question for now and focus on his primary concern. "Are you ready to talk about it? Are you ready to tell me what happened?"

He nodded, a curl of dark hair bobbing. "Yes. Ask me and I'll tell you."

"Why were you in Burbank in April, 1976?"

"Major Tuttle contacted me. He told me he could

get me a job there. I had trouble finding work. Nobody wanted to hire a vet."

He was right. Sad, but true, vets were treated like pariahs when they returned from overseas. "Who is Major Tuttle?"

"He's my commanding officer. Well, not my direct C.O., but he took an interest in me when he saw I was a sharpshooter."

"Did you stay in touch with him after you got discharged?"

Asa shook his head. "I didn't stay in one place. I hitchhiked around the country for a while then I ended up in Vegas."

"How did he know where to contact you?"

"I don't know. He called me. I was in Las Vegas. I stayed at the Circus, Circus hotel. I lived there for six months. Then he called me."

I nodded at the notepad balanced on Chessy's thigh. She hastily scribbled a few lines.

"I didn't know what to do," Asa continued. "Nobody showed me how to live in the real world. I couldn't teach. I didn't know how to get grants or fellowships. I didn't want to work for a university. I didn't want to work for a big company." He shook his head, his face scrunched with sadness. "I didn't know what to do."

Right, again. We received an outstanding college education, but nobody knew what to do with two kids with PhDs who were barely old enough to vote. I was lucky. A family friend recruited me to work at Carnegie Mellon in Pittsburgh. But Asa—I stroked his hand. The Marines recruited him.

"You went to Burbank," I prompted. "How did you

get there?"

"I knew a guy from Vegas who was headed that way. I got a ride with him. I sold my car and cashed out my chips and sold off everything except a duffel bag with some clothes."

"Why did you get rid of everything?"

Asa was silent for a long moment. "I don't know. I think Major Tuttle wanted me to."

Butterfield held up his hand. "Was he taking drugs then?" he asked softly.

"Good question. Asa, were you still taking the drugs the military doctors gave you? Didn't they interfere with your card playing?"

"They didn't bother me when I was gambling."

"Do you know why?"

"I didn't let them bother me."

Butterfield started to speak but I raised my hand for silence. "You mean you had to focus so much when you gambled that the drugs couldn't affect you?"

Asa nodded.

"I see. Okay. Tell me about your trip to Burbank."

"I got there on Tuesday. In the afternoon. I got dropped off at a hotel. I think it was a Holiday Inn. The major picked me up there."

I remembered the transcript from the trial. Harry March was killed on Wednesday, April 7. "What did you and the major talk about?"

"He said he knew someone who wanted to hire me."

"To do what?"

"He wouldn't say. He just said that I had unique skills this person needed. I thought it was cards or mathematics." Asa's hand trembled in mine, the fingers twitching spasmodically.

"It's all right," I said. "No one will ever use you again unless you want them to."

His fingers stilled. "They always want to use us."

"I know." I stroked his fingers gently. "They think because we're smart they can use our brains to get things they want. They never ask us what we want."

He nodded. "It's always a fight."

Chessy frowned and scribbled another note. If she was hoping for an explanation, it wouldn't be forthcoming. Unless someone had our odd background, they couldn't understand. For years we had been manipulated by older people who tried to use our intelligence. I remembered a college professor who tried to convince me that I should let him use my research 'because an older person had more credibility.' Another one pushed me to work for the government, insisting I interview with one of the FBI recruiters.

It wasn't until I met Asa and we fell in love that I saw how my parents and others used me. He and I became a team and I discovered I had validity as myself without seeking validation from another so-called official source.

All this passed through my mind in the time it took to draw a breath. No one would understand. That was part of our special past.

"Where did the major take you?" I asked.

"To a house, north of town. I could see mountains in the distance."

"Was it the major's house?"

Asa shook his head. "No. I don't think so. I think it belonged to someone else. The major didn't act like he belonged there. The house was too fancy. Too modern.

Too rich."

"Can you describe it for me?"

"It had a lot of glass and windows. The outside was dark brown wood with a large main floor. I think there was an upstairs but I didn't go there. The rooms inside were big and there was a big garage, probably big enough for three or four cars."

"Did the major introduce you to someone there? Is that why you went to the house?"

"No. He was alone. But there was someone on the phone. He had a conference phone."

"What did the person say?"

Asa tilted his head to one side, his eyes still fixed on the far side of the room. I could tell a memory-movie was playing in his mind. "The man on the phone said he had a bet with a friend of his. They had set up a target. His friend bet that no one could hit the target. The major told him that I could hit it."

"Where was this target?"

"There was a place outside of town, an old movie lot. They wanted to reenact a scene from a war movie. There was a sniper in the movie. The friend didn't think anyone could make such a shot."

I nodded. It sounded credible, I suppose. "Did they want you to see if you could do it?"

"Yes. The phone-man said he and his friend would be there to watch. They'd pay me a thousand dollars to do it. The major vouched for it all so I said I'd do it."

"What was his involvement in it? Why did he care?"

Asa frowned. "He and the man on the phone were friends. Or maybe not. They may have been . . ." His voice trailed away.

"What?" I prompted.

"Employer? Employee? The major acted like the phone-man was important." His hand, resting on mine, tensed then relaxed again.

Chessy waved a hand. "Name?" she whispered.

"Did the man on the phone have a name?" I asked. "Did he introduce himself?"

"No. The major called him Chairman but he didn't use a name."

That reminded me of something else. "I didn't see any information about the major in the transcript of your trial. Why didn't you mention that he was there?"

"I didn't remember. The major didn't want me to remember."

"Drugs?" I whispered. How did they do it?

Chessy nodded, jotting more notes.

"What happened next?" I asked. "What happened after you agreed to try to do it?"

"The major and I had a drink then we had dinner. A woman brought dinner into the dining room. I think she was a maid. Then he said I could sleep in the guest room. It was on the same floor near the living room. I was tired. I went in and fell asleep."

Was he drugged? It could have been something in his drink or maybe in the food. I glanced at Chessy, who was furiously scribbling notes. She nodded. *Drugs,* she mouthed. *I'll check.*

"What did you do the next day?" I asked.

"After breakfast the major drove me to the movie set. It was like a town, mostly empty. There were large buildings and a street through it all. There weren't any houses, just big metal buildings."

"How far away was it?"

"I don't know. It took us a few minutes to get there. Maybe ten or fifteen."

I didn't know the Burbank area, but back in the 1970s it may not have been as densely populated as now. I'd need to find a detailed map of the area. I added another item to my list of Things To Research at the Library. We also needed pictures of the crime scene if we could find them after all this time.

"What did you do next?" I asked.

"We went up on top of one building that was four stories tall and painted white. There was a staircase on the outside, a black metal one like a fire escape. We went up and the major showed me where the target would be."

I gestured to Butterfield to come closer. I wasn't sure how to ask questions about this part of the event. I didn't know anything about guns. "What do I ask him?" I whispered. "I don't know about shooting."

He leaned close to me. "Ask him what gun he used. What the range was. What the conditions were. Ask him to tell you anything he remembers about the air temperature and the wind and the height where he shot from."

I nodded and Butterfield stepped back, taking the armchair next to Chessy. "Asa, what kind of gun did you use? Did you have one with you?"

"The major had a 300 Winchester Magnum with a good scope. I've used that rifle before." Asa's hand moved, fingers once again twitching.

"What do you mean you used it before?"

"In the Marines. When I went to sniper school. That's one of the guns I trained on. I trained on a lot of them but the Win Mag was the best for long-range conditions."

I swallowed hard. He spoke so matter-of-factly about a killing weapon. I was once again reminded that he was and he wasn't the person I remembered. "What do you remember about that day? How far away were you? Was it hot? Where did you stand on the roof?"

He smiled. "You don't stand when you shoot. You lie down. The rifle is heavy and you use a bipod to support it. A lot of times you need to wait for hours to get the right angle. You can't stand the whole time. Plus somebody might see you. Don't forget, if you're a sniper, someone is looking for you."

"What do you mean?"

"The enemy has snipers, too. I might be targeting them but they might be targeting me at the same time."

My mouth sagged open. "Good Lord," I breathed. "Like a game of cat and mouse."

"Not a game," he said placidly. "Or maybe a game, but a dangerous one."

I nodded even though he couldn't see me. I needed the movement to break my shocked paralysis. "Was it hot that day? Was it windy? What was it like?"

"It was warm and there was a slight breeze, enough to throw off my trajectory. The sun angle was bad. I was shooting from sunny into shadow, and that's always tough. It's hard for my eyes to adjust to targets in shadow. It takes a lot of concentration. We got there at about ten o'clock and the sun was getting high overhead. The roof wasn't too hot, at least. It was a flat roof with a concrete parapet about a foot high with a metal fence."

"Did you hide behind the parapet? You said you had to lie down. How did you do that?"

"There were some old cardboard boxes there. I flattened them out and used them. The gun fit fine under the metal fence. I wasn't hot because it was still early in the day. I hate it when you have to lie out in the sun for a long time. That's when you rig up a canopy or something. Heat can throw off your concentration."

It sounded like he was reciting something from a book. I suppose, in a way, he was. He probably memorized whatever ungodly textbooks they gave him and mentally supplemented them with his own experience.

"Was the other guy there, too?" Butterfield asked softly. "Did he stay on the roof?"

"Was the major with you?" I asked. "Where was he?"

"He showed me where the target was then he had to leave. That was part of the bet. He couldn't be there with me."

I made a mental note to not forget that point. Asa wasn't captured at the scene. According to the trial records, he was tracked down a day later. What happened in the day between the shooting and his capture?

"What did you do next?"

"I got set up. The target was a thousand yards away and I had to aim between two buildings. I had a small field of fire and part was in shadow. I couldn't squint. You can't squint when you're using a scope. I had to use a shade for my head to make sure the sun stayed out of my eyes."

"A thousand yards?" I gaped at him. "That's a half-mile."

He nodded. "A little more than that."

"How could you even see that far?"

"The scope," Butterfield whispered.

"The scope was very good," Asa said. "Probably a Leupold."

I glanced at Chessy, who nodded and jotted a note.

"The major gave me a baseball cap. That helped with the sun angle. I got set up and waited."

"He left you on this roof and told you to aim at somebody coming out of a building a half-mile away. Weren't you worried?" I considered how to ask this question without jarring him from his relaxed state. I had to keep him calm, but a suggestion of guilt might force him back to normal, whatever that was. "How did the major explain it to you? Was it going to be a real person and real bullets? Or would it be a re-enactment?"

"They set up a dummy in a remote-controlled golf cart. I was told I'd see the golf cart coming toward me. In the movie, it was a Jeep."

"What movie?"

"The movie the bet was about. The war movie. I used real bullets, of course. Otherwise it was impossible to tell if the shot was good. They rented the movie set for the day. The men doing it must have had a lot of money to rent a whole movie set to settle a bet."

I barely heard him. The trial transcript had details about the shooting, most of which I didn't understand involving trajectories, angle of impact, wind shear, and line of sight. The bottom line was that Harry March left the movie set and got into one of those little golf cart things they used to drive between buildings on a studio lot. The place where he was found had several buildings clustered close together. Apparently anyone could rent out the studios for a flat fee per day. They were essentially big metal pole barns with an interior structure suitable for film-making.

The D.A. talked a lot about the mechanics of the shooting, with descriptions of the bullet, maps of the firing trajectory, pictures of the rooftop and pictures of the gun. I skimmed most of that information simply because I didn't understand the jargon. Did the jury back then understand? Or did the D.A., a man who went on to run for state office, use the details to railroad Asa into prison?

"Check the D.A.," I whispered to Chessy. "What happened to him?"

"Already noted," she whispered back, flourishing the little red notepad.

"You *are* good." Butterfield's voice was as soft as a sigh.

Chessy blushed and ducked her head.

Asa's hand moved on mine and I was brought back to the here and now. "Did they tell you anything about the dummy? What it would look like? Where it would be?"

"It would seem like a man. That's all I had to know. Like in the Marines. We were never sure who we had to shoot. All we knew was there might be enemies there."

I leaned over my coffee table. "Am I forgetting anything?" I asked Chessy and Butterfield. "Now's the time to ask him."

"How long did he wait? What did he do with the gun afterward? Did the major drive him back to the house? What did he do between the time he left the roof and he was arrested?" Chessy flipped some pages on her notepad. "How big was the bet that was made? What kind of car did the major drive?"

I stared at her in astonishment.

"I have more," she said softly.

I turned to Butterfield.

"What she said," he murmured.

I needed to choose what I would ask. I was afraid that once we got into the actual shooting, he might be startled out of his trance. I would work in Chessy's questions if I could. "How long were you up on the roof?"

"About an hour. I spent fifteen minutes getting things arranged. I had to align the scope and adjust for wind and distance. I wasn't familiar with that particular gun. I had to examine it. I wanted to take a few test shots, but the major said I couldn't. I did the best I could and got into position."

"After you did all that, what did you do?"

"I waited."

Those two words said it all. Waiting. Asa was good at waiting. I could imagine him, laying on the rooftop, unmoving, his unwavering attention centered on the gun scope and the scene below him. He could do that kind of thing for hours. I saw a form of that when he examined a computer program or studied for class.

Or when he and I made love. The sudden memory made my face flush. When we were in bed together, I was the total focus of his world. It had nothing to do with his pleasure and all to do with mine. He was the most giving sexual partner I ever experienced.

His hand moved again, his fingers curling. I forced myself back to the task. "Did you have any warning when the man—the dummy—was coming?"

"Sort of. I was told it would be about a half-hour. Then a black golf cart would drive through the kill zone first. When I saw that, then I knew it would be a few minutes until the dummy came through."

I tried to visualize the scene. Asa, on the roof, focused downward, his gaze centered on the narrow roadway between two large buildings.

"What happened next?" I prompted.

"The black cart came through. A woman drove it. She had red hair. Then a few minutes later the red door opened. I saw a white golf cart start to drive down the lane."

"What did you do?"

"I took the shot."

Chapter Ten

I don't know what I was expecting, but it wasn't that simple statement. I was speechless. For some reason I didn't imagine that he actually pulled the trigger. I thought he got to that point and somehow, some way, he didn't do it.

"What happened next?" Chessy prompted.

"What did you do?" My throat was so dry I wasn't sure I could talk. "What happened to the dummy? What did it do?"

"It was a clean shot. It fell out of the golf cart, which was what I expected. I had a high caliber gun. It would have impact."

I swallowed hard. "Was there blood? Did the dummy bleed?"

"I don't know. A sniper never waits around to check. You need to move on to your next position. I did what I supposed to do. I hit the target."

The target. A human being a half-mile away was dead. Chessy gestured to catch my attention. "Where did he go after that?"

I nodded, cleared my throat then managed to ask, "Where did you go?"

"I did what I was told to do. I left the gun there and I went down that outside metal staircase. There was a car in the street outside."

"Was the major there?" I was starting to get my

equilibrium back. As far as Asa knew, he hit a dummy, not a human being in that car. Just a target. I took a deep breath.

"No. Another man drove the car. He said he was a friend of the major's and he was going to take me to my hotel."

"What hotel?"

Asa frowned. "I'm not sure. I think the major rented a room for me."

I gestured to Chessy to make a note and she nodded, flipping another page and scrawling something.

"What was the man's name who picked you up?"

"He didn't say. He said he was a friend of the major." Asa wrinkled his nose. "The man kept chewing his fingernails. He was very nervous. He drove me to a hotel and that's where they found me. That's where I was arrested." He turned to gaze at me. I know he didn't really see me because his eyes were unfocused. "Can we stop now? I'm tired."

"Of course," I said immediately. I knew when we got to this stage we had to quit. The few times in the past when we pushed beyond this point were disastrous, leaving Asa shaken and distraught. "Why don't you relax now? I need to talk with my friends for a minute or two."

"Okay." Asa clasped his hands in his lap and slouched down on the cushion so he could rest his head against the back of my couch.

"We need more details," Chessy said. "We can't stop now."

"We need to stop. He's done what he can do for now. You have all the notes, right?"

She wiggled the little notepad. "It's almost full."

"Good. We'll review what we have and see what's missing." I turned to Asa. "You're going to wake up when I count to ten but you'll be very tired. You'll need to go in and take a nap. Does that sound okay to you?"

He nodded, his head still resting against the back of the couch. "Yes. I think that's best."

I counted to ten. When I finished, he opened his eyes. "Did it work? Did you get anything?"

"You were great," I said. "We got a lot of details."

"Yeah, man. You talked a mile a minute," Butterfield said.

"Good. I'm glad it wasn't a waste of time." Asa yawned then leaned forward, stretching his hands in front of him. "I'm really beat. Can I use your spare room and take a nap?"

"Of course." I gestured toward the hallway. "You know where it is. Take your shoes off first, okay?"

Asa grinned. "I won't ruin another one of your bedspreads, I promise." He stood and went to the hall, but before he reached the doorway he stopped. "Did I do it?" he asked, his voice hushed. "I don't remember any of it."

I considered how much to tell him. "I think you were set up to kill him."

Asa nodded thoughtfully then he looked at me, his dark eyes haunted. "Shouldn't I remember it?"

He seemed so forlorn, so lost. I sprang up from the couch and went to him. It was the most natural thing in the world to put my arms around him, pulling him against me. "It wasn't your fault." I leaned my head on his chest, hearing the hollow thud against my face.

"It was my fault but not only mine. I've already paid. But other people should pay, too." He rested his forehead against mine briefly then he kissed me, our lips lingering. It was a comforting kiss but I sensed hidden passion there. "They should pay." He went into the bedroom.

I followed and watched him unbuckle the holster holding his gun. He shrugged out of it and set it on the side table, moving the lamp and clock to make sure the gun was stable. Then he kicked off his sneakers and dropped onto the double bed. The room, seldom used, faced the front of the house. I walked around the bed and pulled down the window shade against the encroaching sunlight.

"That's one of my pictures," Asa said.

I turned at his voice. This room had pale yellow walls with a flowered bedspread that matched the cushion on the wooden rocking chair in the corner. He was staring at a large framed watercolor on the wall opposite the bed. It showed a barn in the distance, long rows of green and yellow corn stretching from the foreground to the red structure like fingers pointing the way. "Yes, it is. I have another one in my bedroom and one in my office."

"I threw them all away when I left college."

"And I got them out of the trash. I have six of your paintings. I change them out from time to time." I sat on the edge of the bed and took his hand. "How do you feel?"

"Empty. Tired." He smiled briefly. "Afraid. I never killed anyone before during one of my blackouts."

"This wasn't a typical blackout." I squeezed his hand and stood. "They drugged you."

"Maybe. But I still shouldn't have done it."

"Maybe you didn't. We don't have all the details

yet." I turned to leave but he tugged me back to him.

"Alice, I meant what I said. I do love you. I will always love you." His blue eyes were intent on my face.

"You're remembering the past, that's all. You remember when we were in love. This is different now. I'm different."

He shook his head, his hand tightening on mine. "I know that's what you think but you're not right about this. I've met other women and I've slept with other women. I've only loved you. Don't be afraid. It doesn't matter to me if you don't love me. It's enough to know that you're here and I can see you now and then."

"Listen to what you just said. You said I'm the only one you loved. That's past tense. You don't love me now. You did love me. It's in the past."

"Don't worry." He released my hand and closed his eyes. "We'll talk about it later."

"Asa, you can't just—" His breathing deepened and I knew he didn't hear me. He had the uncanny ability to simply shut off his senses whenever he needed to avoid something unpleasant.

I left the room, pulling the door closed. I leaned against it, trying to gather my scattered emotions. It was years since I saw him and he could still throw my life into total chaos. Why did I care about what happened to him? Why was he important to me?

I thought of the other watercolor, hanging in my bedroom. It was a portrait of me when I was at college, complete with long, curling blonde hair and a pile of books near me. I wore a white blouse and navy skirt and I sat under a tree on a red blanket. I was studying and had no idea he sketched me, watching me from several feet away. When I looked up, I found him staring at me.

He and I hadn't socialized until that autumn afternoon. We were in some classes together, but seldom talked. That day I asked him to join me and he showed me the sketch. We talked and I knew something was different about him, not only his intellect. He was so socially inept. I *knew* I was too young and too inexperienced to be around the other students. Asa knew but he didn't care. It simply didn't register for him.

That day marked the beginning of our relationship. A photograph, stored in the closet in my office, marked the end of it. My parents took the picture of me and Asa at his graduation. He had his arm around me and we were both smiling, both young and carefree. Three months later he was gone. Four months after that was the last time I saw him.

Until yesterday. The homeless Viet Nam vet I set out to rescue financially was a successful businessman, but he still needed rescuing.

He still needed me.

Was that why he had such a hold on my emotions? When was the last time anyone really needed me? Certainly none of my former lovers. Relationships started, flourished, and ended with very little bitterness and often a feeling of relief. I had no children and my siblings and I weren't close. There was no one in the world who truly cared about what happened to me. I didn't need anyone in my life or so I told myself.

God. What a depressing thought.

But now there was Asa. Allowing him to become a part of my life again would open me up to care and worries. It would open me up to hurt. "Who am I kidding?" I muttered. "I'm already part of his life again." I looked back at the bedroom door. "Why are you here?" I whispered. "Why can't I get away from you?"

The door didn't reply.

I returned to the living room. Butterfield had edged his chair closer to Chessy's and they were studying her notepad. "What was that about the bedspread," Butterfield asked when I entered the room.

"Oh. Nothing." Asa once ruined a bedspread when he grabbed me, tossed me on the bed, and we proceeded to have sex without getting fully undressed. My bedspread was never the same. "We should go to the library and do research. If I can get online I can use Yahoo or Lycos to do web searches." I glanced at my home office where my computer and modem sat on my desk. "Something tells me I probably shouldn't use my home internet connection."

"I'm better with a card catalog." Chessy glanced at Butterfield, sitting in the armchair next to her. "I want to get some maps of Burbank back then. Maybe we can find crime scene pictures and map out a route to and from the place. We need to find out about that Tuttle guy. Let's see if we can get pictures of rich houses in the area. Back then there probably weren't too many big spenders. If we can figure out the house where he stayed, we might be able to figure out who was behind all this."

"I need more background information about Senator Hart, too. I want to find out what committees she's serving on and who her aides are. Hold on. I'll make notes, too." I went to my office and grabbed a legal pad then came back to the room.

Butterfield was glaring at Chessy and she appeared exasperated. "What?" I asked. "Did something happen while I was gone?"

"I told her I'm no good with libraries and stuff like that," he said. "I don't know how to use those cards and things."

"I'll show you," she said. "We have a lot to research. You can help."

"I don't read good." He got up and went to the kitchen, pushing past me. "I can't help with that shit."

"Of course you can," Chessy said. "Don't give me that crap. If you can break into a house you can figure out how to use a card catalog."

He stopped in mid-step, wheeled and stared at her. "How'd you know about that?"

She stood up. "I'm a detective, remember?" Chessy regarded me. "When do we start?"

I jotted some notes on my legal pad. "Let's get organized first. I don't want to leave Asa alone. I should be here when he wakes up."

"Then we'll go," Chessy said. "You can stay here with him."

"No way," Butterfield said. "I ain't leaving him alone here. Those Feds might come back."

"Okay." Chessy sat next to me on the couch. "Let's compare notes." She glanced at Butterfield, who stood in the kitchen doorway. "Why don't you be useful? Maybe get started on that jigsaw puzzle."

"You're a bossy bitch, anybody ever tell you that?" He crossed his arms and glared at her.

"All the time. Here." She held up the box holding the jigsaw pieces.

I pointed to the dining room. "Just take off the

placemats and use that table. It should be big enough." I continued writing while I still had ideas rattling around in my head.

"You got any beer?" Butterfield snatched the box out of Chessy's hand and stomped into the dining room.

I caught a glimpse of him through the arched doorway, sweeping my linen placemats aside with one massive arm. "It's only noon."

"What's the time of day got to do with it?" he snapped.

"That sounds good." Chessy handed me her notepad and joined him. "How about pizza, too? Any good pizza places out here in the 'burbs?"

"No anchovies," Butterfield warned. "No pineapple and crap like that."

"Absolutely not," Chessy said. "Meat and cheese."

He opened the box and dumped the contents on my table. "Maybe you ain't so bad after all, Blondie. Maybe."

"Pizza phone number is on the fridge," I said. "Make sure one is only sausage and mushroom. Asa won't eat anything else."

"Yeah, I know. He's a drag when it comes to pizza," Butterfield grumbled.

"Let's get one with pepperoni and onions for us," Chessy suggested. "And get a boring one for them." She went to the kitchen.

I barely heard her. I was busy noting the questions I needed answered and deciphering Chessy's handwriting. I revisited earlier conversations in my head and remembered I also had to prepare for my role as a blackmailer. I stared at the fireplace wall. Beyond it lay Asa, the instigator of all this turmoil, sleeping like a baby while sunlight warmed the room and…

Sunlight.

I turned back to my notes. "I need that trial transcript," I called out. "Let's get a copy of it to use and annotate."

"Now that I can do," Butterfield said. "He's got a couple of copies of it back at the warehouse."

"Warehouse?" Chessy asked. "What warehouse?"

I tuned them out again and focused on my list. I filled three pages with notes and questions then began inventorying items in the box. When I got to the bottom, I found a manila envelope with a pink presentation folder, like the kind used to hold certificates. Inside was a sheet of infant handprints and footprints, the tiny images still so clear I could see the whirls and ridges on the fingerprints. *Woodland Municipal Hospital, Woodland, California* was printed at the top of the sheet in flowing italic letters. I made a note to check the location of Woodland.

The doorbell rang, startling me so I dropped the papers back into the box. "What's that?" I jumped to my feet.

"Pizza," Butterfield said, striding past me to the door.

I checked the clock on my fireplace mantel. One-thirty. As though acknowledging the lunch hour, my stomach rumbled.

Asa appeared in the hall leading to the back rooms. "How long did I sleep?"

I set my notepad on the coffee table. "About an hour or so. How do you feel?"

"Fine." He ducked back into the bedroom and reappeared holding his gun holster.

"Do you have to do that?" I asked.

"Do what?"

"Wear a gun."

Asa watched Butterfield go past me into the kitchen, carrying two boxes of pizza. "He carries a gun. Why don't you yell at him?"

"I'm not yelling." Then his words registered. "Wait a minute. Mr. Butterfield, are you carrying a weapon?"

"You can call me Butterfly." Butterfield poked his head around the kitchen entryway. "Sure I'm carrying a gun. Where're your paper plates?"

"Use the dishes," I said. "Where's your gun?"

"Huh?"

I went to the kitchen archway. "You heard me. Where is your gun?"

He tugged up his T-shirt and turned, displaying a small gun in a holster clipped to his belt on the right side. "Got one in an ankle holster, too, but I don't show my legs to strange ladies, and lady, you are strange." He grinned and opened cupboard doors.

"Next to the stove." I went into the dining room where Chessy sat, staring intently at the tabletop and the jigsaw pieces scattered there. "Is it legal for them to carry guns in Minnesota?"

"Probably not. It's probably illegal for them to carry guns anywhere." She didn't shift her attention from the group of pieces she was rearranging. "They're both convicted felons. Anyone convicted of a felony is prohibited from using firearms. I think it's a Federal law."

"If it's a Federal law, why didn't those Federal agents arrest Skinny when he had a gun aimed at 'em?" Butterfield asked. "You want a beer?"

Chessy held up her glass. "Still got some. I don't know why they didn't arrest him. They're Feds. They have plots within plans within plots. You know about their involvement in the Kennedy assassination, right?"

"Let's not go into that," I said hastily. "Are you hungry?" I asked Asa, who came into the dining room to stand next to Chessy.

"What are you doing?" he asked her.

"Sorting the colors. I think it's an eight-sided puzzle." She remained focused on sliding puzzle pieces around, pushing some into the five larger groups on the left side of the table.

Asa sank down into the chair next to her. "Eight sides?"

"More than four, that's for sure." Asa reached for a piece but Chessy thrust out her elbow, blocking him. "If you're going to play, follow the rules. Straight pieces there." She tapped one group of pieces. "Bright blue and white pieces there. Pastel colors there. Flesh tone there. Everything else over there." She tapped the largest pile.

"Here. Take a break." Butterfield thrust a plate of pizza at her.

"Great. I'm starved." Chessy rolled her shoulders then twisted her head from side to side. I heard faint popping noises.

"I usually sort by shape," Asa said.

"Good luck with that. I tried that but a lot of them are weird shapes. This wasn't cut like most puzzles. See what I mean?"

I moved around the table to stand behind her and Asa. She was right. I examined the piece she held up over her head. It wasn't cut in the standard square-with-indentations, but instead was shaped like . . . "That's the Eiffel Tower, isn't it?"

"Or it's some kind of tower. There are some that are round with curly edges, and a couple that are, like, melty looking and some that are like onions and some that are boxes." She dropped the piece into the "everything else" pile and took up the plate of pizza.

I leaned over the table between her and Asa. "What's this?" I picked up a piece that was gray with lettering on it.

"Some of them are like that." Butterfield slid into the seat opposite us. "Just a gray background."

"It's the reverse side," Asa said. "Someone wrote something on the reverse of the puzzle before it was cut." He started flipping pieces over.

"Hey!" Chessy grabbed his hand.

"If we can assemble the reverse with the lettering that should give us a big chunk of the puzzle."

"Or not." She forced his hand down to the table. "We thought about that, but the lettering is probably a tiny piece of the puzzle."

"At least let me try. I'll flip over all the ones you have sorted. If one has lettering, I'll take it. Otherwise I'll leave it alone." Asa's hand crept forward toward the "everything else" pile of pieces.

"That makes sense," I said. "As long as you return things to how they were, it shouldn't disturb anything."

Chessy took a bite of pizza and chewed, eyeing us suspiciously. "I suppose," she finally said grudgingly. "Just don't fuck it up."

We ate in companionable silence, each of us moving pieces around and sorting according to our own criteria. I finally pushed my chair back. "I need to get to the library before they close to do some research."

"Which branch?" Asa asked.

"The main library downtown would be best, I suppose."

"Let's split up. Butterfly, you take the Jeep and go with Miss Chessy to the Minneapolis library. I'll use Alice's car and drop her at the St. Paul library. I'll pick her up at five, when they close. We should go through all the research material tonight. Let's all meet at the warehouse at six. We need to talk about how to handle Roberta Hart tomorrow, too."

"Wait a minute," Butterfield said. "What about you? What are you doing?"

"I have research of my own to do." Asa went to the kitchen with our empty plates.

"What kind?" I asked.

"You'll see." He came back to the dining room doorway. "Let's get going." He went into the living room and picked up the white box. "I'm storing this away again. Do you need your book bag?"

It held all my backup disks. I wasn't letting those out of my sight. "Yep. Put that legal pad in there, okay? Let me grab a sweater." I ducked into my bedroom and met the others in the hall leading to the garage, Asa with my bag slung over his shoulder.

"Do you have time for this?" I asked Chessy in the garage. "I didn't mean to recruit you like this."

"Like I said, this is my first case. It's good experience." She paused with me by the passenger door of my car while Asa and Butterfield spoke near the driver's side. "Besides, I like them. I think he got a bad break. A little *pro bono* work is good." She went around the car to the garage door. "Let's get this show on the road."

"Man, she is bossy," Butterfield grumbled.

I tossed my car keys to Asa. "My wheels aren't as classy as yours."

"They'll do." We got into the car and followed Butterfield and Chessy in the Jeep until we got to the main road going through town. They turned left to go to Minneapolis and we went right to go to St. Paul.

Asa seemed as preoccupied as I was and I was grateful. Too much had happened too fast and I needed time to process it. The Saturday afternoon traffic was light, which wasn't surprising. St. Paul didn't have a thriving downtown outside of business hours. Besides, it was a beautiful spring day in early May. People would be out in the parks or the lakes, enjoying the weather. I tilted my head to the sun and let the light make patterns on my eyelids.

In twenty minutes we were downtown, at the big three-story brick building housing the Central Library. "I'll pick you up here in a couple of hours," Asa said, twisting in the driver's seat to regard me. "Five o'clock. Don't leave the building until I get back."

"What if I get done early?"

"Just wait for me." He leaned closer. "I'm sure Dodge or White followed us. Don't give them any chance to get you alone outside the building."

"What do you mean?"

"Be careful." He kissed me then glanced at the rear-view mirror. "I'm holding up traffic."

"Asa, do you think they'll—"

He put his hand over mine. "I don't think they'll do anything if you don't give them a chance. Now go."

I got out of the car and turned to talk to him, but he

162

was already accelerating. I barely had time to close the door before he was gone. I went into the main entrance and paused to get my bearings. The library was a big old-fashioned kind with enormous windows rounded at the top, a huge central open area and rows of wooden tables along the sides. The place reminded me of a combination church and library, with the balconies holding the books while the worshipers bustled around below, their feet making shuffling sounds on the marble floor.

I headed for the computers set between massive columns supporting the upper floors. Most of the card catalog was digital now so hopefully I could find what I needed somewhat quickly. Everything on my list of questions started and ended with Roberta Hart. She was the place to begin. I found an open computer and entered a few keywords.

Fifteen minutes later I had a list of reference numbers for information about the Hart family, Roberta Hart the politician, Burbank in the 1970s, the film industry, and general guides to rifles and shooting.

I spied an open public computer terminal and pulled out the wooden chair in front of it. The chair was probably deliberately uncomfortable to remind patrons to limit their time at the terminal. The Rules for Use informed me I had to use my library card number to access the Internet.

I dutifully entered it then the screen cleared and a small digital clock appeared in the top right corner of the screen. I had sixty minutes of use. I checked my legal pad of questions and accessed Lycos to being searching.

Forty-five minutes of computer use gave me a

glimpse into Roberta Hart's current life. Socialite, Republican darling, owner of a townhouse in Washington, D.C., a lake home in Northern Minnesota, and a mansion in Eden Prairie, outside the Twin Cities. Her web site gave me a list of the Congressional committees where she served and I made a note of those to research further.

Her father had been a power in California's banking industry, headquartered in Sacramento. He died a decade earlier and was buried in Placerville, the small town not far from Sacramento where the family lived. A quick check of an online map showed me that Woodland, California wasn't far from Sacramento on the north, so presumably that was where Hart was born, which explained the baby prints I found at the bottom of the box.

Hart's husband, Redmond King, split his time between Minneapolis, Chicago, and New York City. He served on the boards of several banks, supported a few high-profile charities, and was seen with celebrities and other high rollers at All the Right Places. He was in his mid-sixties but appeared to have no plans to retire. His wife spent most of her time in Washington unless she was in Minnesota for a charitable or political event, often the two combined into one large fundraiser for either her or the charity du jour.

I paid for the pages I printed at the main desk and headed upstairs to pursue the books I wanted. We were in the mid-cycle of the Presidential races, that time when candidates were starting to test out the waters. Hart set up an exploratory committee to evaluate her options and I wanted to see if I could find out more information about the people giving her their support.

I went first to the government section to scoop up some congressional publications about Senate committees. Next I headed for the 623 section which had gun books, wedging three books under my arm so I could check the numbers I'd scrawled on a scrap of paper. The Presidential race made me think of Chessy, who was probably expounding her Kennedy assassination conspiracy theories to Butterfield at that moment. If you didn't know she was paranoid about conspiracies, her theories sounded pretty reasonable.

That led me to think about President Clinton, who was starting to try the patience of many Americans. A candidate like Roberta Hart might be appealing to a scandal-weary population. I checked the slip of paper in my hand then reviewed the numbers on the spines of the books on the shelves. I turned the corner of the large bookcase, looked up—

And almost ran into Roberta Hart.

Chapter Eleven

I stepped back into a bookcase, knocking two books to the floor. "What are you doing here?" I blurted.

The reality was more petite than I expected. Roberta Hart was probably my height, five-one, although she wore platform shoes, making her taller. She was very fine-boned and appeared fragile, delicate. Her long, dark red hair was streaked with blonde and piled into a loose bun on the back of her head. Tendrils of hair wisped around her thin face. Her eyes were her most striking facial feature. Large and brown, they were tipped downward at the outside edge, giving her a hooded, mysterious appearance.

She moved closer to me and that's when her other notable physical feature came into view. Roberta Hart had an hourglass figure with large breasts, a small waist, and wide hips. Despite her short height, she was perfectly proportioned so she didn't appear overweight, just lush. Her dark green knit top showed off her assets as did the dark, skin-tight jeans. "Did you really think I was stupid enough to meet you in a public place like the Edina Country Club?"

"How did you know I'd be here?" I edged backward, books clutched to my chest like a shield against her anger.

"Don't be naive. I had you followed. As soon as I

knew you'd be here for some time, I came inside." Her gaze flickered beyond me.

I turned. A man blocked my exit and the bookcases around us hemmed me in. He wasn't tall but was solidly built with a shiny bald head and the sort of intense look I associated with police officers or criminals. His dark brown suit covered what appeared to be a heavily muscled body if his hulking shoulders were any indication.

"I don't have to talk to you." I tried to push my way past Hart.

She grabbed my arm and jerked. Books flew out of my grasp and hit the floor with resounding thuds. "What do you want?" she demanded, tugging me close to her. "Why did you send me this?"

Something white fluttered in front of my face. I grabbed for it, my book bag swinging off my shoulder and hitting Hart solidly in the stomach. She grunted and stepped back, overbalanced, and began tottering on her stylish chunky shoes.

I grabbed the photograph from her and took advantage of her distraction to dart past, leaving the aisle of bookcases and heading for a large wooden table and four chairs set in a small alcove nearby. I dropped the two books I still held and sank into a chair. If she wanted to dislodge me, she'd have to take the chair with me.

I examined the photograph of a girl and boy on a beach blanket. Before I could study it more closely, she slid into the chair next to me on the right and snatched the picture out of my hands. "Where did you get this?" I started to reply but she held up a hand. "Wait." She gestured imperiously, a quick snap of her hand. The man who blocked my exit from the book stacks appeared at her right side.

"Stand up," she demanded, staring at me.

"What?" I twisted to look at the man, who now loomed over me in my chair.

"I said stand up. Leo needs to search you."

I clung to my chair with both hands. "Absolutely not. How dare you. This is a public place. You can't force me to do anything."

"And I'm a public figure." She leaned closer to me. "You have no idea what I can and can't do, Miss Little. I suggest you cooperate."

I stared her straight in the eye. "And I suggest you quit treating me like one of your paid slaves. I don't have to talk to you." I turned away, still holding tight to my chair lest her goon grab me and wrest me bodily away.

"And I suggest you leave her alone."

I twisted in my chair at the sound of that calm voice, coming from the book stacks behind us. Asa sauntered out from among the books. I smiled in relief until I saw his gun, held straight down at his side.

The man saw it, too. He pushed his jacket aside but Asa raised his gun, pointing not at the man, but at Roberta Hart. I froze, for the first time realizing how big a gun was and how ominous it appeared when pointed at someone. I may have been a foot or two out of the firing line, but I had a good view of what she faced.

"You're in a public library," Hart whispered. She appeared frozen, too, her hands clenching the back of her chair. Her knuckles were white and her arms trembled. "You'll never pull that trigger."

"Do you want to gamble with a mad man?" Asa moved forward until he was a few feet away. He stared at her, his blue eyes flat and cold. Then he pulled back his jacket, slipped the gun into the holster and stood next to me. "I told you I had some research to do," he said with a smile.

A second or two later, three people approached us from the left around another bookcase. They were young, probably in their teens, and they were giggling about something until they saw all us grownups sitting there, grim-faced. Their laughter cut off abruptly and they scurried away, disappearing down an aisle of books.

Asa put his hands on my shoulders. "You won't search her and you won't threaten her. If you do, there will be consequences."

Hart stood and moved around the table, taking the seat opposite me. Her man, Leo, followed her, and took up position behind her. I suppose we looked like four crazy figures in a chess game, with the queens facing off and their knights guarding them.

"Where did you get the photograph?" Hart leaned on the table, clasping her hands in front of her. Her fingernails were a dark red that matched her hair color. I wondered if she had both done at the same salon.

"I didn't send you that photograph." I clasped my own unmanicured hands on the tabletop and let my book bag slide to the seat next to me. "I don't know who sent it or why they had my name on it."

Asa's hands massaged my neck gently, working on that tense spot where shoulders, neck and back all met. "Alice was drawn into this in order to draw me out."

Hart stared at him, her head tilted to one side and

her full lips pursed into a pucker, a pose she probably cultivated for press conferences. "And who are you, besides her bodyguard?" The man leaned over and whispered in her ear. She drew back, startled.

Asa's hands stilled then resumed the gentle massage. "Madison Hatterley."

Her gaze flicked to me then back to Asa. "You're the man who killed Harry March."

"There's some debate about that," I said. "Not all the evidence was presented at the trial."

Her stare shifted to me. "That explains you. Oh, yes, I read the story about the genius children, thrown together in college. I didn't know he was back in the picture. I also know you're an entrepreneur who sold her business, I know you're relatively wealthy, and I know you're registered as an Independent voter." One side of her red lips twisted up in a wry smile. "I do my research, too."

"You missed one important point." I reached up and touched Asa's hand. "I'm still his friend. I don't let friends get a bum deal."

Hart leaned back, resting her elbows on the arms of her chair and setting her chin on her steepled fingers. "That means someone sent me something that would lead me to you two. Why?"

"That isn't the only thing of yours we have," Asa said.

She raised her head. "What do you mean?"

He flipped open my book bag and pulled out *Sexy Sorority Slaves*, setting it on the table between us with the cover clearly visible. He reached in again and drew out several pictures, arranging them carefully so Hart could see them.

I tugged on his hand until he leaned over. "The next time you want me to be a courier, tell me, okay?" I whispered. Then I realized what that meant. "Hey. Did you know she'd be here? Why did you put that stuff in my bag?"

"Do you trust me?" he whispered back.

"Of course."

"I'll explain later." He straightened.

I turned my attention to Hart. She was transfixed by the objects on the table. I expected her to grab the videotape, but instead she reached for one of the pictures, a photograph of a young woman in a formal dress and a young man in a tux. The woman might have been her, but I couldn't tell by viewing it upside down.

"Where did you get this?" she asked hoarsely. "It's from my scrapbook and was stolen from me years ago."

"Stolen?" Asa asked. "When?"

I peered up at him. "Don't you mean who?"

He shook his head. "When will tell us who."

"You know who." Hart picked up another picture and stared at it. I couldn't quite interpret the expression in her pale green eyes. Longing, sadness, remorse, excitement all seemed to take a turn until finally she met my gaze, her eyes once again cold and expressionless. "What I want to know is how did you get it from him and what do you plan to do with it?"

Did I say this was a chess match? This was a poker game between two deadly serious competitors, both adept at bluffing. Neither was revealing anything. I had no idea what she meant, but Asa knew. I felt it when his hands tightened, loosened then tightened again on my shoulders. "I have no desire to use the information I have unless it's essential."

"What do you want?" She set the pictures down in front of her, her left index finger moving over the edge of one of them, a photo of a young man standing in front of a body of water. The man was tanned, the sand was light brown, and the water seemed incredibly blue.

"I want to know the truth about Harry March."

She touched one of the other photographs. This one showed a man in front of a car in a parking lot. I don't know why I thought *young man* in one picture and *man* in another one, but there was a real difference between the two.

"Harry showed up in my hometown, pretending to be a scout for a modeling agency." Her mouth quirked up in a half-smile. "I suppose you know the story. Girl falls for guy, guy takes her to the city, guy convinces her to star in the movies."

Hart leaned forward and picked up the videocassette. "And that's what I have to show for my time with Harry March." She tossed the box toward me. I caught it before it could slide off the table. "My father bought him off and brought me home. I changed my life and now I'm a respected wife and mother and a U.S. Senator."

"And Harry March is dead, killed when he tried to blackmail you." Asa's voice was soft but his hands on my shoulders were stiff and unyielding.

"Killed by you." Hart studied the pictures then she raised her head to view us. "Have you ever heard of toxic love? Of course you have." She glanced at Asa. "The genius children, thrown together, so in love. Somehow I don't think it was quite as toxic as—" Her voice trailed away when she viewed the pictures on the table.

"Harry?" I prompted.

Her eyes widened and her cheeks turned a dull red. "Yes, of course. Harry."

Wrong. She meant someone else. Who? I remembered the scrapbook and the love letters in French. Little details clicked into place. The scrapbook and all the pictures. The flowers in an old shoebox.

Roberta Hart, in so many school pictures with one student.

Roberta at the Prom with one student.

Roberta in another picture with *Placerville's Connection to Europe.* "Juan Santiago," I murmured. "A foreign exchange student."

Her shocked stillness was all the answer I needed. "What happened? Did you fall in love with him but he left to go home? Did you leave with Harry because you felt rejected?"

She was silent, her gaze going to the books I dropped on the table then going to the photographs again. "My infatuation with Juan had nothing to do with Harry." One bright red fingernail flicked two of the pictures back at me, one by one.

One slid off the table and I leaned over to pick up the photo of the older man in front of the car. I held it up so she could see it then slid it back across the table. "Is that him? Is that Harry March?" I knew it was, of course. I saw a picture of March in the trial transcripts. He was a tall, tanned man with thick blond hair and the rangy physique of a surfer.

"That was Harry." Hart nodded to my books on the tabletop. "Planning to shoot someone?"

"Not today." I glanced at the books, one about Senate subcommittees and one about guns and forensic investigation. I slid my legal pad over the top of them. It was full of scribbles about Hart's birthplace and Roberta's father. There was nothing there that mattered if she saw it. "You don't seem too upset about Harry March's murder."

"I had a love-hate relationship with Harry. A lot has happened since then. I don't hold grudges." She smiled but it didn't reach her eyes.

"Somehow I don't believe you." There was a small niggling little detail, some *thing* that someone said that stuck in my mind. I struggled to retrieve it, to bring it to light. "What are you going to do now?"

Her fingers tapped out a staccato rhythm on the tabletop. "Let's cut to the chase. You and I know that a woman can't get elected to the Presidency. The country isn't ready for that. I'm going to give it a good run, though. What do you want to make all this—" She creased the photo and tossed it at me, "to make all this go away?"

"I want to know the truth about Harry March's death." Asa spoke very softly but I heard the underlying threat in his voice. *I want to know the truth or else.*

"I don't know what the truth is," she said. "I had nothing to do with his death."

"Wrong answer," he said.

Hart frowned, dark eyebrows drawn together in puzzlement.

"You should have said there is no other truth except that I was convicted and that's that."

She waved a hand. "Whatever. You seem to think there's some other truth and as you said, it's not wise to argue with a mad man."

I remembered what I read on her web site about her

family. "I heard your son is interested in politics as well."

"Jack's young yet." Hart smiled faintly, one edge of her mouth quirking up. "Yes, he's very civic minded. I'm not sure he's cut out for the political life, though."

"Don't you have a daughter, too?"

Her hand stilled. "Yes."

"Perhaps she's more the political type. As you said, the country isn't ready for a woman President yet. But by the time she's ready to make a run at it, we might be ready. Of course, it might be difficult if her mother is exposed as a porn star." I shrugged. "Or not. Who knows how people will feel ten or twenty years from now?"

Hart stood, her wooden chair screeching on the tile floor. Her attention was past me, at Asa, who still stood behind me. "That depends on you. If you try to blackmail me, I'll see to it you're thrown back in jail. And this time you won't get out for good behavior."

"That would expose everything I have about you," he said.

Hart set her hands on the table and leaned forward. "If I'm going to be ruined, I'll see to it that you're ruined as well, and I'll make it my personal mission to ruin your friend here." She glanced at me then returned her full attention to Asa, showing I was insignificant. "I will ruin her in every way I can. And you will sit in jail and know that you caused her damnation."

I stood and leaned on the table, too, facing her down. "What the hell do you think you could do to ruin me?"

She straightened. "Perhaps some of those government contracts your company had were illegal.

My husband is on the board of several banks. Your credit score might suffer. It's possible you were involved with insider trading. You may have misused government property when you were doing some so-called volunteer work for the Veterans Administration. Your home mortgage may have been obtained using fraudulent credit information. There are all sorts of ways I can make your life a living hell, tying you up in court for years to come."

Asa gently pulled me back. "It's a stalemate. She's right."

"She's full of shit," I spat.

"You're not as smart as I was led to believe." Hart walked around the table until she was face to face with Asa. "You, though. Yes, you are smart. You know that I can do what I say and you also know that I would do it. I will stop at nothing to keep my past buried."

"Including murder." Asa stared at her, his voice emotionless.

"I had nothing to do with Harry March's murder." She turned to go.

"You weren't the redhead in the golf cart?" I asked.

She stopped in mid-step and turned. "What?"

I shrugged. "If you had nothing to do with his murder, it must have been another redhead who lured him out that day."

Hart stared at me, her eyes narrowed. "I have no idea what you're talking about. I was giving a talk at the Garden Grove Garden Club that afternoon. It stands out in my mind because I thought it was redundant to have a garden club in Garden Grove."

"What were you doing in California? Didn't you move to Minnesota around then?"

"Miss Little, you should know enough about politics to know it's useful to make public appearances regardless of where your constituency might be located." She picked up my legal pad and skimmed over what was there. "Very thorough. Very—" Her voice trailed away and she frowned at something she saw written there. "Anyway, I'm sure if you do a little bit more research you'll find out what I was doing that day."

"I'll do that." Her instructions-to-an-idiot tone of voice made me long to slap her. Instead I snatched the legal pad out of her hand. "Okay. I guess we're done here."

"There's one other thing." Asa gently touched my arm so I stood on his left side. Away from his gun if he drew it, I suppose. He moved forward until he was a foot away from Hart. "If you harm Alice in any way, I won't kill you. I'll kill someone you love. It may not be immediately, but I will do it. Don't forget what I'm capable of."

Hart stared into his eyes. "I'm not afraid of you."

"I guess what the press says about you is true. You are stubborn and arrogant. This isn't a threat. It's a promise."

"I can't be responsible for what happens to her." Hart backed away from us. "If she has an accident or gets into trouble, it's not my fault."

"You heard what I said. If you harm her in any way, I'll see to it that you pay."

The bulky man, Leo, moved forward when she passed him, blocking us from moving after her. He stared implacably at me, his right hand on his coat lapel, ready to push it to one side. That's when I recognized him. "You look better with a wig," I snapped.

"You know him?" Asa asked.

"His hands gave him away." I eyed the man's ragged cuticles. "He was at the Stand Down. He came in when you left."

"Senator Hart?" A young man approached us from the bookcases on the right. One glance at the guy told me he was a Young Republication. He was so clean-cut he should have squeaked when he moved.

Hart stopped. "Yes? Can I help you?" She was all smiles, stepping forward to meet the young man with her hand outstretched.

"This is an honor. I'm a fan of yours. You're doing a great job in Washington. I can't believe I actually get to meet you." He gave her hand a shake then dropped it, his face reddening. "I volunteered on your campaign, in the Alexandria office."

"I'm pleased to meet you. What's your name?" Hart pulled him to one side, away from us.

I stuffed my notepad into my book bag and grabbed the pictures and movie cassette. A little imp made me turn to her and ask, "Did you want to keep the movie, Roberta? Or did you want me to hold on to it?" I smiled at the star-struck young man, who had his gaze firmly fixed on his idol, the senator.

Hart moved, blocking his line of sight. "You keep it, dear. It's probably the sort of movie you'd enjoy."

"The weather forecast says perfect weather for the rally tomorrow," the fan said when Roberta began moving to the stairs. "I'm looking forward to it. It's such a great opportunity to hear all the important political figures speaking at one event. It's amazing it's going to be here, in Rice Park. How did you manage it? How did you get all those people to come here and speak?"

"I'm surprised he doesn't ask for her autograph," I muttered to Asa while I jammed the movie into my book bag. I slung it over my shoulder and reached for my books, but the guard, Leo, blocked my move.

"Wait here. You don't leave until she's gone." He turned to watch us and watch Hart go down the staircase, the young man keeping pace with her and talking the entire time. She paused at the bottom and peered up at us, standing in the balcony. Then she nodded to Leo and moved out of sight. The guard followed after her, racing down the staircase.

"Now what do we do?" I grumbled. "I don't understand this. None of it."

Asa went to the stairs and I followed. "Now we find Dodge and tell him what happened."

"Dodge? The Fed? You said he was following me, right?" I paused at the top of the steps, which gave me a good view of the lower level. Roberta Hart, her guard, and the babbling young man were exiting through the front doors. "Is Dodge here?"

"I doubt it. He followed you and me. White followed Chessy and Butterfly. When I dropped you off, he stuck with me. I didn't see him when I doubled back to meet you here, but he might have followed me and been nearby. He's pretty good at what he does."

"He's good at lurking, is that what you're saying?"

Asa burst out laughing. "I like that. Lurking."

"I'm serious." I led the way to the computer terminals. "I want to find out about that garden party thing."

"We can do that at my house."

"These are anonymous terminals."

He put a hand under my arm and steered me to the exit leading onto Rice Park, not the front exit I used earlier. "My terminal is an anonymous one, too. Trust me." He took the books from me and set them on a table before we exited.

I glanced around the large open main floor, where people—normal, everyday people—ambled around with no idea what had just transpired. I felt as ignorant as they were. "I don't understand what happened."

"She called our bluff. There is no blackmail scheme." He pushed open the door for me to the double stairway leading to Rice Park. "If anyone tries to blackmail her, your life gets ruined."

The limestone steps were worn in spots from years of foot traffic and I had to watch where I stepped or else I'd tumble. "I don't believe her. Why isn't she afraid we'll expose her? There's a lot of damning information in that box." I hurried after Asa when he took the diagonal sidewalk cutting through the center of the one-block-large city park.

"She knows I won't let anyone hurt you. I can't risk that." He moved fast and I had to hurry to keep up. The small park had a few patrons out strolling, enjoying the sun and warm temperatures but most of the benches lining the walkways were empty.

"Maybe she's bluffing. She can't really do anything she said she could."

"Of course she can." He stopped so quickly I ran into him. "Alice, I could do any of those things she said. I know how to hack a database and change your credit score. I know how to falsify records."

I touched his worried face. "You're a genius, Asa.

She isn't."

"But she can hire as many as she needs to do it." He closed his eyes briefly then took my hand, pressing it against his lips. "I won't take that risk. Besides, what does it matter to us if she's exposed? I got into this mess because I wanted to find out if I was a murderer or not. From what you said to her, you still have doubts." His dark blue eyes searched mine.

"I need to check the trial transcript again. Things don't add up. I've got something buzzing around in my head that won't come to the surface." I caressed his face. "I need to think through all of this. It feels like I've been on a merry-go-round and my head is spinning."

"That might make it easier for me to sweep you off your feet, then." Asa leaned forward and our lips met.

Chapter Twelve

This time our passion was undeniable and not just on Asa's part. I put my arms around him when he pulled me tight against him. I was vaguely aware of his gun, pressing against my arm then I lost myself in the kiss, in the warmth and the emotion and the feeling of—

Love? I pulled reluctantly away from him.

Insane. Any love I once had for him was decades out of date. It was crazy to think that I could fall in love with him in a day or two.

Crazy.

I looked up into his face. The face of a mad man. It might be crazy, but it might be true. I stretched upward to meet his lips again.

"You guys need a hotel room," a dry voice said behind me.

Asa peered over my head. "I wondered if you were following us." He released me and I turned to see Charles Dodge sitting on a bench in the sunlight.

"Of course I followed you." Dodge tilted his face up to the sun. "This feels good after the winter we had."

"Did you see her?" I gestured at the library. "She accosted me. That goon of hers wanted to search me. Isn't that against the law? Can't I sue her or something? I suppose this means we won't meet her tomorrow, right?"

Dodge's impenetrable façade loosened slightly and

his thin lips twitched in a brief smile. "Somehow, I don't think she ever planned on meeting us." He pointed to a sign, a pop-up fabric banner with metal supports driven into the grass. It fluttered in the breeze, one of many scattered throughout the park. Red, white, and blue streamers drifted around it.

"What's that?" I walked across the grass to the sign, holding it taut so I could more easily read it.

Republican Rally for Freedom

Come see U.S. Senator Roberta "Ruby" Hart and ask her the tough questions. She has the right answers for you and for America!

Underneath a picture of Hart was a list of other notable Republicans who would be at the rally, starting tomorrow, Sunday, at two in the afternoon. "That bitch. I suppose if she met me at noon, she could still get here, but I doubt she wants to be seen in my company on the day of a big rally. What kind of game is she playing?"

Dodge joined Asa in the middle of the sidewalk. "If she couldn't get you alone before tomorrow, I'm sure she'd show at the country club. But that was probably a last resort for her."

"Can't you arrest her?" I strode across the uneven ground to join them. "For heaven's sake, she must have to fill out an ethics or moral questionnaire before she runs for public office. She obviously lied on that and who knows what other things she lied about."

Asa put an arm around my shoulders. "Alice gets excitable when she's under stress."

I glared at him. "Who are you calling excitable?"

He kissed me quickly. "You're trembling, you're speaking a mile a minute, and you don't really make a lot of sense. You're stressed. Take a deep breath and chill." He smiled when he said it but I saw concern in his eyes.

He was right. My pulse was racing, I had an insane desire to pace or run or do *something* that involved action. That was the way I reacted to confrontation, something I usually avoided at all costs. Roberta Hart brought out the worst in me, damn her.

"She's done nothing illegal," Dodge said. "Even if she did star in pornographic movies when she was younger, that isn't illegal."

"She was a teenager," I protested half-heartedly.

"She was eighteen. Barely. The most she's guilty of is poor judgment. I'm sorry."

"If that's the case, why are you investigating her?" Asa's arm tightened around me, pulling me closer to him.

Dodge didn't answer for a moment. He stared at the rippling banner then turned to view the other people in the park. "I care about America. I care what happens in this country. Most people don't realize that we are constantly under attack. We are hated and reviled in other countries and we have been for years. For decades, really." His plain Everyman's face softened and for an instant he was notable, like an actor who shed makeup to reveal the true person underneath.

I glanced at Asa, expecting him to be as surprised as I was by this burst of patriotism. Instead I saw dawning comprehension in his eyes. I certainly didn't understand whatever he did. "And what does that have to do with Roberta Hart?" I demanded. "I'm sure she'd insist she's a patriot, too."

Dodge met Asa's eyes. "You know, don't you?"

"I think so," Asa said. "You want proof not only

from her past. You want evidence."

Dodge nodded.

"You were hoping she'd let something slip when she talked to us."

Dodge nodded again.

I turned from to the other. "Would someone tell me what's going on?"

"We need to do more research," Asa said.

"Her place or yours?" Dodge nodded at me. "I hope it's hers. The stakeout there is more comfortable."

"We'll go to mine to meet the others then to hers. If you watch my place, I own the building across the street. You guys can set up in the apartment on the third floor. It's empty." Asa began walking again.

"You own the building across from yours? Really?" I fell into step with him, Dodge on my right side.

"Yeah, the city wanted to tear it down and put up condos. I converted it into rentable studio space for artists. It's a good building." Asa walked to my car on the north side of the park while pulling a leather memo book from his jacket pocket. "Here's the entry code. Feel free to use it." He jotted something with the attached pen, tore off the sheet and handed it to Dodge.

"Thanks. I guess." Dodge creased the page and put it in his suit pocket. "How long will you be there?"

"Not long. Figure we'll be back at Alice's by seven or so." Asa glanced at me. "I know a good place for Chinese takeout. Let's grab some and take it back to your house."

"Don't do anything stupid tonight, like try to get out without us seeing you. We're there to protect you."

I jerked on the passenger door handle but it was

locked. Asa shot me a disapproving glance. "You need to learn to lock things." He slipped into the car and I heard the door locks click.

Dodge opened the door for me and leaned on it after I dropped inside. "Make sure he sticks to the plan, okay?" He spoke to Asa. "You have it with you? The information about Hart?"

Asa started the car. "It's safe."

I fumbled open my book bag and pulled out the photographs and videocassette. "Here's some of it."

Dodge glanced at the photograph, the one Hart creased and tossed at me. "Who's this?"

Asa leaned across me. "I'll fill you in tomorrow. Stay in touch."

Dodge closed my door and stepped back. "We won't be far."

Asa drove north and I expected him to get on the freeway but instead he took a left turn on a residential street. St. Paul's road system always boggled me because of the one-way streets, but Asa seemed to know exactly where he was and where he was going.

I was content to sit in silence, attempting to digest everything that happened to me in—what was it, two days? Today was Saturday and I saw Asa on Friday morning. Good Lord, one day and look what happened, my life was pitched upside-down and inside-out. Prior to this the most exciting event in the past five years had been the sale of my company and moving across country. That paled in comparison to this.

"The reason Roberta Hart came into the picture was because of that box that was sent to me," Asa said after five minutes of driving.

"And because of her connection to Harry March," I

reminded him.

He nodded, eyes focused ahead while he navigated the busy streets around the University of Minnesota. School was still in session, but most students were in the middle of finals and the campus was relatively quiet. "It's all a part of a bigger whole, but how? I thought Harte was the common denominator but I'm starting to wonder if Harry March is, instead. Maybe he's the connecting piece."

"Like the key piece in a jigsaw puzzle. You know the one—when you fit it into place, the puzzle starts to make sense."

He glanced at me, his face thoughtful. "The jigsaw puzzle. What does that have to do with all this?"

"We'll know once we solve it."

"Maybe. Or maybe it's another red herring. Whoever sent that box to me has been manipulating us from the start."

"Manipulating you," I said. "I'm just along for the ride."

"I'm not so sure about that. If anyone researched one of us, they'd find the other. Anybody who checked on me would know about my connection to you and vice versa." He was quiet for several more minutes. "Who sent the box? That's the key piece to our puzzle."

"Let's go through it again," I said. "Maybe the answer is in there."

"I hope so." His hands opened and closed on the steering wheel. "Tell me what I said when you hypnotized me. I need to know."

In the past, I always gave him a brief summary of what I discovered because in the past his blackouts were usually innocuous. That wouldn't do this time. I launched into a recitation of what he told me, making my telling as concise and detailed as possible.

"You were set up," I said while we crossed the Mississippi River to the Minneapolis side of town. "And drugged. I'm sure of it. I need to check the evidence list from your trial. Did they do a blood test?"

"No. They got me a full day after the murder. I doubt it would have shown anything. That's why you asked Roberta Hart about the red-haired woman. You think she might have been there." He pulled into his building and we went through the same procedure as the day before with his key cards.

"I don't know. If she was there, why? Was she needed to get him out in the open?" I shook my head. "Who knows?"

Asa parked in an empty slot next to the blue Jeep. "I don't remember any of it." He stared at the garage wall ahead of us. "None of it. Did I really pull the trigger?" We got out of my car and walked to the elevator. "Who? Who set me up?"

"Tuttle," I said. "Someone you trusted."

We rode in silence up to the third floor. "If he set me up, I'll find him." Asa stalked out of the elevator into his kitchen. "I want answers."

Butterfield and Chessy sat on a couch in the living room, the multi-colored cat perched on the cushion above Butterfield's head. Three sets of eyes regarded us when we entered the room. "Two Feds are outside," Butterfield said.

"I know. I talked to Dodge earlier. I told them to use the apartment if they're going to be hanging out long."

Butterfield began to speak then subsided when Asa

stalked into the kitchen, slammed open the fridge, and pulled out a beer. The big man looked a question at me. I shook my head then sank down on the couch opposite him, which gave me a panoramic view of the river and the buildings on the opposite bank.

Asa joined me, twisting off the cap of the beer and taking a long swallow before sitting down. "What did you find out?"

Chessy picked up a red spiral notebook from the coffee table. "I figured I needed more writing space," she said, waggling the notebook at us. "We dropped by a Target for this and some breath mints."

"You have priorities," I murmured.

Chessy ignored my sarcasm. "I'll submit a bill later. This goes on the expense account." She flipped open the notebook, missing the startled glance Asa and I exchanged. "Okay, here's what I got. We didn't have much luck finding information about Burbank in the Seventies, but I got a bit. The northeast part of town, near the mountains, was mostly undeveloped until the Eighties. There were only a few roads back then. The freeway, I-210, wasn't finished yet." She leaned forward and unfolded a map of Southern California, turning it so it faced us.

I traced a line with my finger from Los Angeles to Burbank, following the path of the big highways. "This highway wasn't there then?" I tapped one fat red line.

"Nope. Only a state highway. Most of the land northeast of there was still undeveloped with a few pockets of homes here and there."

"Were you able to find anything about a house like Asa described?"

"That was cool," Butterfield said, his right hand

angled up to rub the cat's ears. "We found this old book about Southern California architecture. I never would have thought of that, but Blondie did."

"It sounded like a rich guy's house and a lot of times somebody puts together books about expensive homes." Chessy reached to the floor and set a big coffee-table type book next to the map, opening it to the page marked with a slip of paper. "This section has houses in Burbank that might fit the bill. Most are owned by movie stars or movie execs, but a couple were owned by businessmen. They were some of the first rich people in that area."

I studied the two-page spread of photographs. "This one." I tapped a picture on the right-hand page. "That seems like the one you described. It's all windows and chrome and one story and wood." I slid the book across my lap to Asa.

He stared down at the picture, his face unreadable. "I don't recognize it."

I took the book back and read the caption. "Stunning mountain home of Packard Card, millionaire philanthropist and retired business executive."

"I did some digging about Packard Card." Chessy took up her notebook again. "Turns out he was on the boards of a few banks. A couple of the banks were ones that Roberta Hart's father was on the board, too."

"They were friends," I said. "Hart could have used his house."

"If it's the right house," Asa said. "I don't remember it." He sounded tense.

I set the book on the coffee table and leaned back, slipping my arm through his. "It's a start."

"I got the dope on that Major who jacked you

around," Butterfield said. "Once I figured out how that card catalog thing worked, I checked for some military records. There's a lot of crap the government saves about everybody. No wonder people get lost in the system all the time. Anyway, it took some digging but I found out Tuttle retired from the service in 1977. He got a job working as a security consultant to a big corporation out East." Butterfield stared expectantly at Asa. "Go ahead. Ask me about it. Go ahead."

Asa smiled even though I still sensed the tenseness radiating out from his body. "Okay, I'll ask. What corporation was that?"

"Now that's interesting. It took some checking, which mostly Blondie did, but it turns out Tuttle worked for a company that owned a company that managed a company that was owned by Roberta Hart's father." Butterfield tapped Chessy's notebook with one beefy finger. "It's all there, man. All there."

"Where's Tuttle now?" Asa asked, his voice low and harsh.

"Retired. Someplace in North Carolina." Chessy flipped more pages in the notebook. "Yeah, that's the last address I could find."

"I'll find him," Asa murmured. "No problem."

"You guys did a ton of work," I said. "Good job."

"One other thing." Chessy flipped more pages in her book. "I went over the transcript of the trial. There's a diagram of the crime scene and the bullet trajectory. That was one hell of a shot. According to the coroner's report, it was directly centered on the heart." She frowned at Asa. "Not many people could do it."

"I know a half-dozen people who could." He drained his beer and set the bottle on the table, our bodies separating. "So did Tuttle. He had access to the best marksmen in the service."

"What about you guys? Did you have any luck with your research?" Chessy closed the notebook and leaned back. The cat edged past Butterfield to rest near Chessy, sniffing her blonde hair.

I reached for my book bag but Asa said, "We still have a bunch of research to do. We're heading back to Alice's house. We need to check that box of stuff and the jigsaw puzzle."

"You didn't find out anything?" Butterfield asked incredulously.

"Better than that," I said. "We talked to Roberta Hart."

Chessy's eyes widened. "Seriously?"

I nodded. "She followed me there."

"What happened? What did she say?"

"We came to an understanding," Asa said. "If she leaves Alice alone, I leave her alone."

"What? That's it?" Chessy's head snapped from me to Asa then back to me. "You believe her?"

Asa stood. "We need to get more information. Butterfly, can you stop by The Looking Glass and get dinner? You and Chessy meet us at Alice's house. Take her car." He dropped my car keys on the coffee table and went back into the kitchen.

"What's up?" Butterfield asked me softly.

I shrugged. "Not sure."

"I'm sorry, guys, but I can't join you." Chessy handed Butterfield her notebook. "You'll have to carry on without me. I've got some stuff I need to do tonight. What about tomorrow? What time are you leaving to meet Hart? Are you still meeting her?"

"We haven't nailed that down yet," Asa said.

I joined him in the kitchen, where he was changing the black gun in his shoulder holster for a dark gray gun from the box in the cupboard. "What's going on?" I asked in a low voice.

"I want to get going on an idea I have." He examined the gun, removing a part which I assumed was ammunition then reinserting it into the gun with a sharp jab of his hand. "I need to check the contents of that box again. I get the feeling we missed something." He tucked the gun into the holster.

Butterfield and Chessy joined us at the door. "I'll drop her off at her car then get some food and come by the house. You'll be okay alone?" Butterfield's gaze bounced anxiously from me to Asa. "You need me to follow?"

"Dodge or White will be following," Asa said. "We'll be fine. Meet us at Alice's house as soon as you can." He headed for the doorway leading to the elevator foyer.

"Okay, I'll feed Duchess then we'll get on the road." Butterfield watched Asa stab at the elevator button then turned to me. "What's got him pissed off?"

"I don't know," I said. "He seemed fine on the drive over here. You know how he gets, though, when he has an idea he wants to explore."

"Yeah, I know. He gets as skittish as a newbie in a prison shower." Butterfield went to a cupboard and opened the door, rattling it a few times. "Come on, cat. Chow."

The cat jumped down from the couch and trotted into the kitchen to sit on the floor next to the big man.

"Thank you for all your help." I impulsively

hugged Chessy. "Really, you've been great about all this. I can't tell you what it means that you did this work for us."

She grinned and drew the battered little notepad out of her back pocket. "I kept track of my hours. Tell him I'll bill him."

"You do that. I'll see you later."

"Any preference on Chinese food?" the big man asked, reaching into a cupboard for a can of cat food.

"Shrimp or scallops only, no beef or chicken, and not too spicy." I hurried after Asa, who stood by the open elevator door, waiting for me.

"What's your hurry?" I asked while the car moved downward.

"You have Internet access at your home, don't you? A high speed line?"

"Yes, I do. It's as high-speed as I could get out in the sticks. Why?"

"I need to do some searches."

"Aren't you worried about somebody hacking the signal so they'll know what you're doing?" We entered the garage and Asa headed for the BMW sports coupe.

"I can fix that. There's nothing to worry about." He touched the key fob in his hand and the car chirped. "Get in."

I slid into the passenger seat and buckled my seat belt. "What has you upset? What's going on?"

He backed out with a screech of tires. We left the garage in record time, swinging out into the street and heading south before I could get my book bag settled on the floor at my feet.

"Asa, what's going on? Tell me."

He didn't speak for a long moment. "I don't know if

anybody who wasn't in the service could understand."

"Understand what?" I studied his profile when it lightened then darkened as we drove. The setting sun was a brilliant ball in the distance, giving everything an orange glow.

Asa jammed the car into gear and we careened around a corner, then we merged onto the Interstate heading south. "Tuttle." His voice was low and bitter. "He betrayed my trust. He betrayed the trust of everyone he served with. We rely on each other in our unit, our division, our battalion. We're a team. He betrayed us when he sold me out."

He was right. I didn't understand such reliance on another person or other people. But I did understand he was deeply hurt. I put my hand over his on the gear shift. "What will you do about it?"

"I'll find out where he is and I'll kill him." He glanced at me then returned his focus to the road. "It's not revenge. It's nothing that small. This is about trust."

There it was. That word again. "It's always about trust with you, isn't it?"

Asa nodded once, sharply. "Everything is built on trust. Love, respect, understanding. It all depends on trust."

"Killing Tuttle might get you into big trouble," I said.

"Maybe. But I doubt he'll be checking over his shoulder. It's been a long time and as far as he knows, I'm still the crazy guy who needs drugs to get by." Asa's shoulders relaxed. "Don't worry, Alice. I won't involve you in it. You won't be affected."

"Of course I will be," I said. "What will I do if you get caught?"

He shot me a startled glance. "What?"

I squeezed his hand. "I can't lose you again, Asa. Not when I found you."

He drew in a long breath. "I wasn't sure you felt that way."

I smiled. "I feel that way right now. Keep in mind I'm all dizzy from everything that's been happening. Once my feet land on the ground, I might change my mind."

"Then I'll make sure to keep you spinning." He slipped his hand around mine then lifted it to his lips to kiss it. "Promise."

I drew my hand away. "Right now, try to keep this car from spinning, okay? You're driving way too fast for the amount of traffic."

He laughed. "I'll keep you safe, don't worry. I feel the same way. I'm not going to lose you again now that I've found you." He let the car slow down to the speed limit and focused again on the road ahead.

"What were you and Dodge talking about earlier? When we were in the park? Why is Dodge keeping an eye on Roberta Hart?"

"I'm not completely sure. Before I say anything, I want to go through that scrapbook again. And I want you to help me." He held up his right hand briefly before I could ask a question. "You'll see things I won't. You understand the social aspect of what was in that box. You understand the value it might have to Hart. I don't."

"Didn't you save any mementoes from when we were in college? From the Marines? Weren't there souvenirs you wanted to keep?"

"The one thing of value to me in college was you.

And the only thing of value to me from the Marines was the ability I learned to keep my disease under control. Neither of those required a bunch of letters or pictures to remind me." He glanced at me quickly before steering the car through four lanes of slow-moving traffic. "I did keep a picture of you. And the letters you wrote me when I was in Basic Training. I know you kept my paintings. Anything else?"

"I kept your letters and some photographs." I stared out my window at the urban landscape sliding past, remembering college, our past together, the things that used to be important. "The jigsaw puzzle has to mean something. That's why she kept it. That and—" I struggled to remember the other item in the white box that seemed odd to me. "Something else. I can't remember what."

"Why is the puzzle important?"

"It doesn't fit. It's the one thing that doesn't fit. The movies, the scrapbook, all of that. They're similar to each other. But the puzzle is different than all of them."

"Doesn't fit," Asa murmured. "The shapes don't fit." He frowned, eyes narrowed in thought. "What doesn't fit here?"

"What do you mean?"

"What doesn't fit? We know I was set up. We know my C.O. knew Roberta Hart's father. We know someone stole information from Harry March and sent it to me."

"Okay!" I tossed up my hands. "Tell me something I don't know."

"Who sent it and why did they send it? And why aren't we trying to find out about that?" He tilted his head slightly to one side as if he viewed the puzzle from a different angle.

I recognized that look. He knew something or thought he did. He was exploring possibilities.

"That's it. What doesn't fit into the picture?" Asa started to smile. "That has to be it. That explains Dodge's interest, it explains Harry March trying to blackmail Roberta Hart, and it explains why March was murdered."

"What does?"

Asa pressed on the accelerator. "You'll see."

Chapter Thirteen

"Okay, now show me." I stood by my coffee table near the white box, which Asa pulled down from the attic. We arrived at my house in record time. I suspect the only reason we didn't get a speeding ticket was because Dodge somehow fixed it with the local police. Otherwise we should have been arrested for going the speed of light on a freeway.

Asa flicked on the lamp by the couch and pulled the lid off the box. "First let me do some research to see if I'm right."

"Asa!" I grabbed the box lid and threw it at him. "Tell me what you think."

He easily fended off the lid and pulled me to him in a body-pressing hug. "I think you're the most beautiful woman in the world. And don't tell me I'm remembering the past and getting all confused about it." His hands framed my face, pushing back my chin-length hair. "This is the Now Alice and I love everything about you."

I stared into his eyes, which seemed to be examining every nook and cranny of my heart. "I don't know how I feel," I murmured. "It's all confused. I'm angry about what you went through. You could have been killed in prison. All those years lost, all those years wasted."

"I didn't lose them. I needed time to get my head

straight. Butterfly protected me and so did some others. The time I wasted is the time I spent watching you from a distance and not coming forward. I was afraid of what you might say when you saw me again."

I touched his face, running my hand over his smooth dark beard. "What did you think I'd say? What were you afraid of?"

His eyes searched my face. "Go away. Leave me alone. I can never love you. That's what I was afraid you'd say."

I smiled. "Never is a very big word. You know me. I never say never."

Asa smiled, too. "I'm glad that hasn't changed. Now the thing that worries me is your involvement in all this. You might become a target."

"No one can target me if I'm with you. I know you'll keep me safe."

He smoothed back my hair. "For how long, though?"

"Let's take it one day at a time. We have other problems to solve now. I need time to think. I haven't had ten seconds to simply sit and process everything we've seen and heard." I pulled away from him. "I need some mindless exercise."

"While you do that, I'll use your computer. What's your password?" Asa reached into the white box and pulled out the scrapbook.

"I don't use one. Just turn it on." I wandered into the dining room and sat at the table. The colors were different in the overhead light, easier to see than they were earlier in the day, in sunlight. I saw a few that needed to be rearranged.

"You don't lock your doors, you don't use a

password, and you don't lock your car." He headed for my office, shaking his head. "You're lucky you're still alive to tell the tale."

"Until you came back into my life, I didn't know it was important." I said it jokingly, but Asa paused, frowning. "I'm teasing," I said. "Remember? I used to do that to you all the time."

He nodded uncertainly.

"I've learned my lesson. I promise to be a good, paranoid citizen from now on. Go and do whatever it is you're doing and when you know what you're talking about, come back and tell me."

"Now I know I'm crazy. I understood that." He ducked into my office when I pretended to get up out of my chair.

I stared at the puzzle for twenty minutes, my mind a blank with thoughts zigzagging around and making no sense. When I heard my garage door open I met Butterfield at the hallway door. "Thanks for bringing my car back." I stepped aside to let him into the house.

"No problem. Where's Skinny?" He walked past me into the kitchen, setting down a six-pack of beer and a grocery sack full of food that smelled marvelous.

"In the office using my computer. What did you bring?"

"Sea scallops and shrimp for you, Korean BBQ stir fry for me, and steak and broccoli for Skinny. The usual." He went into the living room and dropped a stack of books on the couch. "Blondie thought you might want to go through these. Here's her notebook, too." He handed me the red notebook then bustled around my kitchen, pulling containers out of the sack. "We get this take-out at least once a week. This place is great."

"You and he have been together a long time." I left the notebook on the counter before pulling plates out of the cupboard.

"I've known him about twenty years." Butterfield opened a container of spring rolls and arranged all the containers on the opposite counter. "He had a rough time of it in prison at first. The drugs were bad. And he didn't exactly fit in."

Prison. Asa in a prison. The thought was as mind-boggling as him in the military. I leaned against the sink, suddenly weak. What did he endure? What was it like? I stared at Butterfield and knowledge—real understanding—suddenly washed over me. If it wasn't for this man, Asa would most likely be dead. If not dead, he'd be so badly beaten or abused it might have pushed him right over the edge and warped whatever sanity he retained.

I lurched forward and wrapped as much of Butterfield in a hug as I could. He peered down at me, startled, containers of rice held up over my head. "What's wrong? Are you okay? You're crying. What's wrong?"

"I'm fine." I backed away, wiping at my tears. "Nothing's wrong. I wanted to thank you for helping— for saving—for being there." I fumbled out some silverware to put on the counter next to the plates and containers.

"Just luck, I guess." He eyed me cautiously when he set the rice down next to me. "Skinny helped me a lot, too. I got my G.E.D. in prison and I even took some college courses. I need to take a few more and I'll have a Bachelor of Arts in History. Imagine that. Nobody in my family ever even finished high school and all I need to do is finish these two correspondence courses and I'll have a college degree. Of course, it took me longer than most folks because I have trouble with reading. I got that dyslexia thing."

"History? Really? That's great." That was almost as mind-boggling as imagining Asa in prison then I immediately chastised myself for such an uncharitable thought. Looks certainly could be deceiving and Mr. Butterfield continued to surprise me.

"Yeah, Skinny and me, we helped each other a lot." He rearranged the cartons on the counter, putting them all in a straight line and avoiding my gaze while he did so. "He wants to stay here tonight with you," he blurted. "You know that, right? Are you okay with that? Because if you aren't, you'd better start figuring a way to let him know."

Oh, good heavens. What was this, true confession night? I stared, unseeing, at the sack, emblazoned with the image of a girl in front of a mirror. *The Looking Glass. Come in hungry and leave satisfied.* I felt like that girl, hesitating on the brink of stepping into the unknown.

Butterfield watched me, frowning. He had an investment in Asa, as great as my own if not greater. He had a bond, too, and I had to honor that with honesty. "I feel backed into a corner with him sometimes." Now I moved things around, straightening the silverware into a tidy row. "He doesn't really love me. He loves the past."

Butterfield crossed his arms and stared at me. "You have been his mission in life for years, since he got out of prison and got clean. He knows you and he loves you."

I remembered Madison's single-minded devotion to me during our youth. That passion was exhilarating and frightening, to be the focus of so much affection. "He's lonely. His illness makes him focus on one person and—"

"If you don't care for him, tell him. Don't run away and leave him hanging. He told me that if you didn't love him, that was okay. It's enough to know you're safe and someplace in the world. It wasn't until he got that crap in the mail that he thought he had to contact you."

"What? Why?"

"It's been bugging him for twenty years. Did he kill that guy or not? And if he did—why did he do it? You're the one who can help him figure it out." Butterfield leaned into the hallway. "Hey, food is here. Get your skinny white butt out here!"

"I'm busy," Asa called back. "I'll eat later."

"Oh, I've heard that before." Butterfield took a plate and began ladling food onto it. "If I don't put it in front of his face, he'll forget to eat."

I smiled at his grumbling but made sure he didn't see my amusement when he left the kitchen and went into my office. I filled my own plate and went into the dining room, clearing a spot at the table to fit my dishes and the glass of wine I poured for myself.

Butterfield soon returned and went into the kitchen then came out and took the chair opposite me at the dining room table. He opened one of the cans of beer he brought then noticed me watching. "You want one?"

I touched my wine glass. "I'm fine." I savored another bite of the succulent food. "How did it go with Chessy today? It seemed like you and she got along pretty good."

"Yeah, she's okay." We ate in silence for a few minutes then he said, "She's kinda crazy, though."

"You mean the government conspiracy thing? She's not alone. A lot of people have problems with the government."

"Nah, not just that. She's messed up. She's got problems with the adoption thing."

"What adoption thing?" I skewered a shrimp, dabbing it with rich wine and butter sauce.

"She was given up for adoption when she was little and was in and out of foster homes. As soon as she graduated from high school she began digging around for info about her birth parents. I guess what she found was pretty bad." He burped softly. "Sorry."

"She told you all this?" I sipped my wine.

"Not directly. When she was doing all the search shit at the library, she let it drop that she did that kind of stuff before, when she tried to find out about her parents. She made some crack about letting sleeping bitches lie." He frowned and jiggled a puzzle piece into another one.

"Stop that. It doesn't fit."

"It should. It's the right color."

"It's got to be color and shape. Not just one."

He grumbled something unintelligible and fiddled with more pieces.

Asa appeared in the dining room doorway. "Do you have any music?"

I pointed to the Bose stereo system and the CDs near it. He went into the living room and knelt next to the CD bookcase.

"I've seen this before," Butterfield whispered.

"He'll play a bunch of loud music and bounce ideas off me. This is how we roll."

I doubted Asa was bouncing anything off the big man, but I didn't say it. A brick wall would do when Asa was deep in study mode. He disappeared back into the office while AC/DC began to wail.

Butterfield dabbed at his forehead with a napkin. "These guys know how to do spice right. You want to try some?"

"No, I'm getting full." I set my plate to one side and focused on the jigsaw puzzle, sipping wine and relaxing, letting my mind wander. Jigsaw puzzles were good for that.

A few minutes later Asa appeared at my side. "It's the pieces that don't fit." He leaned over the table while Angus Young's guitar riffs filled the room. "Take out any that are normal. The ones that seem commercially pressed."

"Just keep the weird ones?" Butterfield asked.

"Yep. The weird ones are the important ones." He disappeared back into my office.

Butterfield set his plate to one side and bent to the task. We worked in silence, images flickering through my mind while I tested and rejected puzzle pieces. I focused on the mechanical objective of fitting one piece to another. The CD changed and Blind Faith's *Can't Find My Way Home* began to play.

I stared, unseeing, at the puzzle. Was that what was going on with me? Was it blind faith that let me believe Asa? If I used any logic at all, it was crazy to be involved with him again. The connection we had was decades old and I was barely an adult then, not someone who could make good judgments about people.

But my gut level feelings told me this was the right thing to do. It was right and necessary for me to help him. This wasn't just faith in a person I used to know. This was faith in the man he was now, a man I was coming to know better and better every moment.

I took a break and picked up Butterfield's dish and mine, taking them to the kitchen. I sniffed the container with Butterfield's food and drew back, startled. It even *smelled* spicy, with garlic and a pungent horseradish-like aroma permeating the dark red sauce. My father used to grow horseradish in his garden and I remembered how the odor burned my eyes when he processed it. I put the leftovers into the fridge but stopped with the door open when my mind raced. Garden. Garden Grove. Roberta Hart giving a talk to a Garden Club in Garden Grove on the day Harry March was killed.

On the afternoon Harry March was killed.

I went to the dining room doorway. "Where's the trial transcript?"

"On the couch in the living room." Butterfield peered up at me from the table.

"Get it. Where's the atlas? How far is Garden Grove, California from Burbank? You used to live in California, didn't you?" I wiped my hands on a kitchen towel, my mind going a thousand miles an hour.

"California's a big state." Butterfield ambled past me to the living room. "I don't know. I think they're both near L.A. Why?"

"Why?" Asa stood in the hall, watching me, my yellow legal pad and the red scrapbook tucked under one arm.

I spied the white box on the coffee table in the living room. That's when I thought of another odd thing. "Everything in that box is from high school. Everything. Why are her baby footprints in there?"

"It's all sentimental things. Maybe she wanted to keep her baby stuff here." Butterfield nudged the box when he passed it, coming back to me.

"But there's no other baby stuff. No baby book. No photographs. No lock of hair. What if it's not her baby footprints? What if it's her baby's footprints?"

"She had a kid?" Butterfield handed me the trial transcript. "As you ordered, boss."

I tried to glower at him but he was smiling so affably I took the book and muttered, "Thanks. What if she had a baby in high school?"

Asa came into the dining room and set the red scrapbook next to me. "Her report cards don't show any breaks in her schooling. She didn't miss any significant time." He went into the kitchen and returned with a beer, sitting at the head of the table.

"In the summer?" Butterfield resumed his seat.

"Could she hide a pregnancy in high school? I suppose she could but—" I gazed at the white box, trial transcript momentarily forgotten where it sat next to me on the table. "What do we know about Juan Santiago?"

"Who?" Butterfield asked.

"The foreign exchange student she was in love with. We need to find out about him." I opened the scrapbook to search for the pictures of Roberta Hart and the young man.

"Great minds think alike." Asa grinned at me.

I eyed him suspiciously. He seemed entirely too relaxed, too confident. "What were you researching in my office?"

"Did you know there is a small but very powerful organized crime group in Spain? Several of these crime families are in Aragon, which is in the northern part of the country, sharing a border with France. Guess where Juan Santiago was born." Asa nodded at the scrapbook, resting under my hand. "Guess who Juan Santiago's grandfather is."

I studied the faded newspaper photograph of Roberta Hart and the darkly handsome young man. "So? That was years ago."

Asa took a long swallow of beer. "Guess who's stayed in touch with her old friend all these years."

"He's some Mafia guy?" Butterfield asked. "Isn't that, like, illegal? She's a senator. She's not supposed to know Mafia people, right?"

"Wait a minute. Are you saying Roberta Hart had an illegitimate child with the grandson of a Mafia kingpin?" I sat back in my chair, staring at Asa in open-mouthed astonishment. "Where's the kid? Don't tell me she has a child who's running some drug operation in Spain now."

"I wish I could tell you that, but no, I don't think that's true. I'm not convinced that Juan Santiago was the father. I think that's why Dodge is interested in Roberta Hart. Didn't you do some research about the different Senate committees she serves on?"

"Right there." I pointed to the legal pad next to him on the table. "Second or third page. I couldn't make much sense out of them. They all sounded important."

"If we had an idea who it was, we could compare the baby fingerprints to the adult fingerprints." Butterfield slid another puzzle piece into place.

"You can't compare a baby fingerprint to an adult's. Fingerprints change over time."

"Wrong. They don't change. They just get bigger over time." When I shot him an astonished look, he added, "A guy I knew inside was busted because he kidnapped this kid and kept him for, like ten years. Fucking pervert. Anyway, they had the kid's baby prints and they compared it to the teenager's prints when they finally caught the creep. They were the same." Butterfield cracked his knuckles. "That asshole did not have fun in prison, believe me. Criminals got some morals, you know?"

I shook my head. "I didn't know."

"Well, we do. Rapists and child molesters get what they give." He crossed his arms on his chest. "Enough said in mixed company. You know, you had the right idea about this puzzle," he said to Asa. "Once we got rid of those goofy pieces it got easier."

The 'goofy pieces' were all in a pile off to one side. Butterfield was focused on the 'regular' puzzle, the one with the machined pieces. It appeared to be a landscape. He had one side nearly completed and one corner, with several other blocks of puzzle put together, waiting to find their final place.

"When do you think she had this baby?" I turned over the oddly cut pieces, sorting them by color.

"I think after high school. From what I could find out about Juan Acevedo Parades Santiago, his father was a businessman. His maternal grandfather was a criminal. His father and mother led somewhat separate lives. He was raised by his father but he spent summers with his mother and her family."

"How did he end up in Placerville, California?" I

asked. "That's a small town. Did they have a foreign exchange program?"

Asa nodded. "Back in the Sixties and Seventies, there were several different exchange programs. Youth For Understanding, The American Field Service, International Student Exchange, Outward Bound—they all had placement services to match foreign students with American families and vice versa. Parents usually paid to have their child spend a year in another country with a host family. Most of them tried to match small-town to small-town, which is how Santiago ended up in Placerville. His father lived in the suburbs outside one of the larger towns in that part of Spain."

"Wait a minute," Butterfield said. "You're saying a Mafia guy let his grandson come to the United States? From what I've seen in the movies, that ain't gonna happen. Think about *The Godfather.* There's no way some Mafia leader lets anybody in his family travel halfway around the world. What if the kid got snatched or something? Some rival family could hold the kid for ransom." He finished his beer and went into the kitchen for another one.

"It's possible the grandfather did send someone with him or hired someone in America to keep an eye on him. That's a good point."

"He probably hired local muscle," Butterfield said, taking his seat again. "Maybe those Mafia guys have, like, a you-scratch-my-back policy. From what I've heard, they're like big corporations. Maybe they had a California branch and they had guys from there keep an eye on the kid."

"A California branch," I repeated. "You make it sound like a college campus."

"You know what I mean." Butterfield wiggled another jigsaw piece, trying to make it fit, but gave up when he saw me frown at him. "What happened to the Santiago guy?"

"He went home, he went to college and from what I can tell, he went into business with his father. The records were pretty sparse." Asa watched me sort the oddly shaped puzzle pieces. "Are they all different?"

"Yes and no. Some are long and skinny, and some are short and fat. Most of them are rounded. There aren't any sharp corners." I put pale pink ones into one pile, red ones in another, yellow and purple in another.

"This puzzle is easier. Those are all raggedy." Butterfield inserted another piece and leaned back triumphantly. "See. I've got one side mostly all done and you haven't even started."

"They aren't random. There're similarities. Some have an indentation on the left side, some on the right. Some have an outcropping on the top, some on the bottom." Asa stared down at the puzzle pieces and began to sort them.

"Stop it," I said, slapping his hand. "I've got mine sorted by color."

"And I'm sorting them by shape." His fingers darted in and out of the cardboard pieces, deftly rearranging them.

"See what I mean?" I told Butterfield. "He sorts by shape."

Asa stood back. "That's it. You sort by color. I sort by shape."

Butterfield stared at the jigsaw puzzle. "She just said that, man."

"That's not what he means." I looked up at Asa.

"What is it?"

"I search for the way everything fits together. I consider facts. You think about the colors, the emotions of the people involved." Asa stared at me. "Why did you think about the baby footprints? What was the context?"

"I don't remember. Everything in the box had to do with high school and being an adult. Why would a baby thing be in there?"

"Why did you jump to Juan Santiago?"

"The pictures. She had a lot of pictures of him."

"That's how your mind works," Asa said. "You see the colors. I see the shape. When do you think she had the baby?"

"Not in high school." I said it with certainty, although I wasn't sure how I knew. "There was nothing in those pictures to show a girl who was worried or frightened. She was still innocent in those pictures. He was her first love." I sorted through my memories of the objects in the box. "Harry March. I'll bet he was the father. The baby folder was at the bottom, with the pictures of Harry and the other things from that time of her life."

"Maybe somebody else repacked the box," Asa said.

"Maybe. If someone unpacked then repacked it, they might follow the same order."

Asa nodded. "The person who sent the box to me." He sat down again and sipped his beer. "Who sent it and why? Why did someone want me to see what's in that box?"

"You need to give it all to Dodge," I said. "Dump it on them. Let them handle it."

"Maybe." Asa rearranged some of the oddly shaped pieces, frowning when they didn't align. He reached for some and I shot him a warning glance. He carefully took only pieces of one color and worked with them.

"What did you want with this?" Butterfield tapped the road atlas next to him at the table. "Something about Garden Grove?"

"Roberta Hart said she was in Garden Grove giving a talk when Harry March was killed. How far is it from Burbank?"

"Why, you think she killed him?" Butterfield missed my exasperated glare because he was flipping through pages in the atlas.

"Of course not." I turned my attention to the transcript of the trial next to my wine glass. "Scene of crime details." I flipped through the pages of typewritten text, some of it blurred by multiple photocopying. "There were two things they talked about. Where is it?"

Butterfield looked up from the atlas. "Garden Grove is, like, right there. Not that far from Burbank. See?" He held up the atlas, open to the two-page spread that showed Los Angeles and the surroundings. "Burbank is here and Garden Grove is here. It's about an hour's drive. Probably more because you've got to go through L.A. to get there and traffic is crazy. There's no fast or easy way to do it, but figure an hour, maybe an hour and a half."

I flipped through the pages of testimony, witness statements, ballistic experts, and examination and cross-examination by different lawyers. "Here. The forensic technician is describing where they found the gun." I read through the text then I held out my hand to Asa. "Give me my notepad."

He handed it across the table. "What is it?"

"According to this report, the bullet came from a four-story building a half-mile away." I glanced at my legal pad. "That's consistent with what you told me. The shooting happened on a movie studio lot, with large buildings that could be rented. You had a hard time lining up the shot because of the sun. It was morning and you were shooting into shadow."

Asa picked at the label on his beer bottle. "Those kinds of targets are tough sometimes. It all depends on how dense the shadow is and the angle of the sun. Morning sun in Alaska is a lot different than morning sun in California."

"Makes sense, I guess." I checked my notes again. "March came out of a door and got into a golf cart to drive to the lot where his car was parked. He was driving between two buildings when he was hit."

Asa froze, his body so rigid I saw a vein pulse in his throat. When he tried to pick up his beer bottle it slipped out of his hand. Butterfield caught it before it could spill on the table. "You're saying I did it? You said earlier you weren't sure. I did it? I pulled the trigger?"

"I said I had to check some facts." I tapped the notebook. "You were there. You were on that roof and you had a gun with the right kind of scope. You aimed and you shot at someone in the same location where March was shot."

Asa blew out a long, trembling breath. "I was hoping I didn't do it."

I walked around the table and set the transcript in

front of him, open to the page I wanted. "You didn't hit him. March was killed at two in the afternoon. You talked about being there in the morning. You were set up."

Chapter Fourteen

"You were there. You handled the gun. You got everything arranged. And you did shoot someone, but I think you really did shoot a dummy. Or else you fired a blank. How does that work? Does it really shoot a bullet or does it only make a noise?"

Asa shook his head. "That's not possible. I'd know the difference. It had to be a real gun." He took the bottle from Butterfield and drained it with one deep gulp.

Butterfield eased another puzzle piece into place. "Yeah, remember. He said the dummy fell out of the golf cart. He must have hit it."

"Well, you can't go around shooting in the middle of a movie studio lot and not be noticed," I said. "Someone must have heard or seen gunfire in the morning."

"Unless the set was closed." Butterfield tapped in another piece. "Wow. I'm getting this bad boy done."

"What do you mean closed?" I flipped back through my notes in the legal pad.

"Maybe somebody rented the place for the morning. There were four or five buildings there. From what it sounds like, the guy who set it up was rich as sin. Why not rent the whole place? A lot of production companies do that. I knew a guy who used to do security for production companies. They'd rent these big buildings and station guards all around it so nobody could spy on what they were doing."

"Really?"

"Oh, yeah. Movie making is big business. They try to keep all the stuff they do secret. And think about it, if this guy was into porn, they probably had security all around the place. Maybe somebody did rent it all for the morning." Butterfield leaned back in his chair, which creaked under his bulk. "This is hard on my neck, bending over like this. You need another beer? A wine?" he asked Asa and me.

"Yes, please." I handed him my empty wine glass. "It's on the counter."

"What about you, man? You look like you could use another beer."

Asa shook his head. "I'm fine. I'm trying to grasp this." His face was pale and his shoulders were so tense it made my shoulders hurt to see him.

"Well, a beer won't hurt and it might help." Butterfield went into the kitchen and I heard him rummaging in the fridge, humming along to the Eagles and *Hotel California.* "It sounds like you were set up to take the rap for murder. They probably had you on some heavy-duty drugs." He came back into the room and handed me my glass and set a bottle of beer in front of Asa.

"Let's go over this," I said. "Roberta Hart has a crush on a foreign exchange student when she's in high school. He leaves to go home and she's left behind, lonely and restless, wishing she could be with her boyfriend but instead she's stuck in Placerville."

Asa took a quick swallow of beer. "This is what she does," he said softly. "She figures out what people feel."

I ignored him and continued, skimming through the scrapbook, my notes, and the transcript, the jigsaw pieces forming a backdrop for all of it. "Harry March comes to town and sweeps her off her feet. He tells her she's pretty enough to be a model and she believes him. Maybe she had an argument with her parents about the Spanish boyfriend. Maybe they tried to lay down the law. Whatever happened, she decided to run away with Harry."

"I'll bet it was a Daddy's Little Girl thing." Butterfield fitted a long segment of pieces into his puzzle, the outline of a barn clearly taking shape. "You know, she's graduating from high school, she wants to have some freedom, Daddy wants her to go to college and be a sorority girl, he's glad the boyfriend is gone. She decides to kick up her heels and show him."

Asa and I both stared at him in open-mouthed astonishment. He raised his head. "What? I watch TV and movies. I know how these things go."

"Okay," I managed to say. "Yes, that's probably some of what happened. She and Harry hook up and Harry introduces her to sex." I turned my head to avoid seeing Asa, who was the man who introduced *me* to sex years earlier. "One thing leads to another and suddenly she's making pornography movies."

"And she gets pregnant." Butterfield shook his head ponderously. "Stupid, really. I mean, there's the pill, there's condoms. I mean, stupid."

Once again, I avoided Asa's amused look, knowing he was remembering my first missed period and our panic. I went on the pill but becoming sexually active made me irregular for a month or two. I continued using the pill for years until I finally decided I really didn't want to have children. Then I had a tubal ligation and never worried about birth control again. Sexually transmitted diseases were another matter completely but given my lack of male companionship, I wasn't worried.

"You don't think she had an abortion?" Asa asked.

I shook my head. "Good girls didn't do that back then. No matter what she got into with Harry, I'll bet she had the baby. That might be when her father got involved. You said he grabbed her and had her hospitalized, right?"

Asa nodded. "I found some old records from a small town near Sacramento."

"Woodland, California," I said, consulting my notes. "That's where the baby's prints were filed or at least that's the name on the folder."

"The kid would be, what—thirty years old now? Twenty-something?" Butterfield finished the lower border of his puzzle.

"Depends on when he or she was born but yes, around that." I sipped my wine, leafing through my notes. "Maybe Roberta got smart. Maybe she knew she had to grow up and settle down. By then she probably knew she had no future with Harry or the kind of life he led. Her father was rich and he could make the bad things disappear."

"What does her web site bio say about the time between high school and college?" Asa asked. "You know how it is with public officials. I'll bet her life has been examined every which way since she ran for office."

I set down my scribbled notes. "She was overseas

on a cultural exchange program in France from the time she graduated until she went to college, two years later." I leaned back, smiling. "I wonder if Daddy asked Santiago's family for some help with that one."

"I wonder if the State Department keeps records of who leaves the country and when. None of that was computerized back then. And her passport would be expired by now and renewed. Any record of her travel would be on the old passport."

"I didn't find a lot of details about that, only a sentence or two in her official biography."

"We can ask Dodge to dig into that for us," Asa said. "We may as well put him to use. In fact, maybe it's time to hand all of this off to them. There's enough in that box for them to use to let Hart know she'll be watched from now until she leaves office."

"There's no firm evidence of anything, though. The tapes are damning, but there's nothing tying her to the murder and nothing to show that she and Santiago still have a relationship." I went back into the living room and bent over the box, rooting around in it. I finally found the baby folder and pulled it out. "There's nothing here that could be—"

Two loud cracking noises came from the front of the house. "What's that?" I started toward the front door. "It sounds like something hit the house or—"

Asa leapt out of his chair, pushed the other dining room chairs out of his way and dove at me. I was so astonished I stood there, staring at the front window, baby footprint folder still in my hand. The room went dark and the instant Asa wrapped his arms around me, light and sound exploded across the entire front of my house. It was like the front porch was wrapped in a nuclear explosion or a bomb or—

We hit the coffee table, knocking the box off and scattering the contents around the room. I landed on my back on the table, all breath knocked out of me. Asa covered me with his body, his face pressed against mine and keeping my head down. I couldn't hear anything, only a buzzing sound, annoyingly loud and so persistent it was painful.

Asa raised his head and I did the same. I saw his lips move but I couldn't hear anything. He put his hands on either side of my head and stared intently at me. *Take cover.* He enunciated clearly enough that I could understand what he said.

I nodded. He removed his hands and one was smeared with blood. I ran my hands down the sides of my face and my left hand came away bloody. Asa slid away from me and pulled his gun, all in one movement. I rolled off the coffee table, wedging myself between it and the couch, reaching up for one of the couch pillows. I pressed it against my face then examined it. The blood was centered near my forehead. I pressed the pillow against the spot and peered under the coffee table at the remains of my living room.

The front of the house was gone. Where the front window used to be was a void, a circle of light and heat and flame. Pieces of my porch furniture mingled with my living room furniture in a tangled heap in the center of the room. The only noise I heard was the buzzing, that dryer-machine-finished noise barely loud enough to startle and annoy.

I sat up and stared stupidly around me. The flames lit the scene. Asa picked his way through the rubble to the dining room, crouching and moving his gun from right to left in a controlled arc. I glimpsed Butterfield in the back hallway, his gun drawn, too. He disappeared into my office.

I discarded the pillow and crawled out from under the coffee table. My book bag was on the floor. I stuffed the baby folder into the bag then grabbed Asa's little computer, which lay next to it like a discarded toy. My telephone and end table were gone, somewhere in the mess that was my home.

I jammed the computer into the bag and crawled to the dining room, the denim bag dragging with me. It snagged. A leg from my armchair was wedged under the remains of the television. My bag was hung up on a piece of the television. I tugged on the bag and got it free. That's when I saw the mantel and I remembered.

My gas fireplace.

The flames would reach it in a minute, if not sooner. I lurched to my feet, swinging the book bag's strap onto my shoulder. A figure appeared to the right of the central fire, darting through what used to be my front door and what was now a jagged tear in the wood exterior.

Leo Griffin was clearly lit by the flames next to him and by the ones licking their way up overhead, into my arched ceiling. He was dressed all in black, like a silhouette painting come to life.

I ran for Asa, who was entering the hall leading to my bedroom and the garage opposite it. We need to get out! I shouted but I couldn't hear a word. We need to leave! The fireplace, the stove—gas!

He gestured for me to get down then continued forward.

I grabbed his arm and pointed frantically to the

living room. Fireplace! I screamed.

He peered past me, put his hand on my shoulder, and pushed me down. I crouched and turned. Smoke hid everything then Griffin emerged out of the fog, a shotgun or some other kind of big gun braced on his shoulder, aiming at me.

I froze. All I could think was *I'm going to die and I don't know if I've even lived yet.*

Asa stepped in front of me, raised his gun, and fired. Griffin's head exploded then his body flew back, the smoke-fog separating to enfold him.

Sound filled my head, a booming noise that made me whimper when pain encompassed me—my ears, my face, my back, my legs, my arms. Asa grabbed my arm and jerked me to my feet. "We'll make a break for it through the garage. They'll be covering the back porch."

I stared beyond him to the darkness of the dining room and the porch beyond that. "There are woods behind the house. Maybe we should hide there."

"They'll expect that. Butterfly!" Asa shouted over one shoulder. "Evac!" He tugged me to the garage exit.

I slipped away from him and went into the dining room, scooping up my notes and the scrapbook. Loose pages fluttered out of the book and I snatched them up, jamming them and the bulky scrapbook into my bag.

"The puzzle." I tried to grab puzzle pieces but Asa pulled me away.

Butterfield emerged from the smoke, saw what I was doing, and went into the kitchen. He came back with the paper bag from the restaurant and swept the puzzle pieces into the bag, a few of them scattering on the floor.

Smoke surrounded me then suddenly I was through a door and in the garage. I had faint emergency lighting here, battery-powered wall lights that came on when the electricity went out. The northwest corner was where I had my tornado shelter, a storage closet big enough for me, a few jugs of water, and my emergency suitcase.

I headed for that spot now, but Asa grabbed me, dragging me to the side door. "Let go!" I screamed, almost dislocating my shoulder when I wiggled away from him.

I think he was so shocked by my scream that he let me go. I ran to the closet and reached in, grabbing the Samsonite hard shell suitcase. I dragged it to the side door, unable to get it properly situated on its wheels. Butterfield descended on me, holstering his gun and jamming the sack with the puzzle into my arms. He swept up the purple suitcase in his right hand and me in his other arm, pressing me hard against his side.

He got to the side door in three long strides, kicked it open then set me down. I thought maybe my ribs cracked when I staggered, trying to get a deep breath without pain. Butterfield tossed out the suitcase and followed it, gun drawn. Asa followed him, facing in the opposite direction. When he was satisfied it was safe, he gestured to me.

I clutched the paper bag against me like a shield, stumbling over the doorframe into the side yard. My nearest neighbor's house on the west was hidden behind a row of pine trees that separated us, but lights blazed in the houses across the street. Asa grabbed my right arm and dragged me to the intervening trees. "We need to get to cover."

"This way." Dodge materialized out of the

darkness, his body blending with the shadows. The white of his face and shirt were faintly visible in the flames over the house.

"How many?" Asa still held his gun, now pointed down at his side.

"Three. Two got away. I've got men after them. White was hurt." Dodge gestured urgently to my back yard. "Come on. We'll get you out."

"I got the one that came inside." Asa shoved me toward Dodge. "Butterfly, cover them. I'll follow."

"Wait, I need—" I reached for the suitcase, my book bag swinging on my shoulder and dragging me to one side.

"I got the damn suitcase." Butterfield grabbed the bag and shoved me ahead of him. "Go. Get your butt movin'."

I managed a quick glare at him. "I'm going. No need to be pushy." I hurried after Dodge, who was heading for the end of the pine trees and the drop-off to the ravine behind my house.

Butterfield barked out a laugh. "Sorry, Alice. You don't mind if I call you Alice, do you? I figure we're on a first name basis by now."

I didn't bother replying. It was all I could do to keep Dodge in sight. He faded into the night like some kind of ninja. I tried to keep to the path he used, but I must have strayed because I stumbled often, twisting my ankle more than once.

We made a left turn at my neighbor's house, keeping close to the property line and the woods. The ravine was on my right, a steep drop-off that rose again on the other side of the small stream at the bottom. The houses at the top of the hill on King Street were glimmers in the distance.

"Where are we going?" I hissed to the dark figure ahead of me when he went right, into the woods bordering the ravine.

He didn't answer and I wondered belatedly if this was such a good idea. What if the government was behind all this? I paused and Butterfield ran into me. "Keep moving, Alley Oop," he muttered.

"For heaven's sake." I tripped on a branch and scrambled to keep my balance. "This is crazy. This is stupid." My house was on fire and I was fleeing with two known criminals. I was embroiled in a government investigation, the FBI or God knows who were involved, and everything I owned was gone.

I think that's when it really soaked in. I stopped and turned. All that remained of my life was blazing in the distance. My adorable little house with the cute back porch. My car, my computer, the dishes my mother gave me. The furniture I carefully acquired through the years. All of it gone, all of it in smoke or ashes.

Asa stopped in front of me. "I'll make this up to you." He touched my face gently, but even so it hurt.

I grimaced and pulled away from him. "No one can make it up to me. No one." Tears blurred the leaves and forest debris in front of me but I continued forward. I couldn't stand to see the destruction behind me.

I don't know how long I sloughed ahead, one foot in front of the other, crushing the paper bag to me with my arms crossed across my chest. Trees surrounded us and we moved uphill, zigzagging along a path seen only to the man leading us. My body was a mass of pain from bruises, cuts, and torn muscles. My soul was a mass of pain from confusion and fear and loss. I moved like a dumb creature, an automaton, one foot in front of the other with unquestioning obedience.

Butterfield put a hand on my shoulder, pulling me to a halt. Asa moved ahead to confer with Dodge and I gazed around me for the first time in hours? Minutes? I wasn't sure. We were near someone's detached garage, a house not far away from it. Three cars were in the driveway. I didn't recognize the house. We must have gone around my neighborhood and come up the ravine to the next street.

"Let's go." Asa waited for me, his eyes scanning the darkness.

I walked past Dodge but he stopped me with a hand on my arm. "Are you okay?"

I glared at him. "That's a stupid question. Of course I'm not."

Dodge gently tilted my head to one side. "Your face. You're bleeding." He pulled a handkerchief out of his back pocket and handed it to me. "Facial wounds bleed a lot. Keep a compress on it until you get there then bandage it."

"Get where?"

"Are you okay otherwise? Do you need a doctor? I can send a medic over to check you. That might not be a bad idea." He pressed something on his ear.

"Send a medic where? What's happening?"

Dodge turned aside and spoke softly. "Send a medic to the tea party. Wait outside until they get the signal." He faced me again. "Someone will meet you there. They'll take of you."

"Meet me where? What tea party?"

"No medic. We'll be fine." Asa pointed to the cars in the drive. "Go on, Alice."

Dodge looked like he might argue then he shook his head. "If you need us, you know how to contact us." He turned back the way we came. "We'll be watching. Don't worry. It's safe." He disappeared into the shadows surrounding the woods.

"I've heard that before." I stumbled after Asa and Butterfield, who stood next to the dark sedan. "Now what?"

"We go to the warehouse," Asa said, getting into the car.

"Are you serious? We'll be sitting ducks there."

Butterfield opened the front door and pushed me, none too gently, into the passenger seat. "It's a fucking fortress. We can hold off an army there." He got into the back, tossing my suitcase in first. It landed with a solid clunk against the far door.

"Yeah, but we need to get there in order to get into the fucking fortress." I watched Asa, who was backing the car down the drive.

"Dodge has that covered." He moved the car into the street. "We'll be followed going there and he's already got agents in place."

"He had agents in place here and my house got blown up." I pulled my bag off my shoulder and set it on the floor under my feet with the crumpled paper sack containing the jigsaw puzzle pieces. Sirens wailed in the distance, getting closer. "It's all gone. All the evidence."

"Everything?" Butterfield asked from the back seat. "Didn't you get anything besides the stupid jigsaw puzzle?"

Asa made a turn onto another street. I recognized the area. There was a strip mall nearby where I got pizza now and again. The Interstate wasn't too far away. I turned to see Butterfield, but it hurt so badly I stopped halfway. "I'm sorry. I was busy trying to get out of a burning house. I guess I wasn't thinking straight. All I got was the puzzle, the scrapbook, and the baby folder."

"Damn it. We should have gotten the tapes. Damn it. What about Chessy's notebook? Did you get that?"

I leaned over to rummage in my book bag, but when I did, blood dripped off my face. "Crap. I forgot." I pressed the hankie against my forehead. "I don't know if I have the notebook or not. I grabbed whatever I could."

"Damn. She had a lot of stuff in that notebook."

"You got out alive." Asa's quiet voice cut through our bickering. "That's the most important thing."

"What good will it do me?" I leaned my head on the window, keeping the hankie against the left side of my face. "They'll come after me again."

"No they won't. They got what they wanted. They eliminated the evidence."

"How did they know I had it? How did they know you hid it in my house?"

Asa glanced once at me then faced the street again, his mouth twisted into a bitter line. "They were probably watching us. A high-powered night scope can show a lot. There might be a line of sight from the woods at the back of your house. You don't have any curtains on the dining room window."

"I didn't think I needed any curtains on those windows." I struggled to keep from shouting. "There's a bunch of woods and a hill and more woods back there. I didn't there'd be a fucking sniper out there."

"I'm sorry," he said in a low voice. "I think you'll

be safe from here on in. They got what they wanted."

"They wanted to kill me. The damn FBI were in the woods behind my house. Did you see how useful that was? Holy Jesus, there were fucking agents all around my house and somebody still managed to blow it up. Why the hell do you think we'll be safe in a warehouse in downtown Minneapolis?"

"Hey, Alley Oop, back off," Butterfield said. "Chill."

This time I did turn. Butterfield sat sideways on the seat, peering behind us, gun in hand. "Is someone following us?"

He glanced at me. "Not that I can see. Calm down. Relax. We got this covered." He resumed peering out the back window.

"Yeah, right. Excuse me for not believing you." I twisted back to the front again. "Son of a bitch, that hurts." I pressed my hand against my ribs on the left. "I think you broke my ribs."

"I didn't squeeze you that hard," he said dismissively.

"You picked me up and swung me around like a sack of potatoes," I muttered. "I'm lucky I can still breathe."

"I'm to blame for this," Asa said. "I should never have gotten you involved."

I started to agree with him but stopped myself in time. I knew that tone of voice of his. He was heading into a funk, a deep depression. I'd seen it before, when he failed at something and couldn't understand how it happened. His expectations about himself were so high that when he didn't match them, it made him spiral. I had to snap him out of it and the best way to do that was to counter his self-pity with anger.

"Don't take all the credit," I said. "That's just like you. You always want to be the center of attention, the guy who gets things done."

"Hey," Butterfield snapped.

"You shut the fuck up." I glared at him in the mirror. "He's a grownup. It's time he acted like one instead of like a prima donna. I made a choice to get involved with him again."

"And that was a big mistake," Asa muttered.

"Well, unlike other people in this car, I'm an adult and I accept responsibility for my actions. I got involved with you and it caused me a shitload of trouble. Now we need to figure out how to go forward from here. Work on that, genius."

Asa nodded, his hands opening and closing on the wheel. "This won't happen again."

"Damn right it won't." I closed my eyes and leaned my head against my window. I wasn't sure if I'd ever feel safe again.

Chapter Fifteen

Asa parked the sedan in the slot where the Jeep sat before. "What happened to your car?" I asked. "Is it still at my house? I didn't see it when we left." Granted, I didn't check for it, but it must have been in the driveway.

"That was one of the explosions you heard," Asa said.

"I didn't hear any explosions." I got out of the sedan and reached back in for the paper sack and my denim bag.

"You didn't hear the explosion?" Butterfield got out of the back seat, dragging my suitcase after him. "What the hell do you have in here? It weighs a ton."

"I didn't hear anything except a buzzing sound." I reached for the suitcase but Butterfield lifted it out of my reach. "I have important papers and other irreplaceable items in there."

"Like what, a bowling ball? You must be deaf if you didn't hear the explosion." The big man peered over the top of the car at Asa, who walked to a door near the elevator. "Wait up. I'll check the ground floor." He hurried around the rear of the car and set my suitcase near Asa.

"What explosion?" I asked Asa while Butterfield went through the door. "Where's he going?"

"He'll check the ground level and make sure our

security alarm is set." Asa pulled out his gun. I inched away from him, taking baby steps. His grim face relaxed slightly. "The gun doesn't bite. It's safe."

"I'm sure it is. I'm just not comfortable with them."

"It's a tool, Alice. Like a hammer or a piece of software or a lamp." He kept his gaze fixed on the slightly opened door, the gun held down at his side.

I inched back further. "It's a deadly tool."

Asa glanced at me. "It depends on who's holding it. A hammer is deadly in the hands of a murderer. Is that what worries you? That I'm a murderer?"

"Don't pull logical bullshit on me," I snapped. "I have enough stress in my life right now without quibbling about weapons and their uses."

Butterfield opened the door. "All set. Come on." He picked up the suitcase and went back inside.

"Aren't we taking the elevator?" I asked when Asa ushered me ahead of him.

"Not tonight. It's disabled for now. Go upstairs and wait for us on the upper landing." Asa pointed ahead.

I followed Butterfield up seven concrete steps, making a right turn on a small landing then going up ten more to another landing. The stairs continued upward but were much narrower and rougher, less used.

Butterfield tapped a code into a pad next to a big gray metal door, opened it, and went inside, taking my suitcase with him. The door closed behind him with a solid clunking noise. "What's in there?" I asked.

"Access to the apartments." Asa stood on the landing below me, staring back the way we came.

"I don't understand. Do you think someone is inside?"

"We're making sure no one is and making sure no

one can come in. It only takes a minute."

I wanted to ask another question but the door opened. "Come on in," Butterfield said, swinging it open. "Sorry for the mess. I didn't expect company."

I entered an apartment like Asa's, with a kitchen on my right and a dining room opening into a living room straight ahead. Unlike Asa's apartment, this one was decorated in bright colors, vivid yellow and red, and blue. Soft overhead lighting showed plump overstuffed couches and ferns hanging from hooks near the window. The room was a tropical paradise.

Butterfield waited for us on steps leading upward, the three-legged cat next to him. "You can wait here or at the top of the steps." He went upstairs swinging my suitcase, the cat darting after him.

"Is this his apartment?" I asked Asa, who followed me, locking the door and tapping on the keypad next to it.

"Same floor plan as mine." Asa smiled briefly. "Different tastes." He nodded to the stairs. "Go ahead."

I didn't budge. "Are you pissed off at me for what I said?"

He drew back. "No. You were right. We need to figure out what to do now."

"Why are you acting like I've got the plague or something?"

Asa frowned. "I'm not sure what to do."

I smiled. "Welcome to the real world." I thrust my book bag at him. "Here. Be useful. Carry this. It's heavy." I followed Butterfield up the stairs.

Asa passed me when I got to the top. "Wait here." He set my book bag near my suitcase, which was next to the dining room table then he went into the bedroom

I used the night before.

I glanced down at the cat, sitting on the top step. "What are they doing?" I asked her.

She peered up at me and yawned. I took that to mean there was no danger. I went into Asa's kitchen and scanned the bottles in the wine cooler set into the wall near the fridge. I pulled out a bottle of Riesling as Asa and Butterfield emerged from the bedrooms on opposite sides of the apartment.

"Make yourself comfortable," Butterfield said, walking past me to the keypad near the doorway.

"Thank you, I will. Where's the wine opener?"

Asa joined me in the kitchen, holstering his gun. "It's a twist off." He pulled a wine glass out of the cupboard and handed it to me. I eyed the bottle skeptically. "It's a winery in California," he said. "I have a part-share in it. We found twist-off is better for whites."

"The only twist-offs I've seen are for Ripple. But I'm not picky. I'm thirsty." I opened the bottle and half-filled the glass. "After that trick you pulled on me, I don't trust you. You try it first." I handed him the glass.

"You opened the bottle yourself."

I crossed my arms and glared at him.

Asa took a swallow and handed the glass back to me. "Nice and crisp. Are you hungry?"

"Nope." I filled the glass and went into the living room. I caught a glimpse of my reflection in one of the framed pictures on the wall. "Good God, I look like a refugee from a B movie." My hair was a tangle, blood coated one side of my face, and my blue-and-white knit top was spotted with blood and grime. "I am sick of these clothes. I've worn them for two days."

Asa walked past me into the room opposite the bedroom where I slept the night before. He re-emerged carrying a powder blue T-shirt and a pair of black gym shorts. "Here. We can do your laundry."

I took the clothes then went to my suitcase, kneeling to open it. Butterfield leaned over the kitchen counter, watching me lift out the zipped plastic bag inside. "I thought you had a bowling ball in there," he said. "Or maybe a set of weights or something."

"Nope. It's stuff I can't replace. The suitcase itself weighs a lot because it's nearly indestructible." I took my wine, Asa's clothes, and my zipped bag containing underwear and makeup into the bedroom where I stripped out of my dirty clothes.

I ran a damp washcloth over my face and body, then redressed. The T-shirt was loose and the shorts were tight, but it felt marvelous to be clean. I brushed out my hair and dabbed on makeup. The cut on my forehead was handled with an adhesive bandage from a box in the medicine chest.

I came back into the living room, dirty clothes in hand. "I'll toss these in," I said, going to the laundry room.

Butterfield pulled them out of my hand. "You sit down before you fall down." He bustled to the stairs.

"Wait. Where are you going?"

He paused on the top step. "I'll take care of this. Don't worry." Butterfield went down the stairs, the cat following.

My suitcase was moved to a small nook near the laundry room. I rummaged through the manila envelopes inside, pulling out my legal documents. I took two of the envelopes and my wine into the living room, where Asa stood in front of the window, hands clasped behind his back. He had taken off his denim jacket but still had the gun holstered in the leather holder near his arm. I set my wine glass and the envelopes on the wide slate coffee table and joined Asa at the window. "Where's Mr. Butterfield going with my clothes?"

"He's taking care of your laundry," Asa said, staring intently at the building opposite us. "He'll stand guard tonight."

"What?"

"Just in case."

"Is it dangerous to be out here like this? Aren't you afraid someone will see?"

"Dodge has men over there and probably in a perimeter around the entire block." He nodded at the building across the street. "The window is bulletproof glass. Hart knows by now that we're still alive and she probably knows we're here. What she doesn't know is how much of her things were destroyed."

I peered at the warehouse across the street. The windows were dark. Were men there, watching us? I walked back and sank down on the couch, picking up my wine glass while I went. "Why did she do it? What did she have to gain? You said yourself we had a stalemate."

"She's a politician. She doesn't trust anybody." Asa touched a button near the windows and a thin film slid down, blocking out the view.

I sipped the wine, shivering at the taste of the chilly liquid. Asa noticed and plucked a pale brown afghan from the back of the couch nearest him. He came to me and held it out.

"Sit down," I said, touching the seat next to me.

He hesitated. "You were right. There's no way to make this up to you."

"You can try," I suggested. "You can start by giving me the afghan."

He dropped on the couch and unfolded it, draping the cloth over my bare legs then picked up a remote control from the coffee table to light the gas fireplace. I tugged the cotton blanket higher, tucking it around me.

"You're right," he said softly. "I don't know why Hart did it. It doesn't make sense. I wouldn't do anything to her if you were left alone. Instead she came after you."

I leaned forward and picked up the manila envelope, pulling out the legal papers I'd need to file an insurance claim for my house and car. "And she said *you* were the mad man. She's acting crazy, too." I verified the details of my insurance policy. "I wonder if this covers arson. Knowing the insurance company, there's probably some hidden clause about that."

"Are you sure you want to do that?" Asa asked. "Rebuild?"

Of course, I began to say, but I stopped. "What are you saying?"

"What happened tonight raises the stakes. We'll need to talk to Dodge about his take on what went down, but I think you need to be prepared to go into hiding."

"What?" I let the papers drop to my lap.

"I did what you told me to do. I thought it through to the logical conclusion. Hart can't be sure we won't expose her. She'll try to come after us again. I can disappear and you may need to do it, too."

"I can't just go away."

Asa unbuckled his gun harness and set the weapon on the coffee table. "I did."

"But—" My protests died before I could voice them. I had no one to miss me, no one I was close to. I could vanish without causing undue worry for anyone.

"It's a possibility," he said. "Just don't discount it."

I leaned back and it was the most natural thing in the world to snuggle against him, his body warm against mine. "This would be romantic if I wasn't scared silly," I said.

"Are you?" He turned his head to stare into my eyes.

"I'll never be scared as long as you're there," I whispered. "I know you'll always watch over me."

"And I know you'll always be there for me. I let my fear keep us apart when we didn't have to be. I'll never do that again." He drew me to him. "Please. Let me love you."

Do I need to tell you what happened next? We were old lovers but more importantly, we were friends. I knew what he needed and he knew what I needed.

We needed each other.

At some point, probably after we had peeled off clothing and blankets, I peered around. "Good Lord, if Mr. Butterfield sees me, he'll go blind."

Asa pulled me to him. "He's in his apartment. He's a smart man. But I wouldn't mind moving to the bedroom. It's much more comfortable than the couch."

I laughed softly and sank into his embrace. "You're lucky to have him for a friend."

"I'm a lucky man in more ways than one."

Our lovemaking was built on past memories and

new experiences. My last love affair was years in the past and I was tentative until Asa pulled me on top of him, his hands on my breasts. Then I remembered those riotous days of youth and for a few moments I relived them, reveling in the feeling of a man under me, a man who appreciated me and enjoyed me for who I was, how I was. He loved me, now and forever.

It was a giddy feeling.

I awoke once in the night, sitting upright and panicked when I didn't know where I was. Smoke was strong in my face and for a brief instant I was caught in the explosion again. Asa pulled me back to bed with a murmured something that I didn't quite hear but I understood.

I was safe.

A ringing sound woke me again. The room was light but not bright. I lay in a double bed, naked. An empty bottle of wine stood on the bedside table and the pale brown afghan was at the foot of the bed, as was the three-legged cat. She regarded me as sleepily as I felt.

I fell back into the bed, tugging the sheets around me. I didn't know the time, the day, or what the future held. I did know I felt safe, loved, and secure.

I dozed again and when I awoke the cat was gone and the smell of bacon drifted to me from the half-open door opposite the bed. I slipped out from under the covers and walked into the bathroom on my right. This room was similar to the one I used the day before, but this one was larger and the tub was a large Jacuzzi type model. I was tempted to lie down and soak in relaxing warmth but I settled for a hot shower.

When I finished, I explored the large walk-in closet. This was Asa's closet. It held mostly casual clothes, but there were a few suits and a tuxedo in a plastic wrapper. His shoes were all neatly aligned on a rack at the bottom, and a few neckties were arrayed on the wall. One large suitcase was on the floor, tucked in the back. It reminded me of my tornado suitcase, something packed and ready to go in case of emergency.

I left the closet and stared at myself in the mirror over the double vanity in the bathroom. The cut/bruise over my left eye was puffy and a faint purple, but other than that I appeared surprisingly rested and refreshed. I smiled. Nothing like a night of sex to add youth to a middle-aged woman.

I pulled on the fluffy bathrobe hanging on the bathroom door. Sex? No, last night was that and more. Being with Asa reminded me what was missing in my life. That sense of connection to another human being, that feeling of being a part of two. Past relationships never quite had the feeling of completeness that being with Asa had.

I went to the bedroom door and pulled it open. How long would this last? A day? A month? It didn't matter. Today was now and I'd take what I could get.

"About time you got up, Alley Oop," Butterfield said from the kitchen. "Pancakes today?"

Asa turned in his chair to regard me. His long hair was pulled back into a queue at the base of his neck, and today he wore a khaki shirt with dark jeans. His ever-present gun was in a holster on his belt today. The sleeves on the shirt were rolled up, exposing his arm tattoos.

"Thank you, Mr. Butterfield. I would enjoy pancakes, I think."

The big man grinned at me from the kitchen island. "I told you that you can call me Butterfly. One short stack, coming up. Outta my way, cat," he muttered to the calico cat who danced between his legs.

I sat next to Asa at the dining table and took one of his hands in mine. "You need to explain these tattoos to me," I said, running my finger over a dragon encircling his forearm.

He took my hand in his. "I'll do that tonight," he whispered. "If you'll stay with me."

"I can't commit to anything." I examined the green and gold tattoo. I didn't dare meet his eyes. If I did, I'd be lost.

"We'll take it one day at a time, then." He gently touched my chin, raising my face to his. "Will you stay with me today?"

I drew back in surprise. "Of course I will."

"Okay. I'll ask you that every day. All I ask is that you be honest."

I smiled. "That's an easy promise to make."

He kissed me then leaned back. "Now, on to business. I talked to Dodge earlier. White was injured when the Jeep exploded but not seriously. Dodge didn't see who started the fire. The police have been convinced that it's best for his department to handle the investigation."

"Who convinced them?"

"There's a body in the ashes of your house and an autopsy will show that the fire didn't kill him. I need to answer for that, but it might get complicated if I have to answer to local law enforcement. Let's just say that some inter-agency cooperation is strongly encouraged."

"What do you mean you'll have to answer for

that?" I put my hand on his arm. "You won't go to prison again, will you? You saved my life. You can't go to prison again."

He put his hand over mine. "It won't come to that. Dodge wants to see us this morning. We'll make our official statements to him, answer a few questions, and that should be it."

"But you're a felon. Good God, you probably shouldn't even have a gun, right?"

"Special license. Don't worry about it." He released my hand and picked up his coffee mug. "I think you could say that Dodge and I have a love/hate relationship. He helps me when it suits him and I do the same. Right now it helps us both to quietly handle what happened."

I absorbed that information. It made sense in a crazy sort of way. "Did they get the ones who ran away?"

"No. They lost them on the freeway. The license plates were from stolen cars." Asa tapped the table, frowning.

I moved aside when Butterfield set a plate in front of me. "This is most impressive," I said, viewing the small pancakes neatly arrayed on the plate with three slices of bacon nestled next to them.

Butterfield beamed at me, his round face creasing with laughter. "I had six brothers and two sisters and I was the oldest. One thing I know how to do is cook. You dig in, Alley Oop. We got a busy day ahead of us."

I hesitated, my knife poised over the butter dish on the table. "We do?"

Asa poured me a cup of coffee from the carafe sitting next to his empty plate. "Indeed we do. We're going to a political rally today." He put the metal pot down with a thump. "I need to have a brief discussion with Senator Hart."

I set down my silverware. "Oh, no you don't."

He covered my wrist with his hand, pinning my arm to the table. "I gave her a clear warning. We will not run for the rest of our lives. She needs to know I mean business."

I looked into his dark eyes. "Don't do this because of me."

Butterfield wiped his hands on an apron that barely encompassed his girth. "Oh, Alley, this ain't for you. This is for us. Nobody goes around blowing up our friends. No, indeed." He shook his head ponderously then went back to the kitchen. "No, siree. This is personal. They don't fuck with our friends. Nope, they don't." He smiled down at the cat sitting near Asa's chair. "Right, Duchess? We don't take that kind of shit, no we don't."

Asa released my hand. "What he said." I started to protest but he shook his head. "This isn't negotiable, Alice. I won't let this haunt us. Now eat up. We have a busy day ahead."

Butterfly left shortly after that on some mysterious errand while I finished breakfast. I changed into my now-clean clothes and returned to the living room. Asa gestured to me from the kitchen. "Come here. Let me show you something."

I joined him and watched him open the gun safe over the fridge. He pulled out a box, reached inside, and withdrew a small gun. "Here."

"No, I can't. I don't know how—"

"That's the first thing we'll work on once this is all

over." He gently pressed the gun into my hands. "That's the safety. Click up to release it. I'll give you a full clip of ammo. Hold the gun in both hands. Aim for the biggest part of the body. Squeeze the trigger and hold on to the gun. It'll buck." He kept his gaze on me while he spoke, his dark eyes intent on mine.

"I can't use this." I tried to hand it back but he shook his head.

"We'll work on target practice later. For now, know how to use it if you have to."

I held the small black thing. "It's heavy."

"It's all metal. It's a good gun, small enough to scare somebody but still safe."

I turned it over in my hands. "How do I know if it's loaded?"

"Good question." He showed me how to take out and insert the magazine full of ammunition. "Always check your weapon. Never make any assumptions. Keep the safety on if you're not using it. Don't even think consciously about pulling the trigger. Squeeze, very gently."

I sighted down the barrel. My hand trembled slightly, enough to be distracting. "How do you do it?" I whispered. "How do you stand so still?"

"Deep breath," he said softly. "Deep breath, hold it, aim, squeeze. No conscious thought between each step. Just be. Just do."

"You sound like Mr. Miyagi." He looked at me blankly. "He was a movie character," I explained. "*The Karate Kid.*"

"I don't think I saw it. When did it come out?"

"In the Eighties, I think."

"I was in prison. I sort of lost the Eighties."

Now it was my turn to stare blankly at him. "I keep forgetting that."

One corner of his mouth quirked up. "Not very easy for me to forget."

"You said we'd work on target practice when this was over. That's what you meant, wasn't it? When you asked me if I'd rebuild—will it ever be over?"

He reached into the box and pulled out a small holster. "Clip this at your waist. We'll get you a real harness later."

"Asa."

He finally faced me. "No. It won't ever really be over, not until she dies."

"Are you going to kill her today?" When he didn't answer, I said, "Don't do this for me. Please. I couldn't bear to lose you now that I've found you. You can't get close enough to her to kill her without getting caught."

One corner of his mouth quirked up in a smile. "Now you're thinking like a criminal."

I pulled his face to mine. "Now I'm thinking like a woman in love."

He pulled me to him in a hug. "I'll do whatever it takes to keep you safe."

"That means keeping you safe, too."

He released me. "Show me you know how to use the gun."

We stepped through his instructions several times, with me showing him I knew how to use the safety and how to holster the weapon. By the time we finished I didn't feel proficient, but at least I was relatively certain I wouldn't shoot my own foot. I clipped the gun to the waistband of my jeans and covered it with my knit top.

Butterfly returned with several shopping bags and,

to my surprise, Chessy. Today she was dressed in a yellow dress with a darker yellow jacket and matching low-heeled pumps, making her appear like she was ready for a garden party. All that was missing was a pair of white gloves.

"I looked at the sizes in your clothes," Butterfly said with a grin, opening the bags and dumping the contents on the dining room table. Jeans, shirts, sweaters, bra, panties, slacks, and socks all tumbled out.

"Where did you get this?" I picked up a red-polka-dot knit shirt. "It's Sunday morning. Isn't everything closed?"

"Nope. There're a few open spots. She helped." He jerked a thumb at Chessy, who grinned.

"Most fun shopping I've ever had," she confessed. "He paid and I picked out. We're a helluva team." She enfolded me in a quick hug. "I saw what happened on TV. I was scared. I thought you guys were goners."

"The TV news?" I asked.

"All the local stations. It's not often a house gets a Molotov cocktail thrown at it."

"The media reported that?" Asa asked sharply.

Chessy pulled out a chair and sat. "Maybe not in so many words. They implied it, I guess. What the hell happened? Was it her? Senator Hart?"

"I doubt she was there throwing explosives at me," I said.

"You know what I meant. One of her stooges, then? Her minions?"

"That's what we're going to find out." Asa went into a closet near the entryway and returned with a small suitcase and a navy sports coat. "Why don't you pack up your purchases while Butterfly and I talk?" He didn't wait for my answer but walked into the living room, pulling on the jacket.

"He's kind of bossy," Chessy murmured, shooting a glare at Asa's back.

I quickly folded the new clothing and set the packed bag next to my tornado suitcase. "He's got a plan. He's focused." I dug into my book bag and pulled out Asa's small computer, setting it on the dining room table. The baby folder from the white box slid out with it. I would need to get a purse sometime. All my regular sized purses burned up in the fire.

"What's that? It's from that box, isn't it? Did you save some stuff?"

I jammed the folder back into the bag. "I saved some things but not much. Thanks for all your help on this, Chessy. Butterfly shouldn't have called on you. It's probably best if you stay out of this from here on in. We need to talk to the authorities and it might not be good for you to be involved."

"He didn't call me, I called him. He said you were going to that rally thing and I figured you might need somebody there incognito." She swept her hands over her demure dress. "Can I pass for a young Republican? Come on, I wouldn't miss this for the world. You might need some backup."

I was pretty sure truer words were never spoken.

Chapter Sixteen

"We'll meet Dodge at a hotel not far from the rally," Asa said. "I probably can't get within a block of the park. I'm sure my picture was given to every police officer in the area."

I breathed a sigh of relief. We were on our way to St. Paul in the black pickup truck. Traffic was light but it was Sunday morning, so that wasn't a surprise. Plus the May weather continued to be pristine, with a gentle breeze, warm sun, and low humidity which meant many people were heading to the lakes, not to the urban center.

We had three hours before the rally would start. Butterfly and Chessy would follow us later and wait for us at the library. "Chessy's a poster child for the Republicans. She'll be able to go to the rally and not raise any eyebrows."

"Butterfly is hard to explain, though," Asa said wryly.

"His innate charm will probably give him entrance. Besides, they don't dare turn away a black man. It would be bad politics."

"Well, the rally doesn't matter. Hart is at the hotel. Dodge made sure I'd get a chance to see her."

My stomach plummeted. "What? Are you kidding?"

He glanced at me. "Don't you remember? I have no

sense of humor."

"Damn it, Asa, this is serious. You can't confront her."

"I'm not going to confront her. You and I are going to give our statements to Dodge then I'll have a chance to talk to Hart."

He sounded totally calm, totally reasonable. "Just talk, right? No guns."

"We'll have to go through a security scan in order to get in to see Hart. Even if I wanted to shoot the bitch, I won't get the chance."

I began to relax. Maybe Dodge did have it under control. Maybe we would finally get some answers. I sorted through all the questions rattling around in my head. There were too many to focus on. I fell back on an old trick, letting my mind bounce from one thought to another, trusting that my subconscious would dredge up the pertinent details I needed.

This all started because Asa needed me to hypnotize him in order to find out what happened. Now we had our answer about Harry March's murder. Everything else was secondary to that. Asa wasn't a murderer. He was framed. His military friend framed him. The box of evidence was a red herring, something not important but it became important because of the churn it created. That box had to come from Harry March, but Harry March was dead. The box came to Asa years after Harry March's death. It must have been held for a certain length of time by March's estate.

"His child," I said. "Harry March's child. The child sent you the box of evidence. We need to see Harry March's will. It might name his child."

"Why would someone do that?"

"Let's play this out," I said. "Harry March had a son with Roberta Hart."

"A son?"

I waved my hand. "A son, a daughter. It doesn't matter. Let's say he had a son who was adopted by someone at birth. Harry decides to blackmail Roberta but he knows it might go sour. He writes a letter to his son, telling him what's going to happen."

Asa shook his head. "The child would only be ten years old or so at the time."

I thought furiously. "Maybe Harry left a letter in trust for the child, to be read when the child was older. Harry is killed and all the blackmail evidence vanishes. Roberta can't find it and her minions—" I grinned. "Good word. Anyway, her minions can't find it."

"Until the child grows up and gets the letter that Harry left," Asa said. "That explains the time lag. That explains why none of this surfaced until relatively recently."

"The child wasn't old enough to do anything about it. Or didn't get the letter until now. Maybe the son researched his father's murder and came to the same conclusion that we did, that you were set up. Maybe the son wanted to get revenge on his mother for abandoning him and for the murder of his father. You were the logical person to involve. You were motivated to reopen the murder of Harry March. And if the son researched you and found anything about you, he'd know you had the ability to reopen it."

"But I needed you to help me." Asa stared straight ahead, his eyes narrowed. "If someone watched me, they would see I was trying to find you. I was watching you." His hands clutched the steering wheel so tightly his knuckles turned white. "I sucked you into this mess."

"Yes, but we were set up. For what purpose? What kind of revenge?" I stared at the road ahead. "Is that it? Does someone want you to kill Hart? It would make sense, I suppose." I formed quotes with my fingers. "Murderer strikes again." I turned to face him. "The house fire. What if Hart didn't do it? What if someone else did? What if someone is trying to push you into killing again?"

Asa didn't react immediately then he nodded. "That's possible. Someone might be trying to manipulate me into either exposing Hart or hurting her. Who is it?"

"Maybe Dodge knows," I said. "I get the feeling he knows more than he's telling."

Asa nodded again. "There's something there, something on the edge of my mind. Dodge said something." His voice trailed away.

I didn't speak, afraid to disturb his train of thought. After a second, he shook his head. "He said something at your house when we first saw him there. I can't remember it."

We neared downtown St. Paul from the north. Yellow tape was already wrapped around the parking meters and sawhorse barricades were on the sidewalks, probably to be moved into place in a couple of hours.

Asa drove east then south, to a Hilton hotel five blocks from the park. He parked on the street east of the hotel and we walked to the main entrance. As we approached, Asa pulled a leather wallet out of his jacket pocket and had it open when we reached the glass doors.

A tall man in a business suit stepped out. He appeared as bland and unremarkable as Charles Dodge. Where did they get these clones? Was anonymity a job requirement? "I'm sorry, sir," he said, his voice as unremarkable as him. "There's no entrance to this hotel until after the rally."

Asa handed him the wallet. "We're here to speak with Charles Dodge. You can let him know we've arrived."

The man took the wallet and disappeared back inside. "What is that?" I whispered. "Some special badge or something?"

"Something like that." Asa held up a hand before I could ask another question. "We're being watched, videotaped, and recorded."

I peered up at the doorway, which normally would have opened automatically for us, but didn't see a camera. Two tall shrubs were on each side of the door and I suppose they might have held recorders.

"They're very good at long-distance surveillance," Asa whispered, leaning close to me.

The man returned with Asa's wallet. "This way, sir, ma'am." He opened the glass door and we entered the lobby of the hotel. It was like any other busy hotel except all the people bustling around were in business suits, most were men, and many had gadgets affixed to their ears with long curly wires disappearing into the back of their suit coats.

Dodge came across the long entry foyer to meet us. Like everyone else, he wore a dark suit, blending in with his surroundings. "Thank you for coming," he said to me. "This is strictly a formality. I realize what a trauma this must be for you." He stopped in front of

Asa. "Your gun, please." He held out his hand. "And your book bag, Miss Little."

Asa pushed his coat aside and pulled his gun from the holster on his belt. I handed Dodge the denim bag. "What are you going to do with it?"

"Just procedure. Please come with me." Dodge passed three men who prevented access to the ornate front desk. I wondered if the hotel had any guests who wanted to check in or out. If so, they were going to be delayed.

Dodge set my book bag on a small conveyer belt set up on a table. It was like a miniature airport scanner and sure enough, the bag trundled through a dark rectangular opening. Dodge went to the other side and paused near a man seated at a nearby wooden desk. He gave the man Asa's gun. The man jotted something on a slip of paper, attached part of it to the trigger part of the gun and handed the other half of the paper to Asa. Dodge scooped up my bag, handed it to me, and began walking through the large lobby.

We hurried past deep armchairs under skylights and big tables where newspapers and magazines were all scattered about. Several people sat in different parts of the lobby, but the whole atmosphere was hushed, in part because of the thick area rugs and in part because most people appeared to be speaking in low voices.

Dodge went to the opposite side of the lobby and passed through an oak door with *House Manager* etched on a brass plate in the center of the top panel. He ushered Asa and me into the room then closed the door.

Dodge went around the oak desk that occupied most of the tiny room. "Please, have a seat." He gestured to the two wooden chairs in front of the desk then seated himself. "I'm sure you understand, but I'll reiterate. You're here to give your statements and you met me here as a convenience for me and for no other purpose. We'll get a statement from Mr. Butterfield, too, at a later time. Your statements are the primary ones we need for the investigation."

"Do we need to write it down?" I glanced at the desk, which was devoid of any paper or pens. "Or dictate it?"

Dodge pulled a small black rectangular device from his inside pocket. It made a soft whirring noise when little wheels turned on top of it. "We'll tape it then have it transcribed for you to sign. Miss Little, perhaps you can wait in the next room. I'll speak with Mr. Hatterley first then have you come in and give your statement." He nodded to a door on his left, near the center of the room.

"We won't be separated," Asa said quietly. "I won't have her held for ransom."

I gaped at him. "What?"

Asa stared at Dodge, who returned the stare with equal impassivity. Dodge finally nodded, a slight dip of his head. "An understandable concern." He turned to me. "Miss Little, let's start with you. Tell me in your own words what happened last night at your home in Richmond, Minnesota."

I began with the fire, but Dodge stepped me through the evening starting with arriving at the house, eating dinner, and working on the jigsaw puzzle. "I went into the living room to get something and that's when the buzzing noise started," I said.

"Buzzing?" Dodge kept his attention totally on me. I think he didn't want to see Asa's reaction to my words.

"There was a big flash of light and the front of my house exploded. And all I could hear was a buzzing sound for a few minutes." Despite the warmth in the room, I trembled, probably from delayed shock. I rubbed my arms, trying to get warm.

"Temporary hearing loss," Asa murmured.

"Maybe. I'm not sure what it is. Asa pulled me to the floor." I hesitated, not sure how much to tell. "I grabbed my book bag then we left."

Dodge patiently questioned me for details about what I took, where the door was, what the fire was like. I was as vague as I dared, mumbling something about a notebook and a few photographs, not a real lie because there were photographs in the scrapbook.

"What about the man?" he asked. "The one who threatened you."

I nodded like a bobble-head doll. "Yes. He came through where the front door used to be. He had a shotgun or a rifle or something like that. He aimed it at me and Asa shot him. The man fell down and we ran." I was panting, almost hyperventilating.

"That's enough," Asa said. "That should be all the details you need."

Dodge regarded him with the same calm impassivity he'd shown me. "Do you care to add anything?"

"Griffin had a double-barrel sawed-off shotgun aimed at Alice's head. She was on the floor, stunned by the blast. I did what was necessary to save her life." Asa took my hand and squeezed it. My erratic breathing immediately slowed to normal. "The blast was designed to spread maximum fire. They probably used an accelerant. I didn't smell gasoline, but I wasn't in the room when it blew." Asa squeezed my hand again. "Alice was in that room. She's lucky she wasn't killed."

I saw the rage building in him, that fierce, hot anger that made him so unpredictable. "Luck has been with me a lot lately. It brought you to me."

He smiled, the anger controlled for the moment. "After what happened, I wasn't sure you'd feel that way."

"I'm sure your insurance company will have questions, Miss Little." Dodge shut off the small recorder and pocketed it. "We'll handle all the details."

"Why? Why would you help me?"

Dodge clasped his hands on the desk. "We haven't been totally honest with either of you." His pale blue eyes swept over Asa then me. "We knew about Hart's past association with Santiago and that they remained in touch through a third party. And we knew Hart was possibly being blackmailed. We didn't know what kind of threat, though."

"That's it," Asa said. "You said Hart expected a call from a woman. That's why Hart thought Alice was the blackmailer."

Dodge nodded. "We were monitoring some of her calls, but not all of them."

"Monitoring?" Asa leaned back in his chair, our hands slipping apart.

Dodge smiled faintly. "A year or so ago it came to our attention that Senator Hart's past was not quite what she painted for the media. Certain information came our way. We began a discreet investigation which revealed her ties to Santiago and to the March murder. That brought you to our notice." He turned to Asa, his bland face like a smooth mask. "Then you began searching for Miss Little and that made us wonder if she might be our blackmailer." He switched his attention to me and his face relaxed. "Once I met you, I know you weren't the woman we were wanted."

"I don't know whether to be relieved or mortified," I said. "I'd like to think I can be perceived as at least a tiny bit dangerous."

Dodge smiled, the first real smile I think I saw from him. "Your life has been turned upside down and you still are on your feet. That makes you very dangerous indeed, Miss Little. You're a survivor." He pushed back his chair.

"That's it?" I asked. "A man is killed and that's all you need to know?"

"Yes, it is." Dodge faced Asa over the desk and an unspoken message passed between them. "And now, as you requested, you'll have the opportunity to talk to Senator Hart. I hope you don't mind if I listen in."

"Covertly or overtly?" Asa asked.

Dodge didn't answer. He picked up the beige phone sitting on the desk and tapped three numbers on the dial face. Then he replaced the receiver and stood. "I'll be outside if I'm needed. I'll escort you back to your car when you're done."

"That's not necessary," I said.

He smiled again. "Oh, yes, it is." He left, leaving the door open.

"Okay, what's going on? You and he are in cahoots."

"Cahoots? That's a word I haven't heard in a long time. He and I have an understanding, that's all." Asa stood and tried to move past me, but my knees were inches from the desk. "There isn't enough space in this room."

I got up and moved around the desk. Asa kept his hand on my back, nudging me along. I reached the other side of the desk when I noticed movement in the open doorway.

Roberta Hart stepped into the room and closed the door. She was dressed in casual summer chic, patriotic blue striped top, navy pants, and red platform shoes. Her mass of tumbling red hair was held in place with a red-white-blue striped bow.

"I'm glad to see you escaped injury," she said, leaning against the door. "The story was on all the news stations last night." Her gaze went to Asa, standing to the left of the desk. "I was also glad to hear you wanted to talk to me. We need to set the record straight between us."

Asa stepped forward and aimed a gun directly into her face, the guest chairs separating them. "I told you if she was harmed I'd kill someone you love."

"You turned your gun in," I said, stepping back. "Where did you—" Then I remembered. I slapped my side where the holster was clipped. "You son of a bitch, you set me up."

"I needed a gun and I didn't think Dodge would search you. I was right." Asa continued staring at Hart. "I meant what I said."

"I wasn't responsible for this." Hart's already pale complexion was now pasty white. "You can't blame me for this." Her gaze bounced frantically around the room.

Asa walked forward. "Her home is gone. You tried to kill us."

"I had nothing to do with this." She spoke very carefully, enunciating the words. "I had nothing to do with Harry March's murder and I had nothing to do with last night."

"I saw your man there. I shot him." Asa kept the gun aimed steadily at her face.

"Leo was watching you. He didn't cause it." Hart moved to one side, putting some distance between herself and the door, which also put distance between herself and the gun. She was getting ready to grab the door and take a chance on running.

Asa saw it and moved to the left, closer to the door. "He came into the house with a shotgun. That's not surveillance."

I struggled to control my trembling while fear and adrenaline drained out of me. "Asa, I'm okay. Don't do anything because of me."

"Your house is gone. They ruined your life."

"It's only things. I have what's important." I approached him, careful to stay on his left side, away from the gun that was pointed, unwavering, at Hart. "I have you." Was it love that made me say that? Reaction to fear? Need? I didn't care. I reached for him.

He held up his arm, blocking my hand, his eyes still fixed on Hart. "I'll make a deal with you. In exchange for your life and the life of those you love."

"What are you talking about?" She sounded angry now. Fright could do that to a person. I should know. It's what always happened with me.

Asa walked forward. Now two feet separated her from his gun. "I can kill you at any time. I can kill the people you love at any time. And I will do it unless you do what I say."

She cringed, leaning back until her shoulders touched the wall. "I'll have you arrested. You can't threaten a government official. You won't get away with it."

"I am getting away with it." Asa stared at her over the barrel of the gun. "If you don't announce your retirement from politics after this term, you will be charged with treason. Your association with a known criminal will be made public knowledge. Your past life in pornographic films will be exposed. All the circumstantial evidence we have will be given to the media."

Hart froze, her eyes widening. "You have nothing."

Asa smiled. "Are you willing to gamble on that? I was willing to gamble that you would leave us alone in exchange for our silence. I lost that gamble when Alice lost her home. Therefore, I've raised the stakes. Are you willing to bet everything you love that I'm bluffing? Because if you do, I can tell you right now, you'll lose. I will see you destroyed and I will come after someone you love."

A bead of sweat rolled down the side of Hart's face. She stared at Asa, her eyes so wide I saw the whites surrounding her pupils. "I can't retire. I've set up an exploratory committee for the Presidency."

"Find some excuse. Retire or be exposed. I'm offering you a chance to live. That's more than you gave Alice when you had her house set on fire."

"I didn't do that. It wasn't my fault." Hart sounded desperate.

"That's the problem with lying. No one believes you even if you tell the truth. What will it be?"

"I need to think. I can't decide something like that now." Hart looked around as if she'd find an answer somewhere in the room.

Asa lowered the gun, clicked on the safety, and bent over, tucking the gun into a holster at his ankle. "Wrong answer. If you cared about the people you love, you'd agree to anything. That tells me you don't love anyone enough to save them." He turned to me. "Let's go."

I grabbed my book bag from the floor near the desk. "I'm sorry, Senator Hart," I murmured. "Truly I am." I reached for the doorknob.

"Wait." She moved against the door, blocking me from opening it. "What guarantee do I have you won't change your mind in the future and expose me?"

"You have no guarantees," Asa said. "You have my word. All I want is what you want. I want the people I love to be safe. Get out of politics and your secret is safe."

"What about you?" Hart glared at me. "What do you get out of this?"

"I get my life back." I tugged on the door, forcing her to move to one side. "Just leave us alone and everyone stays safe."

She stared at me. "You're a fool if you think you'll be safe with him."

I took a step forward to stare her down. "You're a fool if you think otherwise."

Hart threw open the door and stalked out, brushing past two security guards stationed in the lobby. Dodge materialized from behind a rack of tourist pamphlets and joined us to watch Hart plow through the crowded lobby. "I take it your talk went well," Dodge said.

"It was productive," Asa said. "Senator Hart is seriously considering retirement. I think that's a wise choice, don't you?"

Dodge nodded. "Probably very wise." He led the way through the lobby, back to the man sitting at the table. Asa collected his gun and we all walked outside into brilliant May sunlight. Dodge turned to us. "What now? I mean, after I get you back to your car."

"I think it's time we retired, too. If ever we needed a government cover-up, now's the time," Asa suggested.

Dodge smiled. "I'll see what I can do."

"I don't know if I can," I said. "What if—what if things don't work out with us? This is no way to build a relationship, Asa."

"Build one? Or rebuild one? We were together for three years, Alice. You know me and I know you." He smoothed back my hair, his hand lingering on my face. "I love you and I think you love me, too. You're afraid of the future and I understand that. This isn't the early retirement you planned." He stared intently into my eyes. "I can promise you that I'll love you, respect you, and care for you all my life. All I ask is that you give me a chance."

"But what if—" There were so many *what if* questions I didn't know where to start.

"I'll make sure you can vanish, alone if that's what you want. I can give you a new identity if that's what you want." Dodge turned to Asa. "I know you can do that, too, but maybe she'll want to use us instead."

Asa moved away from me. "All I ask is that you consider doing it with me."

I was conscious of Dodge's amused gaze. "I'll consider it." I reached into the pocket of my book bag. "I'm going to call Chessy. There's no need for her to come to the rally now that we've already talked to

Hart."

Asa grinned. "I wish I could see her in action, though. She'd probably be hell during the question and answer period." He moved ahead to walk with Dodge while I followed, retrieving the number on my phone and placing the call.

"Where are you?" Chessy demanded. "Is everything okay? What happened with Hart?"

"We worked out a deal with the Feds," I said, trailing behind the two men.

"She gets arrested, right? They'll charge her with—what? Murder?"

"No, it doesn't work that way. They don't have enough evidence. But we worked out a deal where we go free and she'll be punished. Maybe not as much as I'd like, but it's a deal."

"What? That's not fair! After all you've been through? She has to pay!"

"She will. This is her last rally as a Senator. She'll retire soon."

"That's not enough for what she's done."

I was gratified at Chessy's intense devotion to our cause. "It is enough. We'll be safe from her. She'll never be able to harm us again. It's a compromise, but it's a good one."

"But—" Chessy sputtered with anger. "Alice, you lost your home. You were almost killed and he was in prison and—"

There was no discussing it with her. She was right. It wasn't fair, but it was the best we could hope for. "Chessy, there's no need for you to come to the rally. We're done with Senator Hart. I'll call you later, okay? Right now I want to relax and figure out what to do."

She heard the implicit dismissal in my voice. "No, sure, I understand. Man, you've been through the wringer the last few days. We'll talk soon. Don't worry about it."

"Thanks for everything, Chessy. You were a champ about this. I really appreciate all you did to help us."

"I'm sorry it didn't work out."

We were at the truck, Dodge and Asa waiting for me. "Gotta go, Chessy. I'll call you later." I ended the call and tucked the phone back in my bag then held out my hand to Dodge. "Thanks, I guess. I'm sorry for how this all worked out."

"No more than I am. This has been hard for you. It shouldn't have happened." He glanced at Asa while he shook my hand.

"No one is to blame," I said. "I wish you guys would remember that. I made a choice to help Asa. I accept what came about because of that."

Dodge released my hand. "You're one hell of a woman, Alice Little. You're lucky to have her, Mr. Hatterley."

"I know." Asa shook Dodge's hand. "Stay in touch."

Dodge smiled. "You can count on it."

Asa and I didn't talk much on the drive back to the warehouse. I think he knew I was overwhelmed and he gave me the space I needed. When we entered the apartment, Butterfly met us at the elevator. "Blondie left right after she talked to you," he told me. "She was one pissed off woman. I'll bet she went to the rally just to harass Hart."

"I hope she didn't." I eyed my tornado suitcase. "I

suppose I'd better figure out what comes next."

Asa pulled me to him. "I hope I come next. Let me take you on a vacation. I have an island where we can get away from it all. You'll have a chance to think about what to do."

"He ain't kidding," Butterfly said with a laugh. "That lake really is away from it all. It's so far away, it may as well be on the moon."

I rested my head against Asa's chest. "Right now, that sounds about perfect."

The phone on the kitchen counter rang. Asa picked it up and listened while I went back to my suitcase, sitting next to the dining room table. "Turn on the TV," Asa said to Butterfly.

The big man touched a button on the wall and one of the pictures slid upward, revealing a TV inset into the brickwork. "What channel?"

"Local news." Asa resumed listening to the phone, his eyes on the television.

I walked over to stare at the anchorwoman who was talking excitedly. ". . . before the rally. Senator Hart is listed in critical condition at a local hospital. Senator Gordon is also wounded, but we're not sure how badly. The shooter is still at large and . . ."

Asa listened to whoever was on the phone then he hung up. "That was Dodge," he said. "We need to run."

Chapter Seventeen

Carol Lewis leaned back in her chair. "And you've been running since that day?"

I held up my hand to encompass the island and our home. "Actually, no, we haven't. We did travel rather extensively at first, but we soon settled here. We fixed up the lodge and convinced Butterfly to join us. It's an arrangement that's suited us and it certainly suited him." I smiled, remembering moments from the past twenty years. "He found his wife here, raised a family, and has done quite well for himself."

Lewis peered up at the house. "Does he still ask you every day? He said he would ask you every day if you wanted to stay with him."

I nodded. "We've been taking it a day at a time for twenty years. Every day I say yes. Sometimes it's harder to say it than others, but so far, I have."

"What happened to Major Tuttle?" Lewis checked her notes. "Did he do it? Did he kill him?"

I waved my hand. "Tuttle. What an asshole. We found him. It really wasn't that hard. He had cancer. Asa didn't kill him. Tuttle deserved chemotherapy more than a clean death with a bullet."

"They never did catch the person who fired into the crowd that day," Lewis said. "Senator Hart almost died."

"There were two shooters. Hart was collateral

damage." I smiled. I liked that phrasing. "Apparently someone was after Senator Gordon. Or that's what the officials said. Of course, we didn't stay around to find out. Asa was seen at the hotel. Someone might have connected him to the shooting." I shook my head. "No one would believe he didn't do it."

"Did she believe he didn't do it?" Lewis asked.

"She? Hart?" I shrugged. "Probably not. She was pathologically paranoid, I think."

"That's harsh," Lewis said. "She knew you blamed her for what happened to your house. Why wouldn't she believe you retaliated?"

"Because we had a deal. I even sent her a copy of some of the photographs from the scrapbook, so she'd know we still had the evidence."

"And she was forced to retire from office," Lewis said. "It's a pity, really. She was one of the first really viable female Presidential candidates."

"She was also vindictive, hypocritical, and crooked." I smiled at Lewis, whose cheeks flushed at my criticism. "We can argue politics until we're blue in the face. I hated that woman and I still do. It's a pity she didn't die that day. Now she's grooming her daughter, Jackie, for political office, but I heard there's a problem with her daughter's health."

Lewis nodded, the movement jerky. "Her daughter is quite ill, I think."

"And wasn't there a scandal with the granddaughter? She was a cop, wasn't she? Didn't she get involved in a police brutality case? That's a lot of woes for one person, even an old bitch like Roberta Hart."

"I don't know about that," Lewis snapped.

My phone thumped in my pocket then the tiny audio bud in my ear crackled. "Quit baiting her," Asa said softly. "Time to wrap it up. They're moving in."

"Damn," I whispered. "I hoped you were wrong."

"Is there a problem?" Carol Lewis smiled at me, her blue eyes guileless.

I stared into the distance, at the trees surrounding our expanse of lawn. Sunlight and shadow moved with the breeze. I couldn't see any interlopers, but if Asa said they were there, they were there. "Who sent you?"

"My newspaper, of course. Why?" She shifted position, uncrossing her long legs.

"That's not what I meant. Who sent you to distract us?"

"What?" Her messenger bag slipped off the seat. With one quick move she tossed open the flap and dipped her hand inside.

"I wouldn't do that if I were you." I rested my revolver on the left arm of my chair, inches away from her right breast. She froze. "Remove your hand and whatever is in it," I instructed.

"It's only a notepad. What's going on?" She appeared panicked and I almost—*almost*—believed her.

"Take it out of the bag and put the bag on the ground." I glanced at Dina, who got to her feet, staring at Lewis. "Get back, pup. Sit."

"I didn't come alone." A chair scraped on concrete. "And you have the safety on."

My attention snapped back to Lewis. She had pushed back her chair and was safely away from my shooting range unless I moved. But now she had her gun aimed at me, a Walther automatic pointed right at my throat. She held it professionally, her left palm balancing the butt while her right hand held it steady. I was reassured to see that. There's nothing worse than being threatened by an incompetent shooter.

"It's irrelevant if others tried to land here."

"They didn't try to land. They did."

"Really? How many?"

Lewis' eyes narrowed. "What are you doing?"

I lowered my gun and set it on the wide arm of my chair, keeping my hands in plain sight. "You told me people landed here. I want to know how many and how they did it. There's no reasonable landing area anywhere on this island. Especially not for an elderly woman with a bad leg."

"I didn't say she was here."

"You didn't have to. I know her. I know she'd never trust you to do the job."

"You're wrong." Lewis said it so fast I know my words touched on a nerve, touched on some deep insecurity.

"You forget. I know her. I know how her mind works." I was stalling, but Lewis didn't seem to notice.

"Stand up." She slid forward on the chair and got to her feet, the gun remaining fixed on me the entire time.

I wasn't quite as graceful, using the arms to help me out of the deep seat, turning as I did so. Dina got up, too, and took position at my right side. I glanced at the porch. I was sure he was gone, probably to the cupola. I left my gun on the arm of the chair and stared at Lewis and beyond her, to the house. "What do you get out of this? Money? We can pay you far more than whatever she's paying you."

"You can't buy loyalty. Raise your hands."

"Of course you can. She bought loyalty for years." I put my hands up. "What now?"

"Now we chat, Miss Little."

I turned around. Roberta Hart stood at the top of our dock steps, glaring at me. She wore navy slacks and a blue-and-white striped sweater with matching navy pumps, as though she was getting ready to sit down to high tea.

A tall, thin man with gray hair wearing black jeans and a dark T-shirt was slightly in front of her. Another man, identical except for blond hair, was behind her. They moved around her to flank her when she took a hesitant step forward onto the lawn.

I caught a glimpse of the water between the trees behind her, in the cleared space where the steps led downward. "Where's Mike Butterfield?"

"He's in his boat, tied up and gagged. He hasn't been harmed." The old woman moved forward, leaning heavily on a dark wooden cane. Her limp was more pronounced now, but she was older. I suppose arthritis had set in around the wound. She appeared calm and unconcerned, her white hair cut short and seemingly unruffled by a ride in the boat. Of course, she always excelled at putting on a good front. Her spine could have been broken and she'd probably never show it.

The two men moved around her like moons around a planet, each with a gun drawn, each evaluating the woods, the house, the lawn, the garage, moving in an intricate dance of defense. The blond-haired man had a rifle. He kept it at shoulder level, aiming long. The other had a Glock or some other kind of automatic. He kept it low, his eyes intent on the woods.

Something made me look back at the gray-haired

man with the automatic. He swung to face me and that's when I saw his face in the sunlight.

Dodge.

I opened my mouth to speak, but he shook his head fractionally. I forced my attention back to Hart, trying to process the fact that Charles Dodge was there, guarding this woman. I knew how they got here, of course. The landing was the only way she could get on the island. Mike had a remote control on his boat for the dock. He returned to the lodge after dropping off Carol Lewis. Presumably they got the drop on him either at the lodge or, probably more likely, on the lake. It really didn't matter as long as he was unharmed.

I lowered my arms. "What do you want?" I moved toward Hart and Carol Lewis followed me. I sensed her gun aimed at the back of my head. Dodge moved to flank me on my left and Lewis moved to my right.

Roberta's gaze went past me at the house. "Where is he?"

"You know better than to ask that."

She gestured, one imperious flip of her wrist. Blond Guy moved near me, his gun up. I watched him approach and when he was a yard away, I said, "A trained sniper is watching you right now. You're in his kill zone." I took a step back, away from Roberta.

Her face stilled. "I don't believe you."

"He's made shots far more difficult than this. As I'm sure you're aware."

"Stop." She said the single word without hesitation and without fear. For a long moment we evaluated each other, the sunlight warm on my arms and the heady scent of pine in the air. "You won't kill me," she said.

"Why not? We could weight down your body and

dump it in the lake. Nobody would be the wiser."

For the first time, she seemed uncertain. I saw it in the flare of her nostrils, the way her hand tightened on the cane's head. "I have people with me. You can't get rid of all of us."

"I have people, too." I raised my left hand, my index finger pointing to the sky. Chessy was hidden in the woods on that side of the lawn. I wondered if she'd recognize Dodge. She didn't interact with him much and after all, it was twenty years ago.

A bullet hit the ground near Dodge's foot. He spun, his gun aimed at the trees. The other man dropped to one knee, his rifle raised and pointed at the house.

"Don't," I said. "If you do, you'll die."

The old woman raised then lowered her cane, her hand trembling. "Stop it," she snapped. "They're trying to frighten us. They can't kill us."

"Of course we can. We had a deal. Why did you break it?"

"Me? I told you what I needed. Why won't you help me?" The old woman stabbed at the ground near my foot with her cane. I moved aside, out of the impact zone. Dina snarled softly and Hart apparently noticed her for the first time because she stepped back.

The microphone hummed in my ear. "To your right. I don't have a clear shot."

I inched to the right. "I never received any correspondence from you."

Hart's down-tilted eyes narrowed, giving her a sorrowful appearance. "I asked you for help for my daughter. Why didn't you reply?"

"What?"

"How much do you want?"

"I don't know what you're talking about." I inched away farther, my feet sliding on the grass. Dina stayed near me, her eyes fixed on Lewis, the nearest antagonist.

"Quit lying. You've held a sword over my head for twenty years and now I need it. How much do you want? What will it take to get me those records?"

"We were right. It's the daughter." Asa's voice was soft in my ear. "Her illness."

The baby records that I salvaged from the fire at my house. Hart's legitimate adult daughter was sick with a deadly cancer affecting her liver. They were seeking a living tissue donor, but no family members were compatible. "The records won't help you," I said, stalling for time. "There are no details about where the child is today."

"That's my problem, not yours. I have all the records from the hospital. I need to match the footprints you have to the ones I have and I'll have a chance to save my daughter." Hart stepped forward, her face grim. "I want those records. How much? Why didn't you answer my letter? I had it personally delivered."

"She never got it. I never delivered it." Chessy stepped out from the trees behind Hart. She was dressed all in black, her blonde hair hidden under a black baseball cap. The automatic in her left hand was pointed at me and the one in her right pointed at Hart. She dipped her chin, pressing the microphone on her wireless headset against her raised shoulder. "I'll kill Alice if you try anything. I can't miss from here." Her gaze swept over Lewis, Dodge, and the blond guard. "And if any of you move, I'll kill the senator."

The house was in back of me and everyone else

was arrayed around me, guns drawn. It was like a bad Western movie. Hart glared at Chessy, her trembling hands making the cane wobble.

Chessy glanced past me. "Come out where I can see you." She moved so she had a clear view of the house over my shoulder.

"What did you do, Chessy?" I inched to my left where Dodge stood, the blond guard on his left forming the far end of our ragged half-circle.

"I took the letter. She wants the child she gave birth to in California in 1968. They need a liver donor for the perfect daughter, the one she decided to keep."

"I didn't decide anything of the kind," Hart snarled. "I had to give that child in California up for adoption. I couldn't have an illegitimate baby."

Chessy's gaze went over my head. I peeked over my shoulder and saw Asa standing on the upper deck, outside our bedroom. His rifle was cradled in his arms. "You were right," I told him. "About it all."

He nodded, his gaze focused on us.

"Tell him to put the gun down," Chessy said to me.

"You tell him. You're wired for sound." I was struggling to match the woman I thought I knew for years with the woman I now knew. "You're Harry March's daughter. You sent the box to Asa. You made sure I was at the Stand Down. You set the fire at my house."

Chessy moved forward, her gun aimed at Hart's chest. "It wasn't supposed to get out of hand. All I wanted to do was scare you a little, push you to act. But the car exploded and then the roof caught on fire."

"And Leo Griffin was there," Hart whispered.

"He came in and tried to take advantage of the

situation." Asa's voice in my ear was cool, detached. He was considering our options. We had planned for this, but there were always variables. "I killed him and I assumed Hart was responsible."

I glanced to my right. Carol Lewis still held her gun, now pointed at Chessy. "If you kill her, you're sentencing your mother to death," I said softly. Lewis flinched, her attention riveted back on me. "Hart is your grandmother, isn't she? The daughter who's sick, Jackie—that's your mother?"

"What do you want, Chessy?" Asa asked in our earbuds.

"I want all of you to move there." Chessy nodded at the hill in front of the house. "I want everyone in one spot where I can see you." I turned immediately to walk away. "Not you, Alice. You stay with me."

"Why do I rate?" I asked bitterly.

"Because he's the most dangerous one here." Chessy gestured me closer. "And that makes you important. Sorry, Alice."

"If you take her prisoner, we'll kill you and her," Dodge said.

"You can try," Chessy said. "Before you get off a shot, he'll kill you. Go. There, up the hill." She gestured with the gun in her left hand so quickly I barely saw it.

I moved to stand near her. Hart, Lewis, and the two guards walked up the hill, using the slate path. "Now you, Alice. Not too far in front of me." Chessy holstered her right-hand gun and put that hand on my shoulder, steering me forward while she ducked, her other gun pressed into my back.

I gestured with my right hand and Dina walked slightly ahead of me on the right, her gaze alternating between the people ahead and Chessy behind me.

"What do you want?" Asa still stood on the balcony, the gun in his arms, his voice low and calm in our ear buds.

"I want Hart to pay. She threw me away and she killed my father and she ruined your life and she ruined mine. I spent fifteen years in and out of foster homes because she wouldn't acknowledge me." Chessy spoke softly, her breath warm on my neck. "I tried to make her pay years ago and I failed."

"That was you at the rally that day?" I strained to see the ground in front of me. I prayed I wouldn't stumble and inadvertently set off a fire storm.

"Was that crazy or what? I go there, thinking I want to kill her and some lunatic was there trying to kill Senator Gordon." Chessy gave a short, breathless laugh. "What are the odds of that happening? Of course, given the fact they had all the Republican loonies there that day, maybe the odds were stacked after all."

"Alice never hurt you, Chessy." Asa's voice was reasonable, soothing. "Why now? Why do this now?"

"You have no idea what it's been like." She peered over my shoulder at Hart. I felt Chessy's breath warm on my neck. "He wrote me a letter every year until you had him killed. He loved you. He adored you. You broke his heart when you left him."

Hart stared at Chessy, her hands opening and closing on the cane's head. "Harry was a blackmailer and a thief. He didn't love me. He used me."

"He explained it all in his letters. It was the only thing he could do. He knew you wanted money. You wanted a rich lifestyle. And you didn't mind, did you?" Chessy's hand tightened on my shoulder, making me sag on that side from pain. She didn't notice. "You loved being in those movies. You were a slut but he loved you. He loved me, too. I got all the letters when I turned twenty-five. I got everything from his estate and that's when I found out I had a father who loved me and a mother who was lying hypocrite."

The anguish and bitterness in her voice told me just how much that knowledge ate at her for years. "And they called Asa a crazy man," I muttered. "You're crazy if you think you'll get away with this."

"Why won't I?" She squeezed my shoulder, deliberately this time and I winced. "It's the right place and the right time. It bothers me that Alice will be hurt." Chessy didn't sound very contrite and I fleetingly wondered if all the years of supposed friendship were an act.

"You fooled us for years," Asa said softly. "Not completely, but enough."

Chessy's hand loosened. "What?"

"Alice trusted you. I never did, but she did." Asa's gaze locked on me. "She always was the one who was willing to trust."

"Too bad it's coming back to bite her now." Chessy shook me like a paper doll. "Somebody has to take the blame. The details will be leaked to the media. All about the vendetta you had with the senator and how you killed her."

I nearly laughed out loud. I gazed up at the house. Asa now stood above us, gazing down with his gun still held in his arms. The others were huddled near the porch steps. Dodge had moved to one side, his gaze intent on me and Chessy. "Great minds think alike," I said. "Asa and I did the same thing. The entire story is on file with the U.S. Attorney. If anything happens to us, Roberta Hart is ruined."

Chessy faltered. "Why would you do that?"

"Because you keep forgetting we're very smart people," Asa said softly. "It's time."

I twisted, pulling away from Chessy, praying her reaction time was bad, praying she might have some feeling for me that stopped her from pulling the trigger. I dropped to my knees. "Dina. Protect!" I pointed at Carol Lewis.

The small dog launched herself at Lewis, her powerful jaws clamping on Lewis' left leg right above the shin. The woman fell back, trying to aim her gun at the dog. Dodge dove for her, wrestling Lewis to ground and tearing the gun out of her hands. Dina clung ferociously to Lewis' leg, where blood now sheeted down the woman's shin. The dog planted her feet on the ground, pulled back and tore.

Lewis hit the ground hard, Dodge on top of her and Dina angling for another attack. "Dina! Guard!" I pointed at Hart. The dog lunged for Hart, planted herself in front of the older woman and growled.

Chessy grabbed for me but I ducked and rolled. For an instant Chessy was vulnerable. It wasn't a clean shot, but it was enough. Her shoulder exploded in blood and tissue, boney fragments splattering my face. I heard the shot a second later when I raised my head.

Someone jerked me to my feet so hard I was sure my arm was broken. The blond guard shifted his grip to my hair and pressed a gun to my head, his eyes fixed above us where Asa stared down, rifle on his shoulder.

"I'll kill you," the guard said, tugging my head back, exposing my neck. "Call him off or I kill you."

I tried to pull away but his hold was tight. When I shuffled my feet, they touched some obstruction, and I realized it was Chessy's body. My stomach lurched, and I longed to be sick, longed to drop to my knees and puke. Instead I drew in ragged breaths, trying to form words.

"Tell him," the guard said. "Tell him." He inched backward, his eyes focused upward. The gun didn't shift an inch from where it pressed into the side of my forehead.

I hazarded a glance at Dodge, who was frozen in place, his eyes on me. His gun was in his hand but he didn't have a shot.

The blond guard holding me pulled his gun away slightly so he could whisper in my ear. "He won't shoot. He won't risk you."

I stared into Roberta's eyes. I think she saw my answer before I spoke. "It isn't a risk." I smiled at the house and managed to tilt my head slightly to the left. "Take the shot."

The guard's head snapped back and a nanosecond later I heard the bullet. It blew out his head, snapping his neck. He toppled backward. I screamed, falling with him. I clawed at his dead hand still clutching my hair and finally got free, leaving one clump of brown hair in his fist.

"Dina!" I called. "Guard!"

She ran to me and took up position in front of me where I was sprawled on the ground. I pushed myself up onto my hands and knees.

"Are you hurt?" Asa asked in the ear bud.

"No, I think I'm fine. We'll need the medics, though."

"On their way. I'm coming down. Butterfly has you covered."

I waved to the woods at the edge of the lawn. Butterfly and two of his brothers-in-law stepped out, rifles in hand. The other two men would be at the dock, helping the police and the EMTs. I was glad to see our assumptions were right and the big black man was unharmed. Only his pride was wounded when he allowed himself to be taken captive.

"You knew?" Dodge asked, holding out his hand.

I took it gratefully. My head hurt like crazy, and I had twisted my back when I went down in the melee. I felt every minute of my sixty-six years. "We were almost certain."

"Why did you do it? Why?"

I turned at the stunned voice. Hart was bending over Chessy, not Lewis, her granddaughter. She must have seen my surprise. "You killed her," Hart whispered, staring at Chessy. "She was Jackie's last chance. You killed her."

Dodge picked up the fallen guard's gun and pocketed it then went to Lewis, who sat on the ground pitched forward, her hand clamped over her knee. He took the gun she dropped and tossed it near the porch steps, out of the way then he went to Chessy, pulling Hart out of the way so he could kneel next to the fallen woman. "She's alive. Her shoulder's a mess and she's lost a lot of blood, but she'll make it if we can get her to help fast."

Hart peered around her. "Are you insane? We're in the middle of nowhere."

"The seaplane is on its way." I pointed to the dock where men were coming up the steps. "The EMTs have a launch at the dock. They'll transfer her and get her to Duluth in under an hour."

"I'd better meet them," Dodge murmured. "Try to explain what's going on. Of course, I'm not sure I know, so that might be hard."

"What are you doing here?" I asked. "How did you know we'd need you?"

He smiled. "When I found out that Hart was making a trip to Northern Minnesota, I thought I should tag along. She didn't know my connection to you, so it seemed like a good idea at the time."

Asa stepped out of the porch onto the steps. "I'm glad you did. This might have turned out differently if we didn't have you here. We weren't counting on Chessy turning violent. She was one of those variables I didn't know how to evaluate."

Dodge holstered his gun and took his badge wallet out of his back pocket. "You did a pretty good job nonetheless." He walked across the lawn to meet the police officers hurrying in our direction.

Dina trotted to meet Asa, taking an elaborate path around Carol Lewis to do so. "I was careful. Chessy will live." Asa touched Dina's head. "Good pup." The dog wiggled enthusiastically.

"How did you know it was her?" Dodge stopped and called back to us.

I waved him on. "I'll explain later. Go run interference for us, okay?"

He waved and met the four men racing across the lawn, directing two of them to us and stopping the other two by exhibiting his badge.

Asa walked to me, pausing to glance at the dead guard before wrapping me in a hug. "You're bleeding," he murmured, pressing a handkerchief to my head.

"I'm fine. Just a bit of a haircut."

"How did you know?" Hart asked hoarsely. "How long have you known about her?"

"The jigsaw puzzle," I said.

Hart swayed so badly I thought she might be having a heart attack. Carol Lewis stared up at her grandmother, her tear-soaked face blotchy and red. "Grammy?" she murmured.

"I forgot about the puzzle," Hart said, ignoring the young woman. "I thought it burned in the fire."

The EMTs reached us. "Shoulder wound," Asa said, pointing to Chessy. "He's gone." He glanced at the downed guard dismissively.

"I have a leg wound," Lewis said. "That dog bit me. I'll need to get rabies shots." She acted like a forgotten bedraggled child clamoring for attention.

I touched Dina's head. "Maybe I should make sure she gets shots, too. She might be infected from biting you."

One of the EMTs went to the guard and the other bent over Chessy. Asa and I moved out of his way, Hart following us. Her granddaughter watched, I think finally realizing she'd been a pawn in her grandmother's game.

"Once we put it together, we saw a pretty little five-year-old girl," I said. "We didn't get around to doing that until a few years ago. Harry sent it to you, didn't he? He sent it to remind you of what you left behind."

Hart nodded. "He sent me something on every birthday, that son of a bitch. He never let me forget."

Asa put his arm around my shoulder. "We ran the

picture through some age-forwarding software and came up with someone who was like Chessy. That and the footprints and handprints were all we needed to confirm her identity."

Asa looked beyond me to Butterfly, walking across the lawn to join the huddle of police. "We've known for years. There was no reason to reveal it, though. What purpose would it serve? She appeared content to let sleeping dogs lie." He smiled when he said it, but I felt his anger in his arm around me. "I wasn't going to act unless it threatened us." He gave me a tender look. "Unless it threatened Alice."

I buried my face in his shirt, letting the fear leach out of me. I was safe.

I would always be safe with him.

Thank you for purchasing
this publication of The Wild Rose Press, Inc.

For questions or more information
contact us at
info@thewildrosepress.com.

The Wild Rose Press, Inc.
www.thewildrosepress.com

To visit with authors of
The Wild Rose Press, Inc.
join our yahoo loop at
http://groups.yahoo.com/group/thewildrosepress/

www.ingramcontent.com/pod-product-compliance
Lightning Source LLC
Chambersburg PA
CBHW051527260626
47170CB00003B/823